TWINS OF WAR

Part II: The Sacrifice

DANA LEVY ELGROD

Producer & International Distributor
eBookPro Publishing
www.ebook-pro.com

TWINS OF WAR

Part II: The Sacrifice

DANA LEVY ELGROD

Copyright © 2023 Dana Levy Elgrod

All rights reserved; no parts of this book may be reproduced or transmitted in any form or by any means, electronic or mechanical, including photocopying, recording, taping, or by any information retrieval system, without the written permission of the author.

Translation: Shira Carmen Aji

Contact: dana.elgrod@gmail.com

ISBN 9798340900685

Contents

Prologue 5

Chapter 1 7

Chapter 2 20

Chapter 3 28

Chapter 4 35

Chapter 5 43

Chapter 6 61

Chapter 7 67

Chapter 8 77

Chapter 9 87

Chapter 10 94

Chapter 11 111

Chapter 12... *118*

Chapter 13... *130*

Chapter 14... *140*

Chapter 15... *151*

Chapter 16... *161*

Chapter 17... *172*

Chapter 18... *177*

Chapter 19... *194*

Chapter 20... *202*

Chapter 21... *209*

Chapter 22... *217*

Chapter 23... *223*

Chapter 24... *229*

Chapter 25... *238*

Epilogue.. *249*

PROLOGUE

Sacrifice.
I experienced a life of luxury, and I never knew satisfaction.
I wanted more.
I wanted better.
I wanted everything.
I wasn't afraid to hurt others to get what I wanted. I felt no guilt when I took, and I never gave back.
I thought the world was created just for me and that I was supposed to milk it for all it was worth, until the last drop.
And then the last drop arrived.
My world was cracked, broken, and shattered into thousands of black shards.
The world robbed me of the freedom to be selfish and discarded me like a hollow shell longing to be filled with light.

CHAPTER 1

Many months have passed since the day the ghetto gates were closed and the year 1941 is still excruciating and gloomy. The Germans have carried on with their delusions of grandeur and even invaded the Soviet Union in June, and the world gets darker and darker with each passing day. The Polish soldiers and guards stand like cruel jailers at the gates of the largest prison in the world. No one goes in or out other than the few Polish citizens who pick up the garbage that piles up in the streets and, from time to time, bring in the basic groceries that the Germans provide for their prisoners.

I sit on the chair near the wall of my building and stare at the masses of people with indifference. They're just blurry colors that move in front of my eyes. So many people stretch out their hands asking for charity, walking stooped over, dragging their feet, and begging for a bit of food. None of them approaches me. I pose like a statue in my satin gown, and Dziecko licks milk from a bowl at my feet.

I watch two vendors selling their wares. One peddles books and the other shoelaces. It doesn't surprise me that no customers frequent their stalls. They both sell things that cannot be eaten. My eyes wander to a man in an expensive-looking suit walking towards the restaurant on the street corner. Then my eyes are drawn to the soldiers in their gray uniforms, kicking anyone who dares to walk on the sidewalk near them. The noise of screeching truck wheels is heard in the distance, and the throngs disappear inside the buildings. Only a few elderly people remain in the street, lumbering on toward their destinations. The class disparities in the ghetto are shocking – on the one hand, a group of the "new wealthy" has emerged, made up of those who manage to smuggle goods in and out of the ghetto. They spend their time dining in restaurants and enjoying the cultural life available within the ghetto's confines. On the other hand, are all the less fortunate men, women, and children who live in abject poverty, tormented by constant pangs of hunger.

I look down at my cat and realize that I'm very lucky. I haven't felt hungry even once, and I'm surrounded by friends who care about me. I look all around for Ida, expecting to see her creeping quietly along the walls of the buildings, making herself invisible, and I'm disappointed to discover that there's no trace of her.

She spends too many long hours every day at the school they established in the ghetto, and Peter has set up a stall alongside those of the wealthy vendors. Bruno offered to help me get a job in one of the ghetto's factories, but I vehemently refused. I don't need money to live comfortably. My needs in this prison are minimal. I'm not invited out to restaurants, I don't frequent any cultural establishments, and I don't indulge in shopping sprees. I wake up every day to the same dreary routine of idleness and sorrow, and under no circumstances do I want to work in the company of strangers.

The noise of the truck dies down, and the masses return to the streets. An elderly woman sways in the road and suddenly collapses to her knees and falls forward. People keep walking as if she were just a worthless object that shattered and broke. I look at her fragile skeleton of a body. Her face is pale and wrinkled, her eyes are open, and she's staring into space. I don't need to worry that making eye contact with her will make me feel connected to her. She is no longer of this world.

A few minutes later, the soldiers order two scrawny boys to take away the body, and I direct my eyes to the blue uniforms. I recognize Anton's rugged figure at the end of the street. He doesn't turn to look at me, but I know he watches me as much as he can without arousing suspicion. Even now, he's drumming on the butt of his gun while I involuntarily twirl a lock of hair around my finger.

An angelic voice addresses me in the strange language of the Jews.

"I don't understand," I say impatiently and look down.

"You're so beautiful," the angelic voice declares in Polish.

"Thank you." I finger the lace on the brim of my hat and avoid making eye contact.

"You look like a princess."

I grunt, hoping the little girl will understand that she's bothering me and leave me alone.

"Are you really a princess?" She kneels down and pets Dziecko's fur.

Her body is tiny, and her clothes are filthy. Her black hair is wild, and her skin pale. Her eyes are fixed on the bowl of milk, and her mouth is watering.

My chest tightens, and Dziecko moves back as if sensing her desperation.

It's not your problem, I chide myself. This girl has nothing to do with you.

She doesn't touch the bowl and just keeps petting Dziecko's fur. The cat lifts his head towards me and yowls.

"Are you hungry?" I ask – and immediately regret it.

She nods.

"I'll check if there's any milk left." I bend my knees and cover my mouth with my hands as she picks up the cat's bowl and drinks the milk.

"It's so delicious," she announces with excitement and licks the bowl until it's clean. Suddenly she tilts her head back and laughs. I lose focus, and my eyes meet her playful, black, doe eyes. Her figure, which was just another blurry blot of color moments ago, is suddenly clearly painted in bright clear lines. I'm accosted by a terrible sensation of fear — an intense fear that someone will hurt this pure little creature.

I lower my eyes and nervously rub the back of my neck. My survival instincts are collapsing, and fear threatens to paralyze me. Two soldiers march past me, and this time I'm unable to ignore their presence. I long to shield this little girl from the horrible reality that surrounds us.

The girl notices the soldiers. She wrinkles her nose in annoyance and says, "Don't be scared of them."

"I'm not scared," I lie.

"I forgot that you're a princess." She giggles. "Princesses aren't afraid of evil soldiers."

Her laugh is the most beautiful sound I've ever heard in my life, and her black doe eyes remind me of the wise eyes of my mother, but instead of Mother's harshness and cynicism, I see her childish innocence.

The girl skips lightly across the road and comes back with an empty oil canister. She sets it down in front of me and sits on it.

"My name is Sarah." She offers me her tiny hand to shake. "What's your name?"

"Ania." I carefully shake her hand.

"Princess Ania..." she murmurs, then rests her elbows on her knees and holds her chin in her hands. "Tell me about your kingdom."

My mouth involuntarily stretches into a smile. "How old are you, Sarah?"

"Seven," she tells me as she sits up straight and proud.

I bite my lip. She looks like she's about five.

"I only look small. I'm actually really strong." She shows me her biceps.

"You look strong," I whisper. "In my kingdom, all the children look small but are actually very strong."

"Why are you whispering?" she asks me, also in a whisper, and tilts her little body forward.

"Because we don't want the bad soldiers to find out about my kingdom," I continue whispering.

"Ohhh..." She nods and stares at me in awe. "If I were a princess like you, I don't think I'd want to be here."

"The king sent me to find out the bad soldiers' plans." I smile slyly. "Soon, his mighty army will come and drive them away from here."

"Really?"

"Really." I nod and keep whispering, "My kingdom is high up on a mountain, far away from here." I point toward the horizon. "The sun shines there all year round. It has giant lawns, parks, and..."

"And are we allowed to go into the parks?"

"Of course." I feign surprise at her question. "Everyone is allowed to play in the parks, and visit all the stores, and eat in all the restaurants."

She continues to stare at me, open-mouthed.

"And at these restaurants, you don't have to pay." I wink at her. "Anyone can come in and order whatever they want."

Sarah licks her lips.

"A waiter in a tie will serve you a meal on a porcelain plate. He'll set it on a table covered with a white tablecloth and there will be a vase of beautiful flowers in the center." I drum on my lips with my finger. "Oh... And it's important that you know that the flowers are picked fresh every morning in the royal gardens."

"And... And what do you have to eat at this restaurant?" Sarah scratches her head.

I lick my lips hungrily and elaborate, "Kotlet schabowy, żurek, pierogi, golonka, kaszanka..."

"Milk and meat together?" She gasps.

"In my kingdom, there are no rules." I shrug. "Everyone is free to choose whatever they want to eat."

She sighs. "I wish I could visit your kingdom."

"Of course you can! You'll be my guest of honor." I lift my hand and gently wipe the milk off her upper lip with my thumb. She trembles as though she hasn't been touched in a long time. "You have to go home now." I gather Dziecko up into my arms. "The curfew is about to start, and your parents must be worried about you."

"I live with my grandfather," she says as she stands up and caresses the fur of my coat. "Mother went to heaven when I was born. Grandpa says she was so joyful that I came that she wanted to watch over me from above." Sarah points to the sky.

I swallow the lump building up in my throat.

"And Father went to the war and hasn't come back since. Because of them." She moves her hand to point at the Germans, and I instinctively slap her finger. She quickly buries her hands inside her shabby coat. "Grandpa says that the soldiers who won took the soldiers who lost and that they'll guard them until they get tired and decide to let them go. I wanted to ask the soldiers when they'll get tired of guarding Father, but Grandpa won't let me."

"No, no," I whisper apprehensively. "If you want to visit my kingdom, you must never speak to them."

"But Grandpa looks so sad." She scrunches her nose. "Maybe if he knew when Father was coming back..."

"Sarah," I whisper her name sternly. "Promise me that you will never speak to a German soldier."

She chews the inside of her cheek and doesn't answer.

"Sarah, did you know that you must always obey a princess's request?"

She nods in assent.

"I promise you that when the soldiers from my kingdom arrive, I'll send them to free your father."

Her eyes light up with joy, and she shakes my hand, binding our promises.

"Princess Ania, do you think I can come back to play with your cat tomorrow?"

Logic tells me to refuse her and forget our encounter, but my defenses have collapsed, and I nod. "You can come to play with him whenever you want."

She claps her hands in delight and then turns and scoots away. Within two seconds, I can't see her. She disappears between the blots of color that have instantly turned into living, breathing people. My fear grows. It burns my insides. A terrible fear that something bad will happen to her.

I rub the back of my neck and stare at the back of the man in the blue uniform. Suddenly, as if sensing my distress, he turns, piercing me with a fiery stare. His fingers drum in a constant rhythm on his gun, and I twist a curl around my finger and close my eyes.

The shadow looming over me is not Anton's shadow, and I open my eyes.

"Mr. Stern." I blink in confusion.

"Please, call me Bruno." He smiles at me.

"How can I help you?" I ask politely and don't look away. My concern for the little girl won't go away.

"I would love it if you would agree to come for a short stroll with me." He looks down and takes a step back.

"A stroll?" I ask in astonishment, and I answer, "I'm afraid I'll have to decline. I don't like walking around the ghetto."

"Then we can stay only on this street." He adjusts his hat. "The German patrol has moved on to the next street."

I lean forward and look to the left and then to the right. There's no trace of the soldiers.

"Umm... I'm not sure I'm interested in a walk." I sneak a peek at the blue-uniformed back.

"Then I'll come back tomorrow with the same proposal." He gives me a small smile.

"No." I stand, reminding myself of Ida's words on the first night he came to visit us. In recent months, he's become a comfort in the dark scene around me, and I don't want to lead him on. I continue to keep a polite distance from him. "Mr. Stern, I will join you now, but it will be just this once."

"Bruno." He again insists that I call him by his first name and steps down into the road so I can walk next to him on the sidewalk. He puts his hands in his pockets and keeps a safe distance from me.

"How are you getting along?" he asks casually.

"I suppose much better than other residents of the ghetto." I turn around to ensure Dziecko is following behind us and step down into the road. It's impossible to walk on the sidewalk without hopping over the countless weary, malnourished bodies sitting on it. Men, women, and children waiting for someone to notice their plight. But no one ever notices.

"Here the situation is less serious," he sighs, "But the big ghetto is unbearably overcrowded. I pity the many families living in demolished buildings or under the open sky. The meager provisions that we get from the Germans aren't enough for anything, and people are simply dying of hunger."

"And what does your father, the Great Rabbi, have to say about all this?" I ask irately. "Does he believe that people can survive here simply by having faith in your god?"

"It's nice to learn that in all these months you've been ignoring me, you've been inquiring about me, too." He sneaks a smile at me.

"I didn't inquire about anything," I reply in alarm. "Ida told me."

"You ignited hope in me for a moment there," he says as he keeps smiling.

"You're avoiding my question." I bend down and pick up Dziecko.

"You asked a tough question." He stops at the sight of two boys running past us. An old woman chases after them in tears.

"Help me," the woman shrieks. "They stole my bottle of milk."

We turn around, but there's no trace of the boys.

The woman falls to her knees and cries out, "My grandson needs that milk."

Bruno looks at her, powerless.

I approach him and whisper in his ear, "I can check if I have any milk left in my apartment."

"No." He squeezes my arm and drops it immediately as if cautioning me not to speak. He bends over toward the woman and helps her to her feet. "Go to the public kitchen and say that Bruno Stern sent you. They won't give you milk, but if you get there before curfew, you'll receive hot soup."

Nodding eagerly, the woman breaks into a run.

"Why didn't you let me bring her milk?" I ask him angrily.

"Can you bring her milk tomorrow and the next day as well?" He wipes his brow. "And what will you do when she tells her sister or her neighbor about your good deed and an endless procession of starving people flock to your apartment, begging for your assistance?"

I purse my lips and refrain from answering him.

"I'm not saying we should turn our backs on the dire hardships surrounding us." He looks at me, his eyes pained. "There are quite a few organizations in the ghetto trying to help, but it seems they are only helping us to die more slowly."

"Why don't the leaders of your community raise an outcry?" I sneak a look at the peddler, who's waving his shoelaces. "Why don't they demand better conditions?"

"I'm not a big supporter of the Judenrat, but I have a hard time judging their conduct." Bruno bows his head at a bearded man. "They're trying to create a routine. They've established schools and hospitals, and they even make sure to hold cultural events. But it distorts the realities of the situation and, unfortunately, the moment will come when they realize that the Nazis are misleading them. They are powerless. All they're doing is postponing the end. Every time trucks come to kidnap more Jews and take them to the labor camps, the Judenrat raises money to bribe them. How long will they be able to continue raising the outrageous amounts that the SS command demands?" He doesn't wait for my answer. "Hunger, poverty, and disease will make it so that they don't have anyone left to care for."

I pet Dziecko's fur and keep walking onward. "You see this terrible situation, and you still believe in your god?"

"Yes," replies Bruno without hesitation. "I strongly believe that my people will survive despite these decrees."

"But they aren't surviving." I point to a woman sitting with her legs spread out on the sidewalk, hugging her son. Her expression is grim, and she doesn't even lift her hand to ask for a donation. The child's head is close to her chest, and he's not moving. I feel goosebumps popping up on my arms.

"Since the dawn of the history of the Jewish people, we've had to cope with disasters coming down on us," he replies calmly. "If they haven't succeeded in destroying us until now, they won't succeed this time either."

"Why doesn't your god protect you?" I turn around when we reach the end of the street, and Bruno turns in my wake. "Why doesn't he do anything to save you?"

"The Rebbe says it's a test of faith," Bruno says thoughtfully. "We Hasidim need to pray harder for salvation."

"This conversation is annoying me." I quicken my pace. "And now I'm sorry I didn't give that poor woman some milk."

"This conversation is annoying me, too." Bruno narrows the distance between us. "I would much rather use our stroll to get to know you better."

"There's nothing to get to know," I grumble. "You hold an irrational belief, and I hold another, more practical one. If I had given her some milk, I wouldn't feel guilty now."

"That's not exactly true," he insists. "May I share a short story with you?" He stops walking, and despite my anger, I decide to behave politely and stop, too. "Imagine a situation in which the two of us have been walking for a long time, and you have a glass of water in your hand. If you share it with me, we'll both die. If only you drink from it, you'll be able to reach the village."

"Which village?" I ask as I furrow my brow.

"A safe village." He smiles. "A village where your family is waiting for you."

"America..." I murmur with longing. "It's indeed a long way away. Why wouldn't you also bring a glass of water with you?" I glower in annoyance.

"This is the situation," Bruno shrugs. "What would you choose to do?"

"Share it with you, of course," I answer, rolling my eyes.

"And so readily sentence us both to death?"

"That's a trick question," I complain. "If I were walking with an SS soldier, I would drink all the water and pour whatever remained on the ground to watch him die of thirst right in front of me."

Bruno laughs and shakes his head. "But that's not the dilemma I presented to you."

"Do you expect me to say I'll drink the water and let you die? Is that the correct answer?"

"I don't think there is a right answer." He sighs. "This is the very dilemma that my father's wisest scholars have been discussing since the minute we were imprisoned in this ghetto. The Talmud offers the opinions of two geniuses. One of them insists that we must share the water, and the other reasons that our lives come before the lives of our friends."

"I vote for the first one." Dziecko squirms, and I put him down on the cobblestones. "The second seems to be too selfish to me."

"I think you're the first person I've ever met who dares to call Rabbi Akiva "selfish." Bruno laughs again.

"I don't know this rabbi, but I don't think I would like him."

"I somehow have the feeling that he would have liked you." Bruno studies my face for a few seconds and then looks down in embarrassment. "He would find that even though you solemnly swear that you don't believe in our God, your heart and soul are enveloped in His love."

"Okay, you've convinced me." I defiantly stick out my chin. "I won't give you even one drop of water." I start walking again.

"I won't hold it against you. I promise." Bruno grins, putting his hand on his heart. "But I would love it if you would allow me to come back and accompany you on another stroll."

"I cannot allow it. Look at you, and look at me." I tighten the belt of my coat. "You are so Jewish, and I... I am but a visitor in your world."

"I would be delighted for you to continue visiting my world."

Dziecko walks past us and sniffs the filth strewn all over the road. I look behind me, and for a moment I'm afraid that Ida will see us. "Bruno, did I do something to make you think I want you to court me?"

He offers me a smile, but I can feel his discomfort. "God forbid. I just want to get to know you better."

"I already told you: There's nothing to get to know." I wave my hand in dismissal. "The worlds we come from are just too different."

"Then let me be a visitor in your world."

I shake my head.

"Are you being courted by another man?" he asks cautiously.

I inadvertently turn my head to the side and search the street for the blue uniform. Anton is leaning against the wall of my building and giving me a stern look. I quickly bow my head, "No. I'm not being courted by anyone." My own answer pains me. "I'm not interested in suitors, and my answer is final." I pick Dziecko up and run inside my building without looking at Anton again. The knowledge that the only man I've ever wanted belongs to my sister is unbearable.

CHAPTER 2

I position my chair against the building's wall and already hear the sound of the large oil canister being dragged over to me. Sarah sits in front of me, her eyes shining.

I want to tell her that I've changed my mind, that the open invitation she received from me is canceled. Her black doe eyes haunted me in my sleep, and I awoke drenched in sweat from a horrible nightmare. I tried to protect her from the forces of evil but failed miserably. The fear that has accompanied me from the first second I looked into her eyes threatens to paralyze me, and I feel utterly defenseless.

"Sarah…" I whisper.

She doesn't notice my distress and whistles sharply. A fair-haired girl runs across the road with another oil canister in her arms. She puts it down next to Sarah's and sits in front of me, beaming.

"Bella, I told you my princess was real." Sarah leans forward and tugs at the hem of my dress. She shows her friend the hand-embroidered floral patterns, and they both linger, examining them. "Tell her," Sarah implores. "Tell her about our kingdom."

I clap my hands and sigh. Bella has clear blue eyes, and her smile conveys curiosity. The girl looks like an angel, despite her yellowish skin tone and oversized coat. The look in her eyes pierces my heart. Now I can't help but feel apprehensive about her fate, too.

"Maybe..." I whisper and glance to either side, "Maybe before I describe the kingdom to Bella, I can offer you two something to eat?"

Their little jaws drop in amazement.

"Sarah, did you tell this princess that we have no money to give her?" Bella elbows Sarah.

"There's no need to give me money," I reassure her. "I was sent a special basket from the kingdom." I make sure no one is looking at us and then I pour milk into Dziecko's bowl and pass the bottle to them.

"Real milk!" Bella licks her lips and looks around anxiously.

"Drink it already," Sarah urges her.

Without uttering a word, they take turns sipping the milk and don't waste a single drop.

I unfold the paper package on my lap and reveal a few cubes of cheese and three little round buns. I didn't take into account that Sarah would arrive with a guest, and suddenly the assortment I brought looks too meager.

"Is all of that for just us?" Sarah salivates.

I smile and nod.

They both peek apprehensively right and left before lunging at my knees. Each of them grabs a bun and a few cubes of the cheese. They chew quickly, cramming more and more cheese into their mouths, but instead of looking happy, they look frightened, as if someone might come at any moment to steal their treasure.

I stare at them in shock, and when I realize how hungry they truly are, my shock turns to shame.

The food runs out, and their panic dissipates. They clap their hands soundlessly and hug each other.

"Do you want to share the last bun?" I break it in half.

Bella gobbles down her half, and Sarah buries the remainder in her coat pocket. "I'll save mine for Grandpa," she says with pride.

"Now tell her!" Sarah rests her elbows on her knees and cups her chin in her hands. "Tell Bella about your magical kingdom."

I pick up the cat, put him on my lap and, stroking his fur, let my imagination drift far away to a distant and magical kingdom. I whisper a story to them about a kingdom where two virtuous princesses live safe and protected, and are never, ever hungry.

* * *

Peter and Ida are sitting on the sofa, and I'm sitting on a chair across from them. Dinner is on the coffee table between us, and we're eating together. They are holding a hushed conversation, but I'm lost in thought. I cannot dispel the image of the girls wolfing down the little amount of food I brought them. So far I haven't gone hungry, but I didn't think of myself as lucky. Are they forced to beg for their food while I sit here and eat the abundance in front of me? Do they risk stealing from others?

"Ania." Peter waves his fork in my face.

"What?" I blink in confusion.

"Didn't you hear my question?"

"Ask it again, please."

"I asked how you spent your day today." he says with a smile. "Did Mr. Bruno Stern come to see you?"

I stick my fork into the bigos stew, a dish of cabbage and sausages. "Don't you have anything more interesting than my social life to talk about?"

"To tell you the truth – no." Peter twirls the tips of his mustache and grins. "It's getting harder and harder to smuggle goods into the ghetto, and my stall looks pretty pathetic." He pokes his fork into the last piece of sausage on his plate and sighs. "Even the rice is about to run out. If I have nothing left to sell, we'll have to survive solely on the supplies Anton brings us."

"I'm sure we'll manage." Ida scrapes the little cabbage she has left onto his plate. "I get a modest lunch at school."

Their discussion brings the picture of the two starving girls into my mind, and I'm suddenly overwhelmed by uncontrollable anger.

"Shame on you," I admonish them. "Haven't you seen what's going on out there?" I point to the window. "People fall in the street like the autumn leaves fall from the trees – sick, starving, begging for a bit of food – while we sit here enjoying this abundance." I grab the leftovers from Peter's plate and wrap them in a napkin.

I look up and am met with two shocked stares.

"This place will make me lose my mind," I complain. "I can't disconnect myself emotionally. I swear on my life that I tried."

Ida pulls a cigarette out of Peter's pack and lights it. Her expression is sad. "Ania, do you want to share with us what you went through today?"

"No." I stand up and take the leftovers to the kitchen. I put them in the oven and return to the room. "I think I've had enough of this ghetto. When can we leave?"

Peter lights a cigarette and then stands up and opens the closet. He takes out a fur scarf and wraps it around his neck. "You are right, Miss Orzeszkowa," he announces resolutely. "I believe it is time to leave, but we must dress to the nines, so that we can demand that they open the gates for us." He puts one of my most flamboyant hats on his head and spins around on his toes. "Come on, my lovely ladies. Look at yourselves. You look like miserable riffraff in your nightgowns." He points at us with his cigarette. "I demand that you wear your most beautiful gowns. I have an honorable reputation to maintain in this city."

He looks so ridiculous that Ida and I burst out laughing and rush over to the closet.

We hear the sound of brakes squealing on the street and all three of us freeze. Peter throws his hat and scarf back into the closet, and we approach the window tentatively.

German soldiers jump out of the back of the truck and run into our building. Three seconds later, we hear heavy footsteps in the stairwell. I tighten the belt of my robe and stare at the door. Ida clutches one of my hands, and Peter holds the other.

We can hear doors being kicked in. And screams. And pleading and crying. The terrible commotion is right outside our door.

The image of the two little girls plays in my mind, and fear grips me, paralyzing my limbs. I'm not afraid for myself. I'm anxious about the fate of those I hold dear.

Our door bursts open, and Peter pulls us up against the wall.

The cat dashes to the corner of the room and curls up into a motionless ball of fur. We silently watch the soldiers charge in. They rip the closet doors from their hinges, and three soldiers thoroughly feel the material of each of my dresses. My breath catches in my throat as they rip the sleeves off the coats. Ida squeezes my hand tightly, and my heart pounds even harder. They didn't discover my earrings.

The soldiers bark at us in German, but none of us dares open our mouth. We stand pressed up against each other with our heads bowed. They move on to wreak havoc in the kitchen, and the floor shakes as another man enters the apartment.

Out of the corner of my eye, I notice a blue uniform. My arms tremble, betraying the shock I feel.

"If you have any valuable property here, you better tell me right now." Anton's deep voice sounds tormented.

A German soldier peeks in from the kitchen, and Anton swings his club, hitting the broken wardrobe. The soldier goes back to the kitchen, and Anton tilts his head to the side as if imploring us to answer.

I look down, take a deep breath, and suddenly remember: Father's pistol!

I look up sharply, gesture with my head toward the bathroom, and open my eyes wide.

Anton doesn't need another signal; he rushes through the black door, and I hear the sound of the bathroom furnishings being smashed. The soldiers come out of the kitchen and stand in front of us.

"Jewelry," one of them barks into Peter's face.

Peter shakes his head no, and his head snaps backward from a hard slap.

Ida lets out an alarmed cry, and I close my eyes and pray that Anton finds the pistol I hid behind the toilet.

The bathroom door slams, and I open my eyes and stare at Anton. He is busy buckling the belt of his coat and doesn't look at me but nods his head once in confirmation.

I swallow my sigh of relief as a slap shakes Ida's cheek.

Tears flood my eyes, and I try to prepare myself emotionally for the blow that will surely land on me next.

"Look how they tremble with fear," Anton sneers and comes over to us. "They've probably peed themselves already."

The soldiers snicker, and Anton walks around them and stops in front of me. "These vermin would have snitched on each other already if they had anything valuable here." He pushes me backward and turns toward the soldiers. "We should continue the search so you can return to headquarters with something that will please your commander."

"Heil Hitler!" they shout as they salute, and they leave the apartment.

Anton trails after them, staring at his feet.

We continue holding hands and panting heavily until Peter comes to his senses and runs to close the door. He jiggles the handle for a few minutes before finally giving up and putting the suitcases against the door. He turns toward us and buries his head in his hands.

"In what world do men beat up women and no one raises their voice in protest?" He walks over to Ida and hugs her.

She rubs her cheek and bursts into tears.

I start to assess the damage. The kitchen cabinets are broken, the dishes are shattered, and the rice is scattered all over the counter. I open the oven and sigh with relief when I see the leftovers sitting inside unharmed.

I return to the room with my back straight and head held high. I approach the closet and hang up the dresses one by one.

"I'm afraid she's in shock," Ida whispers.

"I'm not in shock!" I hiss angrily through clenched teeth. "I'm angry. I'm angry at your god for not listening to your prayers." I walk over to her and carefully caress her cheek. "I see you lighting candles every week and hear you praying to him every night, in tears, begging him to save us. Why doesn't he listen to you?"

"He will listen." She avoids looking at me. "He has to listen. Because if I lose my faith, what will I have left?"

I go to the closet and pick up the black coat with the sleeves ripped off. I push my fingers into the wool lining and feel around for the hidden earrings. Without saying a word, I grab my sewing box and sit on the sofa.

"Anton pushed me," I whisper, and my voice is drowned out by the sounds of the commotion taking place upstairs.

"If he hadn't, they would have continued hitting us." Peter sits down beside me.

"He wouldn't have pushed Michalina." I poke the needle into the material and bite my lip. "He would rip his own hand off before hurting her."

"I think he ripped his own heart out when he realized he couldn't protect you."

I quickly wipe away a wayward tear, and Ida, too, sits beside me.

"Leib begged him to join the Resistance in the woods." She positions her hand on mine in a silent appeal. "That was their plan from the minute the Germans broke through Warsaw's defense line."

I purse my lips.

"I think Anton also hoped, as you did, that the Germans would pass over the assimilated Jews." She glances up at the ceiling. The awful screams make her eyes tear up. "He decided to put on the blue uniform and go through the humiliating ceremony of ripping off our nation's flag when he realized that his hope had been in vain."

"I'm sure he hates being here just as much as we do." Peter picks up the two halves of the broken ashtray.

"Anton is in close contact with the Resistance," Ida whispers. "He can take off his uniform and join them whenever he sees fit."

The thought of his going away and leaving me here alarms me, and I cover my mouth with my hand. I won't be able to breathe without him. I feel an intense, searing pain in the pit of my stomach, and I grab the triangular pendant hanging around my neck – the half that completes our star. "He promised her he'd take care of me," I declare firmly to remind myself. "The day my sister returns, he will remember why his heart belongs to my better half."

Peter and Ida exchange a pained look and don't say a word.

CHAPTER 3

I sit on a chair up against the wall of my building and look helplessly at the two beautiful girls who came to visit me, accompanied by three little boys. Their thin sidelocks are tucked behind their ears, and dark circles surround their eyes. The little coats they're wearing reveal skeletal arms and fragile hands. Five exhausted little children sit in front of me on empty oil canisters and look at me, beaming.

"Sarah," I whisper, "if you keep telling people about my kingdom, the bad soldiers might find out I'm a princess."

"I promise I only told them." She puts her hand to her heart. "Misza," she says, pointing to the smallest boy, whose blond hair cascades down onto his forehead, "was sad because yesterday his father was taken to work outside the ghetto. I wanted him to know that the brave soldiers from your kingdom will bring him back to us very soon."

Misza stares at me with wide eyes, and I secure my hat pins and feel myself sweating in discomfort. My desire to reassure him triumphs over my voice of reason.

"Of course they'll bring back Misza's father, too," I whisper and wink at him.

Misza hops onto his short legs and surprises me with a tight hug. The children laugh and clap their hands.

"Shhh..." I press my finger to my lips. "Don't be so noisy. The Germans already suspect there's a princess in their territory."

All five of them immediately cover their mouths with their hands.

"I didn't know you were bringing friends." I smile apologetically and lean down to pet the cat. "I'm afraid I didn't bring enough food for everyone."

"We'll share." Sarah's head bobs up and down energetically. "We don't need much."

I glance around to ensure we're not attracting too much attention and pull the napkin off the plate.

The children emit sounds of wonder.

"You see? I told you I found the best princess." Sarah sticks out her chin.

I pass her the plate with the leftover bigos, a few pieces of sausage, and four buns.

She divides everything equally into six modest piles. "I'm the one who found the princess, so my grandfather gets a share." She wrinkles her nose in an attempt to look angry.

They nod in agreement and storm the plate. Each of them eats only their own portion. They huddle close together. No one can see their humble feast, and yet the children throw terrified looks in every direction.

"Don't you go to school?" I try to initiate a conversation because the children are chewing so fast that I'm afraid one of them will choke.

"We go," Bella replies with her mouth full. "My mother says the brain is our most important organ."

"And you don't get lunch there?"

"We do," Misza answers in a babyish voice. "But, almost every day, big kids come" – he lifts his hand to exemplify their height – "and steal our food."

I tear up.

"Don't the teachers see them doing it?" I whisper in shock. "Don't they help you?"

"We can't snitch." Sarah shrugs. "Once Avrum told a teacher, and then the big kids caught him and beat him up really, really bad. He doesn't come to school anymore."

I groan under my breath and secure the pins in my hat.

"Tell them, Princess Ania." Sarah giggles as if she hasn't just told me a horrifying story. "Tell Misza, Oleg, and Gershon about your kingdom, too."

Oleg and Gershon still haven't said a word. They just sit, staring at me quietly. Their hair is as black as their eyes, and they have tired, haunted expressions on their faces, like old men acquainted with worldly atrocities.

I find it hard to overcome the rage that arose in me following Sarah's story, but when I see their small, innocent eyes staring up at me, I realize that they don't need my anger; instead they need to escape from this damned ghetto – even if only for a few minutes.

I lean forward, stretch my lips in a sneaky smile, and quietly describe the splendors of my imaginary kingdom.

"The Child Whisperer."

I sit up straight in apprehension, startled by an amused, masculine voice.

Bruno is standing over us in his black suit; he has one hand in his pocket, and he fleetingly pats Misza's head with the other. The youngsters exchange shifty looks.

"Tell me what Miss Orzeszkowa whispered to you," he addresses them with a charming smile.

Bella scowls in annoyance. "Not Miss. Prince..."

Sarah elbows her, and Bella stops talking and flushes red.

"Now I *really* want to know." He laughs, and I pick up Dziecko, put him on my lap, and relax in my chair. I don't know why, but Bruno's presence puts me at ease.

"Come on..." He fakes an angry expression. "Whoever reveals the maiden's secrets to me will get a piece of candy," he says and pulls out a chunk of hard caramel from his pocket.

The children's jaws drop, and they gawk at the candy in wonderment.

I pet the cat and wait to see who'll break first.

Sarah is the first to lower her eyes, and everyone else follows suit except Misza. He licks his lips and stands up.

"Misza," Sarah scolds him without looking up.

Bruno kneels and waves a candy in front of Misza's face. "First, tell me." He cups his ear.

"Never!" Misza kicks Bruno in the knee, grabs the candy, and runs away.

The other children burst into laughter and run after him.

I cover my mouth with my hands, trying to stifle my own laughter.

"Miss Orzeszkowa." Bruno rubs his knee and chuckles. "It seems that you've recruited a particularly fierce army for yourself."

Loud screaming interrupts his laughter, and we both look over at a woman being dragged down the street by a Jewish policeman. The Jew is wearing a brown coat fastened with a thick belt, and a black hat protects his head from the rain that has begun to fall. His yellow armband catches the eye.

"What's he doing?" I ask in alarm when I see that he's dragging her straight toward two German soldiers. "I mean, he's Jewish, too."

"There's trash in every home." Bruno spits onto the sidewalk. "They're our trash."

"The children." I stand up and study the busy street. "Maybe I should have made sure they made it home safely."

The woman's pleading screams grow louder, and I anxiously look left and right. There's no trace of the children.

"Stay calm." Bruno grimaces at the sound of the woman's pleas. "I'll make sure the children get home safely." He spins around and disappears into the crowd.

A muscular figure in a blue uniform stands with his back to me. "Go inside the building," Anton orders quietly.

I grab the cat and peek at the hysterical woman. She's sitting on her knees at the soldier's feet and pressing her palms together as if in prayer. She not screaming anymore; she's mumbling apologies. The Jewish policeman is standing behind her and looking at her scornfully.

"Go inside the building." Anton's whisper sounds like a yell.

I can't take my eyes off her.

"I caught her smuggling goods from outside the walls," the Jewish policeman hollers so that everyone on the street will hear.

"No, no!" the woman wails in Polish. "It was just a loaf of bread for my children."

The Jewish policeman doesn't translate her words, and the German soldier draws his weapon.

I take a step forward. How can it be that no one will translate her explanation?

"Go into the building!" The whisper is accompanied by a strong push, and I wobble on my feet.

One gunshot.

One gunshot paints the woman in black and red, and I cry out soundlessly and run into the building.

* * *

I lie on the mattress, hugging Dziecko and listening to Peter's muffled snoring. Ida rolls from one side to the other, and I understand that she can't fall asleep either.

I want to ask her to join me on the sofa so I can share my terrible fears with her, but the faint sound of her crying indicates that she's decided to spare me her own fears.

The door creaks open, and we both sit up in a panic. Peter sits up a split second after us as if he hadn't been asleep at all.

The door closes, and a match is lit.

The three of us stare in astonishment at a face nearly as frightened as our own.

"Oh my God." Peter leaps from his mattress and runs to Olek. He embraces him, grabs his cheeks, and kisses him over and over again.

The cat runs over and sniffs his shoes, and Ida looks at me in confusion.

"That's Olek," I whisper. "Peter's lover."

Her eyes open wide in surprise.

"What are you doing here?" Peter sneaks a wary glance at the door and then turns around to confirm that the curtains are fully drawn.

"I volunteered to pick up the ghetto's garbage." He tiptoes inside. "I bribed a Polish guard to stay here."

"Forever?" I ask, shocked.

"No, no." Olek chuckles and slips off his shoes. "I only have one hour."

Peter claps his hands noiselessly and then pulls Olek onto the mattress. Only when they lie down beside me, do I see that Peter's eyes are full of tears.

"Don't cry," Olek says tenderly and kisses Peter's eyelids.

"I've missed you so much," Peter sniffles. "Not a second goes by that I don't think about you."

"So, do you want to whine or show me how much you missed me?" Olek kisses Peter's lips.

Ida pulls the blanket over our heads and hugs me. "Let's give them some privacy."

I close my eyes and command myself to stop thinking and just fall asleep. I lie on my belly and quietly listen to the declarations of love they heap on each other. After a few minutes, they fall silent, and the mattress next to mine trembles to the sound of their soft moaning.

I listen to them in silence, and the noises of their love slowly but surely succeed in easing my fears. I try to imagine how I would feel if the man I desire were lying next to me on the mattress and consoling me with declarations of love. I pant quietly and feel my blood warm up as I imagine Anton removing his uniform and groaning hoarsely in my ears. I remember every last detail of how my breasts pressed against his chest, how his fingers fluttered over the nude skin of my thighs above my stockings, and how his eyes blazed with passion. I imagine him bending over me and giving me his electrifying smile. I press my thighs together and shudder as an intense pain pierces my abdomen.

He's not yours, I chastise myself. Even in your thoughts, you betray your sister.

The moans from the other mattress get louder, and I cover my ears. I'm struck with a terrible understanding. I'm paying a hefty price for all the years I demanded to be the center of attention. I'm now being punished for all the times I stole my friends' suitors.

I weep into the mattress.

In depriving others of the opportunity to love and be loved, I condemned myself to the same fate.

CHAPTER 4

The cold makes my teeth chatter. December of 1941 could have been a horrible month if it weren't for the sparks of hope ignited by America's joining the war. Temperatures have dropped below zero, and the Germans have demanded that all the residents of the ghetto part with their fur coats. Now, in addition to starvation, people are dying of cold.

Five gaunt, frozen children sit in front of me. They pass the bowl of porridge from one to the other and giggle with delight. Pedestrians pass by, staring at us blankly. Some look on in despair at the bowl going from hand to hand, and some keep walking, pushing one foot in front of the other.

I look around in trepidation and then lift the napkin from the plate, revealing the daily plunder I saved for them.

They smile with gratitude and excitement, despite the meager pickings.

Our supplies dwindle as the days go by. A basket from Anton still arrives every week, but it's hard to survive on it alone when there are five extra mouths to feed. Peter has abandoned his stall and survives mainly on the scraps that Olek manages to sneak to him. Ida returns to the apartment every evening, weak from hunger, as the situation at the school reflects the difficult situation on the streets. The rations that the Germans provide are not enough for anything. And the overcrowding, hunger, cold, and despair are a fertile breeding ground for deadly illnesses that mercilessly strike men, women, and children. A terrible epidemic is spreading across the ghetto, and every day more and more people collapse in the streets.

I had hoped that the diseases would strike the Germans, too, but they look rosy and alive, as if they're immune to the ailments of the Jews.

I pass the plate to Sarah, and she divides the rice and beans into six equal mounds. She puts her grandfather's portion on the napkin and buries it in her coat pocket. When she nods her head in permission, the children rush at the food but are careful not to drop the plate, and they painstakingly avoid peeking at their friends' shares of food.

I take a deep breath and hug Dziecko. I feel so tired. I thought I could go without my meals today as well, but it seems that my body is beginning to betray me after three consecutive days in which I've sustained myself with just three spoons of rice and a quarter of a glass of milk.

"Grandpa asked to meet you." Sarah tells me as she smiles, revealing significant gaps between her tiny teeth.

"Maybe tomorrow," I respond with my usual answer and close my eyes for a moment.

"The princess looks a little sick." Oleg presses his palm to my forehead. "Can princesses get sick?"

"No, they can't." Gershon tucks his sidelocks behind his ears. "Weren't you listening when she explained that the worst sickness in her kingdom is a stuffy nose?"

"Gershon is right." I try to smile. "Princesses suffer from colds from time to time. There's no reason to worry."

"Don't bother her." Sarah slaps Oleg's hand.

"He's not bothering me." I pull his hand to me and examine it. It's filthy, and there's a ton of dirt under his fingernails. I study the hands of his companions and see that they are all in the same state.

"You must make sure to keep clean," I admonish them in a whisper. "Wash your hands very well, so you don't catch any of the diseases raging in the ghetto."

They bury their hands between their knees in embarrassment.

"Don't your parents make you bathe?"

They look mortified, and I regret scolding them. After all, I know that they have no one to care for them. How dare I rub it in their faces?

"What a confused princess I am." I tap my finger on my temple. "I forgot for a second that I got a telegram from the king. He asked me to take care of you."

"The king?" Bella opens her eyes wider in amazement. "The king of the kingdom knows who we are?"

"Of course," I reply in a firm whisper. "He knows each of your names and is grateful to you for making sure the princess's time here is pleasant."

Their eyes spark with emotion.

"The king told all the citizens of the kingdom about the princess's special children. When you arrive, they'll hold a majestic feast for you."

"Miracles and wonders..." murmurs Misza. "Can you please tell us about your kingdom again?" He spots a grain of rice that fell onto his coat and hurriedly puts it in his mouth.

"Of course," I yawn. How is it possible that my tales don't bore them? Day after day, I repeat the same story. Every now and then, I manage to spice up the plot with new descriptions, yet they still look at me with endless curiosity.

I lean forward and begin to whisper to them about the marvels of my kingdom. When I reach the part where my kingdom's soldiers break into the ghetto with drawn swords, the children clap their hands and laugh enthusiastically.

"Shh..." I hush them, "We mustn't attract attention."

"I promise that this time I won't ask you to tell me what she's whispering to you." I hear Bruno's jesting voice behind me.

I sit up straight and smile at him. But my smile fades when I notice how pale he is.

He puts his hand to his mouth in an attempt to block an aggressive bout of coughing and then takes a handful of candies out of his pants pocket. The children look down, refusing to look at him.

"Hearing the laughter of children in a place where everyone is weeping is almost like hearing the voice of God." He stifles another cough with his sleeve and hands me the candies.

I open my fist, and the candies are quickly snatched up, disappearing into the children's pockets.

"Now hurry home." I wave my hand. "It's late, and soon it will be dark."

I earn a group hug that opens my heart even wider, and a few seconds later, the children are swallowed up in the throngs of people.

"Bruno, you look terrible," I address him, concerned.

"That's no way to let a fellow know that you fancy him." He winks at me and coughs to the side, away from me.

I smile. He hasn't hinted at his intentions toward me since our stroll together, and he always makes sure to address me with the utmost courtesy. Ida did tell me, however, that he continues to refuse any matches proposed to him, but I'm sure I haven't done anything to let him believe that I'm interested in him.

"You look a little pale yourself." He studies my face and then looks away, as if he's committed a sin by looking at me.

"I'm just tired." I yawn into my hand.

"It's tiring to whisper stories to children." He smiles again. "How do you manage to feed so many mouths?" He scratches his beard.

"Are you spying on me?" I stand up, annoyed, and suddenly feel light-headed.

"God forbid." He retreats in alarm. "I just asked a question. It wasn't an accusation."

I lean against the wall of the building and exhale in fatigue.

"I understand." He sighs. "You deprive yourself of food to feed them."

"It's none of your business," I blurt out too loudly, but the people passing by don't even stop to glance at us.

Out of the corner of my eye, I notice a blue uniform approaching us. My behavior has made Anton presume that I'm in trouble.

"Forgive me." I put my hands on my heart. "I'm treating you terribly for no reason."

Bruno looks at me the way only one man has looked at me in my entire life. That one man is now standing with his back to us, but I'm sure he's listening to our conversation.

"And to think that Mother and Father allege that you're not worthy." Bruno continues staring at me intently. "Ania, if you would only show me a sign that you'll let me court you, believe me when I say I would prove them wrong."

"I really *am* unworthy," I whisper, hoping that Anton won't hear. "Trust me, an observant Jew like you would never want a nonbeliever like me. I have no religion and no faith."

"Faith isn't measured by the number of prayers you pray." He tilts his head to the side, barely stifling another cough. "Faith is measured by actions, and somehow every time I encounter you, I discover that your faith is even stronger than mine." He approaches me hesitantly. "Please, Ania. Please give me a sign."

I press my lips together tightly and shake my head.

The brawny, proud, smiling man in front of me bows his head in defeat.

"Bruno, believe me, you don't actually want to woo someone like me," I try to console him. "If you knew me, you would despise me. If they had not forced me into the ghetto with you, I would most likely be sitting in my mother's boutique at this very moment, not batting an eyelash at the reprehensible incidents taking place here."

"But you *are* here," he tells me, looking up and giving me a sad smile. "While I sit with my father's Bible scholars to study Torah, you're out here fulfilling its commandments." He puts his hand on his heart and briskly walks away from me.

I land on my chair, depleted, and bury my face in my hands. My conscience torments me because I've just hurt someone important to me.

I hear the rustle of a uniform. Anton stands with his back to me and doesn't say a word.

"I didn't go back to old habits," I whisper, my voice trembling as I look at his broad back. "I swear I didn't do anything to encourage him to pursue me."

"You don't look good," he whispers without turning to face me.

"I'm tired."

"You're exhausted because you haven't been eating." His voice is stern. "I bring you a basket of groceries every week, and you distribute it to others."

"And what do you suggest I do?" I let the tears flow down my cheeks. "Should I leave those children to starve?"

Anton lights a cigarette and blows the smoke away from me. "Who would have thought that this abominable place would be where you finally opened your eyes?"

"I would be happy to close them again." I lean my head back against the wall. "But I suppose that being here is my punishment for being so selfish in my former life."

"You have to eat." Anton takes a few steps over, hiding me from the street. "I'll try to get more groceries."

"I would be grateful if you could." I yawn. "I could give the children more. I could..."

"I expect you to eat, too," he whispers angrily. "I understand that you've formed a special bond with these children, and I understand that you feel the need to take care of them, but I don't understand how you think you can continue to do so if your body collapses from starvation."

His words sound reasonable, but I don't know if I can promise him such a thing. The children are so small and fragile, and it seems that other than me, there is no one to take care of them.

"Anton," I whisper, and his torso stiffens. "Thank you for taking care of me. I don't know what I would do without you."

His fingers coil around the butt of his gun, and I pick Dziecko up and drag myself into the building.

* * *

Peter and Ida divide the stew she made for dinner among us. It's a kind of mix of rice, lentils, and milk and has the texture of a thick porridge.

They sit on the sofa holding their plates and devour it like starving animals.

"Ania, why aren't you eating?" Ida glances at my plate. "I don't remember when I last saw you put something into your mouth."

"I'm not hungry," I lie and take a sip from my glass of water.

"I'll eat it." Peter reaches for my plate.

"Don't you dare touch it." I slap his palm and open my eyes menacingly.

He lifts his hands in surrender and goes back to devouring his own gruel.

I take my plate to the kitchen and put it in the oven. When I come back to the room, I collapse onto the mattress, exhausted.

"You're saving it for your children..." Ida states questioningly. She puts her spoon down on her plate and pushes it toward the middle of the table.

I see that she hasn't finished her porridge and bow my head in thanks.

"What am I missing here?" Peter frowns. "What children does Ania have?"

"Leave some food on your plate," Ida scolds him and gestures at me with her head.

With noticeable reluctance, Peter puts his spoon down on his plate and pushes it toward Ida's plate. "I still don't understand what you two are talking about."

"Haven't you heard that Ania's nickname on the street is 'The Child Whisperer?'" Ida giggles and looks at me with pride. "She's assembled a small army of kids who worship her."

"Ania? Children?" Peter rolls his eyes. "There must be some mistake. Children are noisy little people who constantly run around unproductively. It doesn't correspond with the isolation Ania has imposed upon herself."

"The children in the ghetto aren't loud. Too few attend the schools. How can they learn anything when hunger dulls their senses?" Ida sighs. "They don't run around and make noise, and they don't laugh either. The Nazis have turned our children into old, miserable souls."

"The children of my kingdom are different." I yawn and close my eyes. "They're kind-hearted, brave, and know how to show their gratitude." My body slides down, reclining, and I fall into a troubled sleep accompanied by vivid nightmares.

CHAPTER 5

I hear myself whispering the story of the magical kingdom and I stare into the shining eyes of my children. They finished wolfing down the scant amount of food I gave them and are now listening to me with undivided attention. I'm trying to take pleasure in the happiness I bring them, but I'm unbearably fatigued and the cold penetrates my bones.

I feel Oleg's hand stroking my head and hear Gershon's words of gratitude. Bella and Misza hug me, and the children disappear between the blurry colors of the crowd.

Sarah stands alone in front of me, and I blink laboriously.

"Princess Ania." She holds my hand. "Today you must come with me to visit Grandfather."

"Maybe tomorrow," I whisper, like always.

"Today," she insists and pulls my hand. "Please don't disappoint him. He's expecting you."

I look into her beautiful doe-eyed stare and can't find the strength to resist her. I stand up with strenuous effort, and she clutches my hand and drags me along behind her. If she lets go of my hand, I'll fall to my knees and land flat on my face. The thought of Sarah being forced to see such a spectacle alarms me, and I steal a breath and try to focus my eyes. The pictures of poverty, desperation, and filth are not foreign to me. The streets are overflowing with garbage. People try to keep warm, standing around garbage cans utilized as makeshift bonfires. Children lie on filthy blankets, and one mother implores her daughter to bite into a moldy vegetable. Staggering, the girl looks at her mother with hollow eyes and refuses. My heart breaks, and I quickly look down. As we get farther away from home, I realize that the situation in the ghetto has deteriorated dramatically since my short stroll with Bruno.

I squeeze Sarah's hand in horror.

She continues to lead us through the labyrinth of alleys. I look around at the unfamiliar streets. I've never been here. Crowds of peddlers stand, trying to sell worthless items, their goods set in front of them on the wide road. I feel dizzy and blink in distress. A man asks if we would like to purchase chair legs to burn, and a girl begs us to pay her for a pair of tattered shoes. I look at her feet: she's barefoot. A shiver runs down my arms when I realize that there isn't a single stall selling food in this market, only people offering the meager possessions they have left, so that they won't starve to death.

Sarah urges me to walk faster until we reach a flight of stairs leading to a high, narrow bridge. I lean on the railing, huffing and puffing with every step. Bodies crash into me, and I bend down and pick up Dziecko. I'd heard that they'd built a bridge to connect the "Small Ghetto" to the "Large Ghetto," but I hadn't walked this far from home before, and I never dared cross the bridge into the "Large Ghetto." Peter told us that the situation there was much worse.

We hear malicious laughter coming from the other side of the bridge, and I notice a group of German soldiers bullying those who dare to cross it. They throw the hat of one of the men over the bridge, and another man tries to escape the blow of a club. It's excruciating to think that Sarah crosses this bridge of horrors every day.

Walking down the stairs should be easier, but my knees shake. I stagger with every step and the cat is so heavy in my arms. I get dizzier and dizzier, trying to regulate my breathing, but to no avail. Suddenly Sarah pulls my arm and drags me into an alleyway. I gasp, hearing loud footsteps behind me.

"Don't worry, Princess Ania," Sarah whispers and squeezes my hand. "It's a soldier from your kingdom."

I can't find the strength to turn my head and check who it is.

"He's here because of you." She giggles, pulling me down another alley.

The sound of the steps is loud and clear.

"I know he disguises himself, so they won't find out he's guarding you." She turns her head to smile at the guard that she is clearly imagining. "The blue uniform is a good costume."

I halt, realizing who's following us.

"I won't tell anyone." Sarah smiles at me sneakily. "I know how to keep a secret." She pulls my hand and prompts me to keep walking.

I don't know how many alleys we've gone through, but it's clear to me that Peter wasn't lying. Crumbling, bombed-out buildings accompany us along the entire walk. So many people pass by us, bumping into us with hunched-over backs and tired eyes. Dead bodies lie in the streets, and their stench goes up into my nostrils. A loud clicking of boot heels heralds the arrival of a German patrol, and three Jewish policemen burst into a run, chasing a boy hugging a loaf of bread to his body.

When Sarah finally stops in front of a run-down building, I put the cat on the ground, and lean on the doorframe, panting as if I've just run a marathon.

"Grandpa will be so excited to meet you." Sarah runs to the stairs, and I stare at her, exhausted. I want to tell her I'm too tired and that he should probably come downstairs and meet me here, but she gestures with her hands enthusiastically, and I groan softly and lumber up after her.

I turn my head to the street and blink at the sight of Anton standing there in his blue uniform.

Supporting myself with the railing, I climb up to the top floor step by step. Sarah stands by the door, impatiently shifting her weight from foot to foot. She opens the door without knocking and pulls me inside.

The small apartment is clean and tidy, but the cold wind that blows through it is even worse than the cold outside. Dziecko stretches his hind legs and then curls up in the corner of the room as if he owns the place.

"Grandpa," Sarah shouts and runs over to a man sitting on a chair and looking out the window. On his head is a black hat.

"Sarah," he says her name with his voice full of love and pulls her up to sit on his knees. "You're home early today. Did something happen?"

"No, Grandpa." She tugs on his beard and laughs. "I brought a very important guest."

The terrible vertigo I feel is unrelenting, and I stand up straight in an attempt to look respectable. I expect him to stand up to greet me, but instead, the man takes Sarah off his lap and continues to sit. My face falls when I see that he is sitting in a wheelchair.

"Princess Ania." His black eyes flash with excitement. "I've waited so long to meet you so that I can thank you."

The tailored jacket he's wearing looks too big for him, his skin tone is yellowish, and his beard is sparse. I regret not bringing some food for him.

"Sit down, please." He points to the lone chair next to the table and wheels himself to sit across from me. I quickly survey the room. There are two mattresses, a small closet, and a wooden bookcase full of books.

"Our treasures." He points to the books with pride.

"It's a shame you can't eat books," I say bitterly and lick my parched lips.

"The soul needs food as well." He puts his hand on his heart. "Sarah, offer our guest of honor something to drink."

Sarah pours water into a cracked mug. I'm so thirsty that I don't even check whether the cup is clean and swallow all the water in one gulp.

The man peers at me with concern in his eyes and then rolls his wheelchair over to the bookcase and returns with a small bundle folded in an old newspaper. He unfolds the newspaper, revealing a slice of black bread.

"You look hungry." He pulls a pocketknife out of his jacket pocket and cuts off part of the slice. "Please," he entreats me to accept it.

"Thank you, but I couldn't possibly." I raise my hands, refusing to pick it up.

"You mustn't refuse food from my table when you are a guest in my home," he says firmly.

"But... But it's all you have." I hesitantly accept the piece of bread.

"And that is why I didn't offer you the entire slice." He refolds the newspaper and gestures to Sarah to return the parcel to the bookcase. "Now I understand what you have been doing," he says in a thoughtful tone, stroking his long beard. "You give the children of your kingdom everything you have."

"I only told Grandpa." Sarah bows her head apologetically. "I swear he knows how to keep a secret."

I smile at her, then bite into the bread and murmur with pleasure.

"You mustn't do so again. You mustn't give away everything you have," the man scolds me. "I'm sure you know that in the Jewish religion..."

"I'm supposed to drink the glass of water myself," I interrupt him impatiently. "That dilemma is irrelevant when the ones walking the long road with me are my sweet children."

"You're familiar with the Talmud?" He furrows his brow.

"I'm not familiar with anything." I shrug my shoulders. "The only thing I know is that you share my outlook because just now you shared the only slice of bread you have with me."

"I did so to remind you of another commandment." He strokes his beard again. "According to Judaism, you are not supposed to give everything you have to others. You are commanded to give just 10 percent."

"And if I have too little?" I bite into the bread.

"Still, no more than 10 percent," he insists.

I turn to look at Sarah, who is quietly listening to our conversation. She's sitting on the mattress with her legs crossed, looking so tiny and fragile. My eyes fill with tears.

"You need to take care of yourself so that you can continue to take care of my Sarah." He bows his head. "I'm not as old as I look, but time isn't on my side."

"Of course I'll take care of her." I put the last bit of bread into my mouth and chew intently. Now I understand how much my body needs this. I still feel weak, and my hunger only grows.

"Miss Ania..."

"Princess Ania!" Sarah interrupts him angrily.

"Of course. Of course. Princess." He slaps his head. "I've been so confused lately." He looks at Sarah with an apologetic grin. "I think you should take that adorable cat for a walk while I continue conversing with the princess."

Sarah doesn't protest. She stands up, pours water into the mug, and serves it to her grandfather. Then she picks up Dziecko and they go out, leaving the door open behind them.

"I don't think I properly introduced myself." The man takes a sip of the water. "Yózef Szulc."

"Ania Orzeszkowa."

His black eyes open wide in astonishment. "Repeat your name!" He almost shouts.

"Ania Orzeszkowa." I shift uncomfortably.

The mug falls from his hand and shatters on the floor. His body is trembling, and he clutches his heart as if he's just received a painful blow to the chest.

I stand up in alarm and approach him to try and help.

His lower jaw drops open, and he stares at me. Then, to my dismay, he bursts into tears.

"I'm sorry. I don't know what I did to make you so sad," I apologize, covering my mouth with my hands.

He pulls a handkerchief from his jacket pocket, blows his nose, and wipes his eyes.

"Come here, girl," he commands me quietly. "Let me look at you up close."

I bend down until my face is aligned with his.

"Oh my God," he mutters, caressing my face. "I prayed so hard, and my prayers have been answered."

I grimace in discomfort at the forced intimacy, but when he cups my chin and our eyes meet, I gasp. I know those eyes well. My heart has been torn apart with longing for them.

"You understand now." His eyes tear up again.

"I... I'm not sure I understand," I stutter and sit down in front of him on my knees, waiting for an explanation to calm my racing heart.

"It's not by chance that you chose to take care of my Sarah." He pats my head. "She's your mother's brother's granddaughter."

My heart pounds inside my chest, my body shakes uncontrollably, and I grab onto his knees to steady myself.

"Where is your mother?" he asks anxiously. "Is she here? When can I see her?"

I shake my head no.

"Has something happened to Agata?" He looks terrified.

"No, no," I reassure him. "Mother is somewhere safe, far away from here."

His sigh of relief echoes in the small room.

"And your sister?" He tucks my hair behind my ears and looks at the spot where the beauty mark should be. "My father, may he rest in peace, told me that her birth mark is the only way to tell you two apart."

"Michalina and Father are in America." I wince, feeling a searing ache in my stomach.

"It's a miracle!" He pats my head again. "You are my miracle in this damned place."

"I don't understand..." I open my eyes wide in surprise. "If you are my mother's brother, why have I never met you?"

"You met my father."

"Once." I sigh. "I don't remember him because I was too young, but I know that my grandfather's name was..."

"Simon."

"Yes." I nod.

"Agata decided to end her relationship with us," he says as he turns to look at the bookcase, "As soon as she was allowed to spread her wings and fly, she left us forever."

"But why?" Using his knees to support myself, I stand up and take a step back. "Did you hurt her?"

He frowns in bewilderment. "Agata didn't tell you why she decided to abandon her religion and her family?"

"Mother didn't talk about her Jewish roots." I bite my lip and grab onto the back of the chair. "She detests Judaism and warned me that your people would try to ensnare me in their webs. But..." I rub my face vigorously, "When she was sick, I heard her shout the name Yózef in her sleep. She was tormented by visions of someone hurting you."

"My dear sister." Concealing his face in his hands, he bursts into tears.

"Tell me. Please tell me why Mother hates you."

He gives me a pained look and shakes his head. "My sister doesn't hate me. She hates Judaism, for she believes that the older brother she idolized was hurt because of Judaism."

I sit down on the chair sluggishly and stare at him, exhausted. How did I not see the resemblance between them the second I entered the apartment? The big, intelligent, black eyes, the high forehead, the round face, and the sharp nose. He looks like a male version of Mother.

"I'm seven years older than Agata." He wheels himself to the bookcase, rummages through the books, and then places a small book in his lap. "But our age difference never stopped her from following me around everywhere and demanding my attention." A melancholy smile spreads across his face. "My friends would call her 'Yózef's Shadow.'" He's laughing and crying at the same time. "I scolded her countless times and sent her to go spend time with kids her own age, but Agata doesn't take orders from anyone."

Tears pour from my eyes, and I laugh softly.

"Over time, I stopped trying to send her away and was determined to be happy that she was near." He clutches the book to his heart. "I walked her to school every morning, and in the evenings she would wait for me to finish my studies and walk me home." He falls silent for a moment and closes his eyes.

I wait with bated breath for him to continue the story.

"She was such a curious and clever girl." He opens his eyes and smiles at me. "She challenged me with difficult questions about the Jewish tradition and my strong belief in God. She was never satisfied until I provided her with long, in-depth explanations."

I try to imagine my mother as a little girl, and Sarah's image pops into my mind's eye.

"We lived in a village outside Warsaw, in a small Jewish community. My parents believed that God had chosen to give them only one child, so when Agata was born, they held a great celebration. We didn't have a lot, but we were grateful for what we had."

I'm having a hard time envisioning Mother as a poor Jewish girl in some village.

"Our parents scraped by running a small bakery, and I took care of all Agata's needs. I was her rock. Her big, strong brother. Her invincible brother."

My eyes are drawn to his wheelchair, but I don't dare say anything.

His eyes follow mine, and his shoulders are hunched over. "The day of my seventeenth birthday, I walked her to school like I did every day, and she couldn't stop talking about the party she had organized for me that evening. We walked together hand in hand down the dirt path. Her enthusiasm was infectious. I laughed at her youthful descriptions, and she kept kissing my hand and making me swear that I would never leave her."

He looks at his hand, and I sense that his beautiful story is about to take a dark turn, and I consider running out of the apartment.

"I saw them walking toward us," his expression hardens, "Five boys with iron rods and wicked smiles."

I whimper and hug myself.

"I whispered to Agata to run and hide in the trees, but she refused to let go of my hand. The boys broke into a run towards us, and I leaned down and screamed at her to run away and call for help." He clutches the book to his chest and sighs. "She ran away but didn't call for help. She hid between the trees and saw her hero, her big brother, fight against five bullies – and lose."

Tears blur my vision and I sob soundlessly.

"She heard the horrible words they hurled at me and at our religion, and she heard me crying with pain as their iron rods broke my bones." He rubs his knees. "When the boys left, I tried to crawl into the trees to look for her, but I lost consciousness."

I sniffle, trying to think of something to say that will comfort both him and me, but I'm too overwhelmed with fatigue and emotion.

"When I came to, they told me a week had gone by and that Agata had refused to leave my side even for a second. She sat at my bed with her prayer book and prayed."

I look at the shabby book in his hands.

"The first thing I saw when I opened my eyes was her beautiful little face, staring at me with profound solemnity. She kissed my cheek, put her prayer book beside my head, and said she would never pray again. I assumed it was a declaration made by a girl who'd just undergone a terrible ordeal and that she would heal in time." He puts the book on his knees and scratches his beard. "The days went by, and when I learned how to manage in the wheelchair unassisted, I found the strength to comfort her. I thought that if I could recover and gain my strength again, so could she. But I was wrong." His fingers grasp the book tightly. "She agreed to talk about the ordeal we went through only once. It wasn't even really a conversation; it was more of a one-sided speech delivered by a girl who had lost her faith. She said she understood that I had been hurt because of my religion and that she would never allow anyone to hurt her or her loved ones because of blind faith in a god that doesn't answer her prayers."

"But... but you recovered."

"She said that during the endless hour that those boys were trying to kill me, she closed her eyes and prayed that God would strike back at them. She prayed so hard that her fingernails dug into her forehead." He grazes his forehead fleetingly. "While I lay unconscious in my bed, she didn't stop praying that I would recover and get back on my feet. The doctor examined me and informed my family that I would never be able to walk again. So, she concluded that her prayers hadn't been answered and decided that if God had abandoned her, she would abandon him right back."

I bury my hands between my thighs and rock back and forth. Mother's grief breaks my heart.

"I tried so many times to make her understand that her prayers had been answered. That I was still alive and breathing, and that God chose to take my legs away so I could have more time to spend with her."

"Do you truly believe that?" I interrupt.

"God works in mysterious ways," Yózef smiles as he answers me. "At the time, I thought such an explanation would comfort her."

"And... Did it comfort her?"

"No." Yózef starts stroking his beard again. "She said that she refused to believe in such a cruel and merciless god and that he was dead to her." He looks up, and a single tear rolls down his cheek. "A 10-year-old girl tore her shirt and sat shiva for her god."

A shiver runs down my spine and I get goosebumps.

"My parents thought she'd lost her mind, but I reassured them that it was just a passing phase, and that she would come to her senses. I was wrong." He pats his knees in a kind of silent resignation. "When her seven days of mourning ended, she refused to speak Yiddish and insisted on speaking only Polish. She refused to come to the synagogue and distanced herself from our community and her family members. She condemned herself to total isolation."

"Poor Mother." I sniffle.

"On the day of her 17th birthday, she packed her things and left for the big city without saying goodbye."

"By herself?" I shake my head, not comprehending. "None of you thought to look for her?"

"Of course we did," Yózef answers indignantly. "We asked the people of the Jewish community in Warsaw for help. We sent messengers to Agata, who begged her to return to her home. Mother and Father went to Warsaw themselves, dragging me from place to place in this chair." He grips the wheels of the chair and sighs. "When we got to the house of the seamstress she was working for, Agata came out to us and said she wouldn't acknowledge us as her family. She said that she had sat shiva for her family as well."

"That's absolutely horrible," I said, shifting in my chair restlessly, "After all, it wasn't your fault."

"Of course not," he dismisses. "Your mother didn't see us as the wrongdoers. She disowned her family because she was unable to deal with the pain she felt, knowing that she'd hurt us. She taught herself to loathe everything we represent to protect her heart."

"Then why did she let Grandpa Simon meet us?"

"It wasn't that simple." Yózef smiles painfully. "She didn't even come to my wedding, and she refused to congratulate me when my daughter was born. She didn't even come to her own mother's funeral."

I feel goose bumps starting on my arms again.

"The years passed, and a merchant who passed through the village said that Agata had given birth to twins. He'd seen them crawling around her prestigious boutique in the center of the city. Father left the village that day, determined to meet you."

"I don't remember meeting him," I say, embarrassed. "I only know him from Michalina's stories. She spoke of him as if she remembered him."

"Unfortunately, he wasn't part of your life," Yózef replies. "Agata allowed him to see you only once and made him swear not to ever come near you again."

"It's strange that Michalina spoke so fondly of him," I say, bewildered. "I find it hard to believe that she remembers him. We were so little."

"She didn't tell you?" Yózef looks shocked.

"Tell me what?" I finger my triangle pendant.

"On the day of your seventeenth birthday, my father came to Warsaw and waited for your sister outside her school. If I'm not mistaken, she had just begun her nursing studies."

I widen my eyes in surprise and nod vigorously.

"He apologized to her for storming into her world without her mother's permission and asked to give you two a gift. He brought her two necklaces with triangle pendants and said, 'Family is the most important thing in the world.' Never abandon your sister because..."

"Only when you put the two triangles together will they become the star that will light your way," I say, covering my mouth with my hands.

"Not just any star," Yózef corrects me. "The Star of David." He traces the Star of David armband on the sleeve of his jacket.

I gasp.

"Father knew that even if you never understood the meaning of the connection between the two triangles, as long as you were together, the Star of David would remain close to your hearts and protect you."

I stare at his armband, and the longing I feel for Michalina punches me in the stomach. Tears stream down my cheeks, and I touch the pendant around my neck. Its true meaning proves to me again just how much I need my sister.

Yózef gives me a pained smile, "My father got sick that same evening, and a few days later he passed away. His daughter didn't come to the funeral."

I stand up and circle around myself in bottomless sorrow. Intense emotions overwhelm me, but my body is too weak to contain them.

"I need to leave now," I murmur weakly. "I... I need time to digest your story."

"Ania," he speaks my name harshly. "You received your life as a gift from the Divine Creator. You are not permitted to risk it, and you are not allowed to give it up. I order you to take care of yourself and to remember." – he taps his finger on his temple – "that you won't be able to take care of Sarah and her innocent friends if you can't take care of yourself."

"What kind of gift is this?" I burst into tears. "What kind of life is this if we're destined to be imprisoned in this horrible ghetto?"

"You'll survive," he replies, his face emotionless. "You'll behave wisely from now on, and you'll get through this awful time. And now that you know that Sarah is a member of your family, you'll do everything in your power to ensure that she survives with you and reaches your magical kingdom."

I hear footsteps on the stairs and quickly wipe away my tears.

"Princess Ania." He bows his head to me as Sarah comes into the apartment. Hugging the cat, she looks at us in curiosity.

I peer at her face keenly.

"I need to leave now," I mumble and take the cat from her arms. "Come visit me tomorrow."

"I'll walk you home," she says and begins to follow me.

"There's no need." I lean down and kiss her cheek. "The curfew will begin soon. Stay here with your grandfather and come to see me tomorrow."

I take one last look at Yózef, confirm the understanding between us with a nod of my head, and leave the apartment.

Down in the street, I look left and right, trying to remember how we came.

A figure in a blue uniform approaches me. I look up, and my eyes sink into his soothing brown ones. I take one step towards him, longing to give up and force him to carry me, to protect me in his strong arms, but two men walk toward us, and he turns his back to me and starts walking.

The men cross to the other side of the street, and I hug Dziecko and walk in silence, following his broad back through the web of alleys.

I feel weaker and weaker, and my steps become heavier. Suddenly I can't see him anymore, and I freeze, blinking in confusion. The buildings in this alley were damaged in the air raids and look like ancient ruins.

Out of nowhere, someone pulls me into the doorway of a nearby building, and the cat jumps out of my arms and yowls. I open my mouth to cry out for help, but my mouth is covered by a large hand.

"It's me," he tells me in a soothing whisper.

His arms embrace me from behind, and a feeble moan escapes my lips. I press my palms against the wall, and he buries his face in my neck. His lips brush over my skin as if he's trying to give me his breath.

"I'm so scared," I whisper.

"I know." His arms wrap so tightly around me it's almost painful.

"I'm not afraid for myself." I tilt my head back and rest it on his shoulder.

"You're afraid for her."

"Did you know?" I turn around and look at him, wide-eyed.

"Michalina told me about your Jewish family," he says, taking my hands and pressing them to his lips. "It wasn't hard to find out who they were and where they were in the ghetto."

"She told you, yet she didn't share it with me?" I shake my head in disbelief.

"Maybe she felt you weren't ready to hear such information." He lowers my hands to his chest.

"Even now, I'm not ready." I close my eyes, trying to fight back the tears. "I didn't think fear could hurt so much. My bones ache," I wail softly. "Anton, what other secrets did my sister hide from me? What else should I expect to find out?"

"I don't think there are any more secrets." He caresses my cheek. "I just know that I hate to see you so weak."

Being near him gives me a false sense of security, and I'm desperate for his embrace. My feelings for him outweigh the terror I feel, but within a split second, the burning pain in my stomach reminds me that I'm betraying my sister again. I pull my hands away and push him from me. "Anton, I wish I could have a pleasant conversation with you." My eyes are shrouded by a veil of tears. "I wish I could turn back time and that we hadn't wasted our time together spouting silly declarations."

He caresses my head, and the pain in my heart intensifies.

"I wish I could invite you for a modest dinner that I would cook especially for you." A tear rolls down my cheek. "And I wish I deserved all the times you chose to take care of me and support me."

"I take care of you without expecting anything in return," he replies, his voice shaking.

"Stupid promise." I snivel. "Why didn't my sister warn me when she left me with you that I would have to share your heart with her as well? Otherwise, how can you explain the fact that my heart demands the love you gave her for itself?"

"Ania..." He says my name, his tone one of torment, but I have no intention of waiting to hear his words of comfort. Guilt is pounding in my chest. I take the cat into my arms and run from him, towards the bridge and over it. I keep trotting onward as fast as I can. So many bodies collide with me, and I grind my teeth and carve my way through the masses with incredible difficulty.

I walk down into the crowded road and look around. I still don't recognize the streets here.

A blue uniform overtakes me and stops in front of me. With trepidation, the large crowd clears the way for him. He strides onward, and I stare at his broad back and follow him. Step after step, my heart thumps, bruising my chest. Everyone around us is worried by the presence of this man, while I alone long for him to turn to me and clasp me in his arms, desperate to hear him say that his heart belongs to me. The pain in my stomach intensifies, and I hug Dziecko and whimper into his fur.

The blue uniform stops close to my building, and I walk around him and go inside. I climb up to my apartment, take off my coat, and run, with all strength I have left, to the kitchen. I squeeze the tiny portion of porridge left on the counter into my mouth and gulp down an entire bottle of milk.

My stomach contracts painfully, and nausea rises in my throat. I hobble to the mattress and fall onto it.

My eyes close, and exhaustion overwhelms me.

I powder my nose before the chiffonier and make sure that every ringlet is in place. My golden locks look like a beautiful crown.

"Did we make plans to go out to a restaurant tonight?" Michalina asks, standing behind me.

"Of course. You need to get ready," I reply angrily and study her facial features, so perfectly identical to mine, in the mirror. "You know Mother doesn't like me going out without you."

"I'm sorry, but I need to study." She wrinkles her nose apologetically. "I can ask Anton to go with you. I'm sure he would be happy to."

"No," I shout. "I don't want to be alone with him."

"Are you afraid of him?" She raises her eyebrows in surprise.

"I'm afraid of myself." I lower my eyes. "You asked me to look after him for you, and I..."

"And you what?" She sounds worried. "Did you insult him? Or hurt him?" Unexpectedly, she spins me around to face her and giggles.

"Forgive me; I know you would never do such a thing. You know how much he means to me and how much I mean to him."

"I know." I avoid her gaze. "I think I mainly hurt myself."

"Anushka." Her smile fades. "Can't you hear the commotion outside?"

I shake my head from side to side, not understanding.

"You need to wake up." She grabs me and shakes me vigorously.

I sit up, and my breath catches in my throat as I hear screaming in German coming from the street.

CHAPTER 6

Peter and Ida sit up with their eyes half closed, and we exchange alarmed looks. The loud screams penetrate the walls.

"What's going on out there?" I yawn and rub my eyes.

Peter kneels and pulls back the curtain cautiously. "Oh my God," he whispers, horrified. "It's just a little girl."

Ida rocks back and forth and covers her ears with her hands.

A black screen comes down over my eyes, and my heart pounds like a drum. I turn to the window, pull back the curtain, and see my worst nightmare unfolding in front of me.

Sarah is sitting on her knees before four soldiers. They are pointing their guns at her. She doesn't look down. Instead, she thrusts out her chin in defiance.

I expect to feel my heart stop beating and shatter into thousands of pieces. I expect to feel my breath catch and my body collapse, lifeless. But none of this happens. The weakness from fasting for the past few days disappears, my heartbeat gradually slows down, and my thoughts are clear.

"What are you hiding under your coat?" one of the soldiers barks at her. "What is the stinking rat trying to smuggle into the ghetto?"

Sarah puts her hands on her hips and doesn't reply.

"The rat doesn't understand German," an SS officer spits on the ground. "Translate to Polish."

A figure in a blue uniform crosses the street and stands behind her. He stands tall, his back straight. His face is expressionless, but even from up here, I can feel his distress burning in my heart.

"Tell this stinking rat that if she doesn't explain to us what she's doing here on the street, I'll put a bullet in her head."

Sarah continues to stick out her chin, and only one thought echoes over and over in my mind: My girl needs me!

I jump to my feet and run to the door.

"Ania, what are you doing?" Ida whispers in alarm. I don't answer her, just open the door and run down the stairs, Dziecko limping at my heels.

I cross the street, push the figure in the blue uniform, and kneel beside Sarah. I grab her hand and give her a reassuring smile.

Sarah shoots me an angry look.

I don't need to see his face or hear his voice to feel Anton's storm of emotions. He cannot protect me now.

"What is this Polish woman doing in the ghetto?" The officer addresses his soldiers, pointing his gun at me.

I look down at my fancy dress and realize that my armband is on the sleeve of my coat. The tension coursing through my body has stopped me from feeling the cold.

"I belong here," I reply in German.

The officer's face contorts in disgust. "I wasn't talking to you." He moves his rifle and puts the barrel on my shoulder.

Sarah and I exhale in distress simultaneously. The horrible feeling of fear returns to me, but not for myself. I fear for the fate of my courageous girl.

Anton walks around me and stands between us and the vicious officer.

"I'll translate the girl's explanation," he snaps and then moves aside and spins to face me. He shoots sparks at me with his eyes.

Dziecko limps towards us. He rubs against Sarah's legs and snuggles close to mine. Sarah squeezes my hand in a desperate attempt to reassure me.

"Tell the rat she has two seconds to give me the contraband she's hiding under her coat."

Anton translates.

"I'm not smuggling anything," Sarah grumbles angrily between her teeth. "I brought my friend a gift."

I close my eyes when I realize whom she risked her life for.

"Show him the gift!" Anton orders firmly.

"No!" Her chin goes out defiantly again.

"Sarah," I whisper her name and open my eyes wide, "please show the officer the gift you brought me."

The soldier presses the barrel of his gun to her head, and she groans and unbuckles the belt of her coat. I whimper soundlessly when I see the circular wreath of flowers she sets down on the road.

"I wanted to bring you a crown," she whispers in my ear. "A princess should wear a crown."

"What is this garbage?" The officer says as he steps on the flowers, crushing them.

"The girl is confused," Anton says in a deep, tranquil voice. "She thinks the flowers are edible."

The soldiers burst out laughing, and Sarah looks at me, infuriated.

"What did he say to them? Why are they laughing at your crown?"

"Shh..." I hush her. "You must let the soldier from my kingdom guard his princess."

"Stupid rat!" The officer kicks the ruined flower crown. "She broke curfew, and now she must pay the price."

I bite my lip and hold my breath.

"Ask her what she prefers," the officer snickers. "A bullet in the foot or the hand."

I steal a breath and interrupt. "It was my mistake. I asked her..." I wrinkle my forehead, trying to think of a logical explanation, "I asked her to take the cat for a walk, and by the time she got back, it was too late. I should have insisted that she sleep over at my apartment."

"The Fräulein butts in again..." The officer clucks his tongue. "The Fräulein really wants to be punished." He points the barrel of his gun at me, and out of the corner of my eye, I see Anton pulling his gun from its holster and holding it close to his body. "If you insist, I'll give you the privilege to choose." The officer grins and presses the barrel to my forehead. This is good. I swallow the lump in my throat. His anger is now directed at me. "Whose head should I put the bullet in? The cat's?" He aims the barrel at Dziecko. I gasp and place my hand on the cat's back. "Or the rat's?" He points the barrel at Sarah. My heart stops beating, and I squeeze her hand. Dread sizzles in my bones, and tears stream from my eyes. I open my mouth, but no sound comes out. "The cat or the rat? The rat or the cat?" He moves the barrel back and forth between them, and a black screen falls over my eyes.

"Uh... Uh..." I hear myself mumbling indistinctly. The air refuses to enter my lungs. I turn to look at Dziecko, and his magnetic eyes blaze with love for me. I then turn to look at Sarah. Her expression is frozen. "Uh..." I choke up, a lump of tears blocking my windpipe.

Suddenly my body shakes from the sharp sound of a gunshot, and I feel as if my ears are bleeding from the earsplitting whistle.

"I chose for her," Anton's muffled voice sounds above me. "And now they'll get out of here." Hands grab my waist and lift me into a standing position, and Sarah's hand falls from mine. I cover my ears with my hands and sway forward like a drunk. I see orange fur turn to red and then turn around and notice Ida and Peter peeking out from the entrance to the building. I drag my feet toward them, my head wobbling heavily. Their arms wrap around me, catching me mere seconds before I lose consciousness.

* * *

A deafening yowl grates in my ears, and I open my eyes in alarm. Dziecko is in trouble. I sit up and look from side to side, confused. I'm in my apartment. Peter and Ida hover over me, but I don't feel the soft fur of my cat.

Suddenly last night's events come back to me, and I burst into tears.

"Sarah? What happened to Sarah?"

"The girl is perfectly safe." Ida strokes my head. "She ran away after... after..."

"After the Nazis murdered my baby," I wail in anguish. "I couldn't choose." I cover my mouth with my hands; the guilt is agonizing. It was Anton who made the decision that saved Sarah's life. "I was so stupefied that I couldn't choose. What does that say about me?"

Peter grinds his teeth. "It probably shows that even though the Germans have lost their humanity, they weren't able to turn you into an animal."

Ida sits next to me, wraps her arms around me, and kisses my head over and over. "Ania, it was the most terrifying scene I've ever witnessed in my entire life. Peter and I ran down to the street after you, but we didn't have the courage to intervene. You two sat there in the road in front of four soldiers with their guns drawn, and all I could do was pray with all my might that lightning would burst out of the sky and strike them down."

"All the neighbors from the surrounding buildings watched the spectacle." Peter lights a cigarette and wipes his forehead. "I believe that despite all the disease, poverty, and death that surrounds us, no one can remain indifferent to the sight of a little girl sticking out her chin to these beasts of prey."

I stretch my arms out, waiting to hear the drumming of my cat's feet, but the apartment is noiseless. I bury my head in my hands and burst into tears.

"What did they do with Dziecko?" I wipe my tears on my sleeve. "Did they throw him in the garbage like stinking trash?"

"After the Germans left, Anton picked him up off the road and placed him on a newspaper at the entrance to our building."

"Is he still there? Now?" I lean on my elbows to hoist myself up.

"Not anymore." Ida grabs the cigarette from Peter and sucks on it forcefully. "Your children arrived really early this morning with a baby carriage. They put Dziecko in it and asked us to tell you they were taking him to be buried."

"They are such good children," I sob and stand up. "They're not safe here, and I don't know how to keep them safe."

"It's a terrible reality." Ida nods, pained. "So many children in the ghetto cannot survive the atrocities."

"My children will survive," I answer angrily. "But they must be hungry." Grief has confused me. "They must be hungry now. Please help me find them something to eat."

I run into the kitchen and stare in amazement at the counter, where there is a basket full of nourishing food.

Peter comes up behind me and puts his hands on my shoulders.

"The heart is a very cunning organ..." Peter whispers in my ear. "When Anton pulled out his gun, it was to shoot that Nazi before he could shoot you."

I shudder as a shiver runs down my spine.

"His heart is very selfish," Peter whispers, "if he understood that he'd rather hang in the city square than live in this damned world without you."

I mumble softly and take two large loaves of bread out of the basket.

"Peter," I address him with my eyes still full of tears. "My heart is selfish too, but I need to remind myself every day that I'm not the same foolish, arrogant girl I used to be. I need to remind myself that he's only keeping me safe for her."

CHAPTER 7

I serve each of the children a few cubes of cheese and take one for myself. They chew with their mouths closed, their eyes darting around nervously. A sad way to celebrate the new year, 1942. I lean to the side, move my hand toward the sidewalk, and shudder when I realize that I'm still doing so, even though it's been a few weeks since my Dziecko was murdered.

I sigh gloomily, and then, seeing Sarah's sad doe eyes looking at me, I stretch my lips into a smile. Sarah hasn't said a word about the chilling experience we shared, but the jet-black color of her eyes has become darker since that awful night.

I bend down to pat her cheek and, in a whisper, start to tell the story of the magical kingdom.

When I get to the part where the soldiers of my kingdom stick their swords into the Germans' bellies, the children giggle and clap their hands enthusiastically.

"Shh..." I hush them.

There isn't one person who passes by us on the street and doesn't stop to enjoy these rare sounds for a moment. Even I close my eyes and relish the music of their laughter.

"Who would believe that I would hear the sound of children's laughter again?" asks Bruno in a thoughtful tone. He stands next to us and pulls a handful of candies out of his pocket. The children open their fists, and he distributes the sweets among them. His skin is ruddy again, and he stands upright and looks healthy.

"Is the Child Whisperer feeling okay?" He takes off his hat and holds it to his chest.

"Physically, I feel better since I started eating again." I bite my lip in discomfort. "But emotionally, it's been hard for me to accept that my baby is no longer with me."

Sarah stares at me with torment in her eyes, and I immediately regret what I just said.

"But look at the abundance that I have." I pull her small hand to my lips and kiss it. "When we finally reach my kingdom, we'll adopt a new cat."

All five children gawk at me.

"Bruno is a friend," I whisper to them, grinning slyly. "Where do you think he gets all these candies from? I asked that they be sent to him from the kingdom."

"Ahh..." Sarah studies him with interest, looking him up and down. "So, he also watches over you, like..."

I open my eyes wider, cautioning her; she stops talking and her face suddenly flushes red.

"Like who?" Bruno laughs. "There should be no secrets among friends."

"You should go now, kids." I wave my hands. "And no nighttime visits," I implore in a threatening tone.

I earn a group hug, and after just a few seconds, they're swallowed up in the crowd.

Bruno stands in front of me and puts his hands in his pants pockets. "I'm glad to see that your children are healthy and strong."

"The fear that something will happen to them haunts me." I look in the direction they ran and feel reassured by the fact that I can't see Misza's golden head of hair. They know how to conceal themselves.

"We're learning to live with that fear. It seems that we're learning to live with all manner of horrors."

I smile at him fondly. I've come to see him as a companion in the terrible fate that has befallen us.

"Ania," he whispers and glances to the side. "There's a group of people who are tired of sitting idly by and waiting for the day the Nazis decide to put a bullet in their heads."

"Are you preparing to fight?" I whisper in astonishment. "And what exactly are you going to do without weapons? Throw books at them?"

"We don't throw books." Bruno's eyes cloud over. "Unlike those animals, we don't throw books, and we certainly don't burn them."

"So what's your plan?" I bite my lip and look around to check that no one is eavesdropping on our conversation. "The epidemic broke out here like wildfire in a field of thorns. It isn't enough for the Germans that the cold, disease, and hunger are destroying the Jews," I say, pointing to the corpse of a woman still lying on the sidewalk across the street. "They kidnap men and women into forced labor every day. Soon there will be no one left to fight against them."

"There are still quite a few good Jews left. Those who are hiding, those who work in the factories, and those who have special permits."

I ponder his words, and countless questions churn in my mind. "And what does the Great Rabbi say about this? Will your father support such a fight? Will his followers join in?"

"The Rebbe has ruled that we should bow our heads and focus on studying Torah." His facial expression betrays his displeasure. "Father says that for every Hasid they abduct into forced labor or murder in cold blood, we need to pray harder."

"And you intend to disobey him?"

"Every time I come to visit you, I'm disobeying him." He smiles and lowers his eyes in embarrassment.

His insinuation has flustered me, and I inadvertently twirl a ringlet of hair around my finger.

"We're recruiting anyone who can be of help." He gives me a pointed stare.

I drop the ringlet. "I don't understand… are you suggesting that I join your organization?"

"Additionally."

"And what will I fight with?" I roll my eyes, "A needle and thread?"

"Our organization also needs information." He scratches his beard and bounces from foot to foot. "To tell you the truth, it's rumored that you have ties with…"

"Damned rumors!" I stand up in annoyance. "I don't have ties to anyone but myself."

"Forgive me." He bows his head. "I shouldn't have committed the sin of making false assumptions."

"Extremely false," I cross my arms over my chest.

"Forgive me," he pleads.

I can't continue being angry with him when he looks so distraught. "I forgive you." My lips stretch into a half smile.

"I'll stop pestering you now." He adjusts his hat. "But I'll be back to visit you soon." He bows slightly and turns away.

I pick up the bottle sitting at the foot of my chair, swirl around the little milk left in it and bring it to my lips. Suddenly, filthy hands grab the bottle from me and push me back forcefully. I fall onto my bottom and stare in alarm at an old man gulping from my bottle. A figure in a blue uniform throws him aside and raises his club.

"Don't hurt him!" I shout, and the arm holding the club drops.

The old man licks his lips. His stare wanders back and forth between Anton and me.

Anton quickly stands up straight and turns his back to me, but it's too late. The old man grins, revealing yellow teeth. "A whore of the Polish police. That's what you are." Supporting himself with his hands, he stands and runs away. My eyes follow the thief and encounter Bruno's face. He quickly looks away, but not before I notice his disappointment.

I pick up my chair, bring it inside the building, and climb the stairs to my apartment.

Rage courses through my body, and I'm desperate to vent. I open the kitchen cabinets and slam them shut. What the hell was Anton thinking? I am furious. A Polish policeman protecting a Jewish woman? He may as well turn on a flashlight and point it at the two of us. I raise my face to the heavens and scream soundlessly.

The apartment door opens, and Ida's heels pound loudly on the floor. She runs into the kitchen and looks at me with wild eyes.

"What happened now?"

"They took him!" she shouts.

Ida never shouts.

"Who? Who are you talking about?" I ask, trying to understand why she's so hysterical.

"Ania, they kidnapped him for forced labor." She continues shouting and running circles around herself. "They loaded him onto a truck in the square, and if we don't do something right now, they'll take him away and he'll never come back." She bursts into tears. "He won't survive. He's not strong enough."

"Who did they take?" I shake her by the shoulders.

"Peter!" she shouts, crying.

The blood drains from my face, and I step backwards until I reach the counter.

"What do you mean they took him?" I swallow the lump that's forming in my throat. "But... But he has a special permit. Anton arranged that he..."

"They don't care," Ida interrupts me. "The damned Jewish policemen seized him and shoved him onto the truck when we went by them in the square."

"Has the truck already driven away?" I ask, totally panicked.

"No, but they're abducting every man who passes through the square right now." She falls to her knees. "Ania, what should we do?"

I press my palms to my forehead and try to think of a rational solution. Ida's hysteria is contagious. "What can we do..." I mumble to myself. The likelihood that Anton can help seems illogical. "What should we do..." I snarl, baffled. "Ida, you told me a few nights ago that the Jewish policemen are corrupt." I grab her sleeve and pull her up into a standing position. "If they're abducting people at random, that means there's no list, and if there's no list, that means we can bribe one of the officers and get him off the damn truck."

"And what do you suggest we bribe him with? A bag of rice? Or a loaf of bread?"

I run to the closet, yank the black wool coat from its hanger, and rip off its sleeves. I push my fingers into the wool lining, pull out the two diamond earrings, and run out the door with Ida at my heels.

We stop short when we get to the square, and I stare at the commotion, out of breath. The men in the truck are shouting and demanding to be let go while women and children cry and beg to get their loved ones back.

"Ania. Ida," Peter waves at us from the truck, and I see that his cheek is swollen and bruised. "Please get me out of here." He is crowded between the men, holding on to the metal beam that frames the back of the truck.

The sight of him jailed in the godforsaken vehicle horrifies me. No one who gets on a truck here ever comes back.

"Come with me." I take a deep breath and walk over to the policeman who is pushing the men into the truck with the help of his club.

"Sir." I address him with respect he does not deserve.

"What do you want?" he barks at me.

"I'm afraid there's been a misunderstanding, and we'd love to speak to you and figure out how it can be resolved."

"There is no misunderstanding here. All the men on this truck are going to the labor camps." Abruptly, he notices Ida, and his face twists uncomfortably. "Miss Hirsch." He nods at her.

Ida stares at him and doesn't respond.

Her lack of response seems to upset him, and he pushes me roughly and goes back to beating the men attempting to get off the truck with his club.

I spin toward Ida and drag her to the side. "Listen to me and listen good." I slap her cheeks lightly until she shakes her head and blinks. "Ida, I need you to focus," I scold her, and she nods vigorously. "I don't know what kind of acquaintance you have with that bastard, but from experience, I can say with complete certainty that he has feelings for you."

"Ania," she grimaces in disgust, "I never implied to that bully that I was at all interested in his company."

"That doesn't matter now." I clench my teeth. "You will smile, flutter your eyelashes, flirt, and do any despicable thing you can to get Peter off that truck."

"But... But I'm not like you. I don't know how to do such things."

"You have one second to learn." I put the earrings in her hand and push her towards him.

Ida looks at her clenched fist and then looks up at the truck. I can't see her face, and I can't stand close to her to lend her strength. I can only hope that she understands that this is a do-or-die moment for Peter.

I step back and watch her approach the policeman. I can't hear what she's saying to him, but I can see that he only has eyes for her.

She lifts her hand and plays with an unruly lock of hair. The policeman responds with a small smile.

She tilts her head to the side, and his smile broadens. He takes her arm and leads her to the front of the truck.

Ida leans in, whispers in his ear, and then gives him the treasure that has been hiding in her fist. Before I have time to blink, the earrings disappear into his coat pocket.

The policeman takes her hand and kisses it, and she responds with a slight nod.

She turns around towards me, smiling widely, but after a split second, the smile is gone and she looks disgusted with herself. She walks towards me with cadenced steps, and when she stops in front of me, she doesn't say a word.

I cover my mouth with my hands as Peter gets off the truck and runs toward us.

"You did it!" I hug her, and my eyes overflow with tears. "Were the earrings a big enough bribe?"

"The earrings and my soul," she replies coldly and then pounces on Peter, enveloping him in a tight embrace.

"Thank you, thank you," Peter wails, and we hold hands and run together toward the apartment. We stop, panting, at the entrance to the building, and as we climb the stairs, I see that Peter's shoulders are slumped over, and he doesn't utter a sound. I expect to see him jumping for joy when we enter the apartment, but he just sits on the sofa and holds his head in his hands.

"You should be happy." I sit down next to him and pat his shoulder. "You were saved."

"And what will happen tomorrow?" he moans. "Or the next day?"

"We'll be fine," I reply with false confidence. "As long as we're together, we can get through anything."

"Ania," he looks at me tearfully, "I wouldn't survive in a labor camp! Look at me. I'll lose the will to live, and from there the road to hell will be very short."

"Then stay here. In the apartment." I press his hand to my lips. "Hide here until…"

"Until those animals break in here and take me by force," he sums up the most horrific scenario. "I'm sorry, but I can't stay here anymore."

"Do you have any other choice?" Ida sits down on his other side.

"Olek knows the Polish guard on the other side of the ghetto," he whispers. "He smuggles goods for me through him almost every night. This time I'll run away with him."

"If they catch you, they'll kill you," I cry out.

"We have friends in the Resistance." He lights a cigarette and quickly wipes away his tears. "People like Olek and I have set up organizations all over Europe to save people from our community." He stands up and turns toward the closet, pulling out two coats and putting them on the table. "Olek will hide me until they find a way to smuggle me out of the country."

"Peter, that is so dangerous." Ida smooths out the coats he took out.

"It's no more dangerous than staying here." He puts on one coat, buttoning it securely. "Rumor has it that they plan to close the Small Ghetto and move everyone to the Large Ghetto."

"What's the logic in that?"

"I don't know. I stopped looking for logic when it comes to the Nazis." He takes off the coat and puts on the other one. "Maybe their plan is to cram us all in one place to make things easier for when they decide to burn the ghetto down."

"Peter!" Ida admonishes him. "Why would you say such a dreadful thing?"

"So that you two understand that you need to find a way out of here, too." He raises his voice. "I'm extremely ashamed that I have to leave you here, but I hope you know that if I had any way to bring you with me, I wouldn't hesitate for a second."

Ida and I nod morosely. I find it hard to believe that Peter is actually leaving us.

He rummages in the waste bin and pulls out the bottle of brandy we hid in the bottom on our first day in the apartment.

"I think the time has come for us to enjoy a first-rate drink," he declares and pulls out the cork. "Who knows when we'll be able to drink together again – if ever?"

I leap up, grab the bottle from him, stick the cork back in, and shove the bottle back into the bin.

"Peter, we promised to drink from it only when all three of us can finally celebrate our freedom," I pound my fist on his chest. "And you must swear to me now that you will do everything in your power to make sure that each of us keeps that promise."

Peter bows his head, pulls me to him, and bursts into tears. Ida wraps us both in her arms, and we stand tight, broken, and dejected, clinging to the promise of a drink that will symbolize the freedom that we so yearn for.

CHAPTER 8

The commotion on the street is different today. The rumors about the consolidation of the ghetto have proved to be true. The decision has been made, and the residents of the Small Ghetto carry their meager belongings toward the bridge. Sick, tired, and starving people are trying to find their places in the chaos surrounding them.

The figure in the blue uniform stands up straight on the other side of the street. His hand grips the butt of his gun, and he stares at me. I look down, wrap a curl around my finger and smile a bit. His presence encourages and strengthens me. Three Jewish policemen cross the street and approach him. I can't hear their conversation, but Anton nods and joins them. I keep watching him until he disappears around the corner.

Ida's and my suitcases are already packed, but I refuse to leave. I sit in the doorway of our building, lean over toward my five kids, and begin to whisper the story of my kingdom to them.

"Princess Ania," Misza whispers, scratching his fair hair, "Can you ask your kingdom's soldiers when they are going to bring Father back?"

"Of course." I pat his cheek. "I'm sure it won't take much longer."

Oleg and Gershon lick the flour off the little buns and listen to our conversation in silence. Their long sidelocks and troubled expressions make them look like two miniature men holding the weight of the world on their shoulders.

"Let's talk about your dreams," I whisper and crouch down close to them to try to distract them and myself from seeing the soldiers harassing two women not far from us.

"My dream is that you'll agree to let my grandfather come with us to your kingdom," Sarah responds immediately. "His eyes are bad, and he can't recognize me anymore."

"Your grandfather will be a guest of the king." I trace her nose with my finger. "He'll have a special companion who will read to him from the books he loves so much."

"I knew you would agree." Sarah gives me a wide smile.

"My dream is to eat an ice cream sundae *this big*." Bella motions with her arms to show the size and then bends down and scratches the dirty big toe that's sticking out of a hole in her shabby shoe.

"You'll get an even bigger one." I stretch my arms out to the sides.

"I just want Father to come back." Misza says as he shrugs.

I nod and squeeze his hand.

Oleg and Gershon exchange looks. "Our dream is…" Oleg scratches his head.

"Our dream is to ride a big horse." Gershon completes Oleg's sentence, curling his sidelock around his finger.

"Oh… That's a fantastic dream." I giggle. "In my kingdom, there are black, brown, and white horses. What color do you want?"

They look at me, confused.

"Don't choose now." I wave my hand, dismissing my own question. "You can ride a horse of a different color every day."

The children burst out laughing.

"Shh…" I put my finger to my lips, shushing them.

The clicking of boot heels behind them indicates that I didn't hush them quickly enough. The two soldiers step straight toward us and stand in front of me with expressions of disgust on their faces.

"Run away," I whisper without moving my lips.

The children hop off their oil canisters and vanish into the hubbub of the street.

With a poisonous smirk, the mustachioed soldier tells the other one, "This dirty Jewess sits here like an empress. She thinks we don't notice the way she keeps looking at us. I think she likes us."

"I was just about to go up to my apartment." I stand up, determined not to look at them.

"The Jewess speaks German." The other soldier approaches me and pulls one of the curls on my head. He is almost as tall as Anton. I don't move.

"Take your hat off when you stand in front of us," he yaps right into my face.

I pull out the hat pins without looking at him and take off my hat. My eyes dart to the sides in search of the blue uniform.

"Take off your coat, too." The mustachioed soldier tugs on my sleeve.

I unbuckle the belt of my coat and pull it off slowly. I close my eyes, yearning to hear the deep voice of my protector.

"What a beautiful dress you have..." The one with the mustache leers venomously and runs his hand over the velvet fabric. "A filthy Jewess shouldn't be wearing such a beautiful dress." He spits on my shoes, then grabs my arm and pulls me down the sidewalk.

I let out a cry of panic, and he spins around and slaps me hard across the face. His friend seizes my other arm, and I squirm, trying to free myself from them, but their grip is too strong. I burst into tears as they push me into an alley. None of the people swarming the streets dares to say a word. They look down and keep walking with stooped shoulders.

My back slams against the brick wall, and I yell and flail my arms. I succeed in scratching the tall soldier's cheek, and my head throbs from the punch he throws at me. I try to protect my face and feel the ripping of the material that covers my chest. The cold air pierces my bones.

"I'm Jewish," I shout. "I'm a dirty Jew." My dress is lifted above my knees, and the soldier with the mustache unbuckles his belt. Horrified, I understand what is about to happen. They are about to rob me of the one thing I have not yet given to any man. I flail my arms hysterically and burst into tears under the cold, inhuman eyes of the heartless beasts. Hands touch me, and I wail softly and command myself not to look evil in the face, to disconnect my emotions while they murder my soul. I look down the alley and shudder when my eyes meet the black, doe-eyed stare I know so well.

The shameful understanding that she's watching me suffer such vile humiliation overshadows the horror of what is about to happen to me.

"Run away," I beseech her in a whisper, tears pouring down my face.

Four small figures stand next to her, and my bleeding, throbbing heart bruises my chest.

"Please! Run away!" I raise my voice.

My underwear is torn from my body, and I shut my eyes tightly.

Suddenly, a deafening scream rings out, followed by another and another. I open my eyes and see my innocent children standing at the entrance to the alley. They are holding hands, their necks are extended upwards, and they let out blood-curdling screams.

"Shut them up!" The mustachioed one barks at his companion.

"Get out of here!" the soldier yells, pointing his pistol at them.

The screaming gets louder.

"Get out of here, I said!" the soldier bellows.

For a fleeting moment, there is silence, and then the screaming starts up again. Loud and jarring, it grates the tainted air surrounding me.

The one with the mustache snarls furiously and rebuckles his belt. He punches me, knocking me to the ground, and they both sprint off in pursuit of my guardian angels.

I blink once, and there's no trace of my children. It's as though I simply imagined that they were standing there.

An elderly woman comes into the alley and quickly limps over to me. "Poor girl," she says to me in a motherly tone and pulls me up to a standing position. I clutch the torn bodice of my dress and try to hide my bosom. I stare into her wrinkled face and can only whimper quietly. She takes off her coat and covers my upper body. "Come on. Don't dawdle," she scolds and then holds me tightly and pulls me toward the end of the alley. "Where do you live, girl?"

I point at my building like a sleepwalker trapped in a nightmare.

"Come on. Come on. Before those animals return," She urges me to quicken my pace.

I stumble on the first step, and she pants and pulls me toward the railing. I grab onto it and continue to whimper all the way up to the door of our apartment, which she opens and pushes me inside.

"You're okay now," she tells me while rubbing her knee and grimacing.

"Th... Thank you," I whisper, my body trembling uncontrollably.

"Don't thank me." She sighs and then stands up straight and runs her rough palm over my cheek, "Thank your children. They're the ones who saved you."

I wail in pain.

"Don't worry about those little devils." She smiles cunningly. "When they decide to run away, even the Angel of Death cannot hunt them down."

I try to answer, but a chill freezes my body, and my tremors intensify.

"I need to leave now," she says, looking toward the door, "before the curfew starts."

I nod with difficulty.

"My coat," she says awkwardly, pointing to the cloth covering my breasts. "I won't be able to survive without my coat."

"Of course," I carefully take it off and quickly press the torn material of my dress to my chest.

"You'll be fine," she says, despite the sorrow visible in her eyes. "We'll be fine," she mutters as if trying to convince herself as she leaves the apartment.

I stare at the closed door, and the tremors cause my body to shake as if someone dumped a bucket of ice over my head. I move one foot back and then the other and sit on the mattress with my back against the wall. I press the ripped material to my chest, put my head on my knees and cry soundlessly.

The door opens.

"Ania, your hat and coat were on the ground at the entrance to…" Ida doesn't finish her sentence and shrieks in panic. "Ania, what happened?" Her high heels shake the floor as she runs over to me. "Ania, what did they do to you?" She bursts into tears.

"I'm so cold." My teeth chatter, and I cannot lift my head to look at her.

"What did they do to you?" She cries and covers me with a blanket, makes sure my whole body is swathed, and rubs my arms. "Did they… Did they…?"

"Defile my body?" I complete her question through chattering teeth. "They dragged me down the street, threw me into an alley, and tore my clothes."

Ida's crying intensifies, and even from within my extreme pain, I want to comfort her.

"But they didn't succeed in taking my virtue." I feel for her hand and squeeze it. "My children saved me."

"I'm so sorry." Ida hugs me and kisses my head over and over. "Ania, I'm so sorry."

The door opens again and slams loudly. I don't need to lift my head to understand who has stormed in. I could recognize his breathing and feel the quiet intensity that emanates from him in my sleep.

"I was in the square." Anton's baritone voice sounds hoarse and distressed. "I was in the damned square while they hung the political prisoners." His steps come closer to me and then move away again. "I was in the damn square when I saw your children running away from the soldiers, and I knew something terrible had happened." The steps move closer, and I can hear his teeth grinding.

"Anton," Ida addresses him, sobbing.

"Move away and let me see her!"

I feel her detach herself from me and I force myself to lift my head. The sheet slides down, and I gasp and pin it back on my chest.

Anton's eyes open wide in horror, and he draws his pistol. Without saying a word, he turns toward the door.

"No!" I shout.

"I'll kill them," he says in a chilling tone. "I'll find them and put a bullet in each of their heads."

Ida leaps to her feet and runs across the room. She sidesteps Anton, blocks the door, and spreads her arms to the sides.

"Move before I push you out of the way!" he commands in a thunderous whisper.

Ida shakes her head no. "Ania is humiliated and hurt, but they didn't have the chance to defile her body."

I sob, and Anton growls loudly.

"Anton," she declares harshly, "revenge won't help Ania now. She needs you here by her side. She doesn't need your body swinging next to the prisoners in the city square."

The hand with the gun in it shakes; nevertheless, he takes another step toward her.

I am as hungry for revenge as he is, but Ida's wisdom manages to break through the fog that envelops me. I need him like I need the air I breathe.

"Anton," I call him in a whisper, and he suddenly turns around towards me. His frenzied eyes fixate on me, and the gun falls out of his hand and crashes to the floor. I shudder at the sharp noise, and he bends down to pick up the weapon. When he looks at me again, his expression is dark and frigid.

"We cannot stay here." His voice sounds too calm. He crosses the room, spreads another blanket over me, and sits on the mattress beside me, making sure not to touch me. "Tomorrow, we leave the ghetto."

I sit up carefully, tighten the blankets around me, and stare at him, bewildered.

"I thought we could survive here," he brings his fingers nearer to my swollen cheek and grazes it just barely. "I thought we could be smarter than they are and lay low until the occupation ended." He stares at my face as though he'll find the answers to every difficult question in my eyes. "I thought I could contribute to the Resistance from here, but my contribution is insignificant." He looks away from me and leans back against the wall. "I feel that the Germans are draining my humanity from me with every day that passes. Soon I'll become just like them. A brutal machine devoid of emotion." He closes his eyes and runs his fingers through his hair. "I can't keep my promise to take care of you. Not when we're trapped in this hellhole. Not while I serve the devil."

I'm so cold. My body slides to the side, and my head rests on his knee.

"Are you going to smuggle her out of here?" Ida asks in a whisper and kneels in front of me. "Because if that's an option, then I'm in favor. Don't worry about me. I'll manage."

They both need to know that I will never leave her here alone.

"The three of us will go together," Anton responds resolutely and arranges the blankets over me. "I wouldn't think of leaving without you."

Her sob of relief blends with my own weeping.

"We'll go to the countryside," he whispers and rubs my arm over the blanket. "Before the Germans imprisoned you in the ghetto, I managed to obtain the official documents of three members of the same family for us."

"And you waited until now?" Ida asks the question echoing in my mind.

"Time was working against us." He sighs and puts his hand on my head. "I only received a conclusive answer from the family that lives in the village a week ago. Maria was very worried about her own fate and that of her sister. They only have each other now left."

"Maria?" I ask in surprise and sit up straight. I wrap the blankets around myself, and my torso trembles powerfully.

"Yes, Maria, your maid," he clarifies slowly.

"Maria has agreed to host us?" I feel my body shaking uncontrollably. "But... But I was so mean to her."

"She remembers the kindness your parents showed her."

"Maybe it's a trick?" I lick the corner of my lips, and the metallic taste of blood floods my mouth. "Maybe she's waiting for us to arrive so she can turn us in and get a bounty from the Germans?"

"Michelina trusted her." He avoids my stare. "I want to believe that if she trusted her, we can too."

The searing pain in my stomach is back, and I nod with difficulty. The longing I feel for her – and for the rest of my family – is unbearable. I look at Ida, and I see that she's looking at Anton, her eyes full of hope. I'm thinking about my children – the brave, heroic children who risked their lives to save me. I also want to feel hopeful, but the hole in my heart is too deep.

"You two should escape," I lie down again, resting my head on Anton's knee. "I won't be going with you. I cannot abandon my children."

Ida chokes up, and Anton's knee trembles under my head.

"Ania, the situation in the ghetto is about to deteriorate drastically," Anton whispers angrily through clenched teeth. "If the rumors are true, the consolidation of the ghettos is the last step before they send you all to labor camps."

I purse my lips and don't say a word.

"But there are children and sick people here," Ida pants in alarm. "What will they do with them at the labor camps?"

"We won't stay here to find out," he replies coldly.

"God save us," she murmurs.

"Your god isn't doing a very good job of keeping the children safe," I say, my voice shaking. "I'll stay here and keep them safe instead of him."

"I understand the special bond you have with them," Anton's voice softens, "but you can't really keep them safe. Not in this cursed place."

"You don't understand," I say, sniffling. "When the soldiers pushed me into the alley, I prayed that you would come to help me. You didn't come, but they did. They are no less a part of my heart than you are."

"We leave tomorrow night," Anton says as if he didn't hear me.

I squeeze his thigh and say nothing, but my decision is final.

CHAPTER 9

Ida and I sit on the sofa in silence. There's nothing left to say. It'll soon be dark, and I'm determined to stay. She, on the other hand, is determined not to leave without me.

Small, lively steps are heard from behind the door, and after a soft knock, it opens.

I stand up in surprise when my five children burst inside, pink-cheeked and panting.

"Princess Ania," Sarah giggles and gives me an exaggerated childish bow. One after the other, all the children bow down to greet me.

"What are you doing here?" I ask, concerned. "Is someone chasing you?"

They look at Ida suspiciously and remain silent.

"You can speak freely," I whisper. "Ida's a good friend of mine."

She offers them a rueful smile, and I feel her pain.

"The Guardian of the Realm sent us," Bella blurts out and then looks at Sarah, waiting for permission to continue. When Sarah nods, Bella giggles and continues. "He told us that the Princess must leave for the kingdom tonight."

"I'm not leaving." I cross my arms over my chest.

"He said you'd say that." Misza shrugs. "We don't want you to leave us either."

I open my mouth to protest again, but Sarah beats me to it and says, "He explained to us that if the Princess doesn't leave, she might get hurt like..." she blushes, "like how she almost got hurt yesterday."

"I'm not afraid for myself," I say. But my words are only half true. My fear paralyzed me yesterday. "I'm afraid of you staying here without me."

"But he said that if you get hurt..." Oleg steals a breath and continues talking quickly, "the soldiers from the kingdom won't be able to come."

I look down.

Sarah comes up to me and grabs my hand. "He said that if you leave with him tonight, he'll make sure that other guards from the kingdom will bring us to you very soon. He promised."

"He promised you that?" I raise my head in astonishment. "Anton never makes a promise..."

"... that he cannot keep." Sarah finishes my sentence and nods. "Gee, he really knows you! He said you would say that."

Ida buries her face in her hands and bursts into tears.

"Why is that woman crying?" Gershon scratches his head and walks over to her. "Is she hungry? I have a piece of candy in my pocket."

"No. No. I'm not hungry." Ida wipes away her tears. She holds his hand and kisses it again and again, and he scowls awkwardly. "I'm not hungry. I'm just happy to learn what wonderful kids Ania has."

"Princess Ania!" Bella admonishes her.

Ida nods vigorously and dashes to hide in the bathroom.

"Sarah." I kneel down and take her hands. "Are you sure the guard said he promised? Or did he use a different word? Maybe he said he would try or make an effort...?"

Sarah doesn't even blink before answering, "He said he promised!"

My heart pounds. A dangerous hope seeps into me against my will.

"So... Maybe I should wait here with you until the kingdom's guards can get us out together." I sink my teeth into the fresh wound on my lip and taste the metallic flavor of blood.

"No!" Misza shouts. "The guard said that because you are so big" – he stretches his arm up – "they can't bring us out together."

I pull Misza into my arms, hug his tiny body, and sniffle.

"I don't understand why he didn't come here to tell me this himself." I continue to resist the doomed hope.

"You're a funny princess." Bella clings to me. "The guard needs to get your carriage ready."

My eyes go to Misza's light curls, continue on to Bella's magical smile, and from there to the pale and emaciated faces of Oleg and Gershon. I steal a breath, and my eyes plunge into her black doe eyes – eyes that seem wiser and tougher to me with every passing day. Eyes that symbolize my past but, more than anything, my future. Pained, I smile at Sarah and tears cascade down my face. Parting from them is unbearably difficult. If we don't part ways directly, my heart won't allow me to abandon them.

"You must leave now." I embrace Misza and Bella, and the tears won't stop. "But you also need to promise me something very important!"

Five little faces look up at me in curiosity and nod.

"Promise me that no matter what happens, you'll stay together." I tell them as I give them a stern look.

"We promise," they reply in unison.

"Promise me that you won't get into trouble, promise me you'll hide if you come across any danger, and promise me that you'll wait for the kingdom's guards together. Promises must be kept!" I wave a finger threateningly.

"We promise." They put their hands on their hearts.

"You can leave now." The lump building up in my throat is getting bigger and choking me.

"Wait." Sarah smiles, and I see that her eyes are moist with excitement. This is the first time I have seen the pain and fear they feel, and the walls are starting to close in on me. "Tell us about your kingdom one last time."

I swallow the lump in my throat and lean forward. I whisper the story of the magical kingdom to my children and promise myself that it won't be the last time.

* * *

I run barefoot against the walls of the buildings. Raindrops land on my head, and I try to adjust my eyes to the absolute darkness that rules in the streets. The silence hurts my ears. Anton walks in front of me in his blue uniform, and I hear Ida's frightened panting behind me. Neither of us dares to speak. We move towards the gate under cover of darkness, knowing full well that even the slightest sound means a death sentence for all three of us. The only possession I took with me was the bottle of brandy that I pulled out of the trash bin and am now concealing under my black coat. Ida took her prayer book and hid it in her coat pocket. We carry our shoes in our hands and cling to the walls whenever Anton gestures with his hand.

The gate is so close. I see the Polish street lights beyond it. My heart is beating so hard that I'm afraid the guards will hear it. Ida presses against me from behind and breathes into my neck.

Two German soldiers armed with guns stand on one side of the gate, and a Polish policeman stands on the other side. Anton signals to us with his hand to stay put. He lights a cigarette and walks straight toward the soldiers. I can't hear what he says to them, but when he points in the direction of the square, they break into a sprint and go by without even noticing us. Anton quickly walks up to the Polish officer and offers him a cigarette. When he accepts it, Anton tilts his head forward and slams it into the man's nose. The policeman clutches his face in shock, and Anton comes up behind him and slits his throat with a knife. Rivers of blood drip down his shirt, and his body collapses, limp. I feel no sorrow for his violent death. Anton sits him with his back to the gate, and it looks as if the policeman sat down there at his own initiative and dozed off for his own pleasure.

Anton waves his hand, gesturing for us to join him, and we hold hands and run to the gate. Across the street, a black automobile signals with its front lights, and Anton opens the door to the back seat and pushes us inside. We lie folded one on top of the other, and he spreads a blanket over us.

The front door opens and closes, and we start moving. Silence reigns in the vehicle. I have no idea who is driving, and I have no idea what our destination is. My arms clutch Ida, and I'm afraid to breathe. At this moment – even if it only lasts for a few seconds – we are out of the ghetto. We are free.

I don't know how long we've been lying curled up and silent, but I guess it's been at least a few hours. My knees ache, and the bottle slams into my ribs every time the car goes over a bump. Suddenly the vehicle slows down, the tires screech on a gravelly surface, and finally we stop.

Our door opens.

"Get out. Quickly," Anton orders in a whisper. Ida wriggles over me and then I carefully push myself out. Anton's arms envelop me for a fleeting second. A second more precious than gold. He grasps my arms and examines my face momentarily, and the worry line on his forehead deepens. I look away at the sound of clopping hooves and see that waiting for us on the dirt path is a brown horse hitched to a wagon.

The car is still parked beside us, but the driver's face is hidden under a wide-brimmed hat.

"Change your clothes," Anton orders and pulls a large burlap sack from the trunk. He hands us faded brown dresses, woolen coats, and tattered hats, and for Ida, he adds a gray headscarf.

We turn our backs on him, take off our dresses and change clothes. When we turn back around, Anton is no longer wearing the blue police uniform. He's in brown trousers, a gray flannel shirt, and a cloth hat that he wears tilted to the side. He looks like a handsome Polish man from the countryside.

Anton nods with satisfaction at our new appearances and then gathers the clothes we've taken off as well as our yellow armbands. He shoves everything into the sack and throws it back into the trunk. Still hugging the bottle to my body under my woolen coat, I blink as the first rays of sunlight peek through the treetops. A cool breeze whips into my face, and I take a deep breath. The air smells so different – unsoiled by disease, death, and despair. This is the pure scent of hope.

The vehicle's wheels crunch over the dirt road, and soon it's engulfed in a large cloud of dust. The gelding stomps his hooves boisterously, and Anton approaches it and calms him down.

"We have to hurry," Anton says in his deep baritone and helps Ida up onto the front bench. He turns to me and gives a magnetic smile that makes my heart skip two beats. "The royal carriage awaits you, Princess." He kisses my hand, leads me to the wagon, and, holding my waist, lifts me up to the back of the cart. I sit down between the large sacks and sigh laboriously. My hope is being crushed under the weight of grief. The thoughts of the children I left behind won't let me be happy.

Anton leaps onto the bench, shakes the reins, and the horse begins to canter down the path.

"Maria's brother and his new wife were killed during the air raids on the city," says Anton, spurring the horse forward. "They came to Warsaw to sell wares and were forced to remain when the siege of the city began."

I remember the family photo Maria showed me and bow my head in sorrow. The only anchor left in Maria's life is no longer with her.

"I have their documents." Anton pats his shirt pocket. "From now on, my name is Władysław, and Ida's name is Izabella. Repeat after me!"

We mumble the names over and over again.

"Ania, your name is Katarzyna," he says without looking at me, "You are her..."

"... dead sister," I complete his sentence. "She was the first to die of the disease."

"I destroyed the record of her death." Anton peeks at me. "If she were alive, she'd be about your age. I took her documents out of the archives, and now she's alive and well, and we'll make sure she stays that way." He's quiet for a moment and then adds, "Maria says you look a lot like her."

I slide down and lie between the sacks and touch my cheek. My fingers flutter over the absent beauty mark. There is only one person in this world that I look like: my better half. She abandoned me and is now safe and sound in America. I feel around under my coat, making sure that the bottle is still close to me. A simple bottle of spirits that symbolizes a far greater promise.

A burning sensation in my stomach makes me shudder. I close my eyes.

CHAPTER 10

Big drops of water land on my face, and I sit up in a panic. The sun is hidden behind massive gray clouds, and heavy rainfall accompanies our journey. I try to shield my face with my hat, but it, too, is soaked.

"Ania, you're awake." Ida smiles at me.

Anton gives her a stern look.

"Sorry... Um... Katarzyna." She blushes in embarrassment. "Maybe we can switch places? I'd love to stretch my legs a bit."

"Of course." I rub the back of my neck and try to remember her new name. "Izabella?"

She nods in approval, and Anton pulls on the reins until the wagon stops.

He holds her hand as she hops to the back, and I take her place on the bench. The horse drinks water from a muddy puddle, and Anton gets down from the wagon, grabs a handful of hay out of one of the sacks, and feeds it to the animal.

I stare at him, standing straight-backed on the path, totally exposed under the heavy downpour, his quiet intensity surrounding him like a fortified wall. Only when he looks at me do I detect the worry line etched into his forehead.

He sits back on the bench, clicks his tongue, and shakes the reins.

The raindrops hit my face. "Don't you think the horse needs a rest?" I protect my face with my hands. "And maybe you do as well?" I ask him cautiously.

"We still have a long way to go," he says, looking into the distance, "The horse and I will rest when we reach the village."

I look at the woolen coat he's wearing. It is drenched from the rain.

"I'll make sure you're warm when we get there." He puts a protective arm around my shoulders and pulls me close.

"I swear – I haven't felt this warm in a long time." I let my head rest on his shoulder. "As far as I'm concerned, we can keep driving until the occupation ends."

A raspy laugh erupts from his throat, and I tense up. I can't remember the last time I heard him laugh. I would give my life to keep hearing the sound of his laughter.

"I've missed you." I press my nose to his neck and sniff. "I've been missing you for such a long time. I missed how safe you make me feel."

"We're not safe yet." He holds me close. "We won't be safe as long as the Germans are on Polish soil."

"But now I feel safe." The raindrops whipping at us mercilessly no longer bother me. "Now I feel invincible."

From his sigh, I understand that he doesn't share my sense of security. "I've missed you too." He presses his chin to my head. "I missed you every day. I was so close to you, yet it felt like an abyss had opened up in the ground between us. Agonizing over your safety practically drove me crazy."

"An abyss undoubtedly opened up between us," I mumble and breathe into his neck. "It's strange that before I was imprisoned in the ghetto, you were the only person I had left, and it was while I was there that I found solace in two dear friends." I peek at Ida, who is fast asleep. "Yet despite everything..." I pause, attempting to choose my words wisely. "Yet despite everything, even in the ghetto, I felt as if you were mine alone." I return to burrowing my face in his neck.

"You weren't wrong," he gently squeezes my thigh. "From the moment you were locked in the ghetto, all I cared about was your safety. I was your own private guard."

I purse my lips and ignore the stomach pain. He is what I need right now, more than anything. I try to remember when I realized that he was no longer just my sister's man but my pillar. I wither in his arms as the concerns about whom I left behind shatter my momentary sense of peace.

"Your promise." I sit up straight and stare at his profile. "Your promise to rescue my children from the ghetto. You intend to keep it, don't you?"

"I never make a promise I don't intend to keep." He clicks his tongue, urging the horse to speed up.

I close my eyes and imagine my children sitting behind me in the wagon, watching me with their innocent eyes as I lean down and whisper the story of the magical kingdom to them. My concern for them sits like a heavy boulder on my shoulders.

"I'll bring you your children." Anton squeezes my forearm. "I still don't know how or when, but I promise I'll get them to you."

"You are indeed the Guardian of the Realm," I whisper into his neck. "It's your job to bring them to me."

* * *

The wagon comes to a sudden stop, and my eyes open in alarm. I'm curled up in Anton's arms, but I force myself to sit up. My whole body aches, and the rain pummels us continuously.

"What happened?" I whisper in panic and look around. The landscape has changed. The woods look so far away, and all around us are sprawling fields. I have trouble seeing the horizon. Darkness envelops us, and the sky is gloomy and starless. I touch my triangle pendant involuntarily.

"We're nearing the village," says Anton, getting out of the cart. The horse drinks from the puddles of water that have accumulated on the narrow path and eats some hay. "We should probably try not to attract the attention of the neighbors." He points toward the horizon, and I squint and make out a cabin at the field's border. "I'll lead the wagon, and you two keep quiet."

Ida comes to sit beside me and grabs my hand. Neither of us emits a sound.

Anton walks beside the horse. He feeds him and pats his hide. The sound of the clopping hooves echoes in my ears, along with the beating of my heart. I sit tensely, ready for SS soldiers to break out of the darkness at any point and shoot us.

The wagon wheels screech on the dirt path, and Anton points to another cottage on the horizon. The cabins may be far away, but the total silence that abounds amplifies the noise made by the wagon and the horse.

After what seems like an eternity, Anton leads the horse to the left. We cross a desolate, muddy field that has seen better days.

I blink vigorously when I spot a small light flickering out of the darkness. Little by little, a two-story wooden house comes into view. On one side of it is a barn, and on the other side, a well. At the back of the cottage, there is an awning surrounded by a fence, and at the front, the ground is paved with stones. A safe haven in the heart of the wasteland.

The wagon stops near the barn, and I notice two thin figures standing at the doorstep of the cottage.

"You can get down," Anton says quietly.

"Miss Ania!" Maria's delicate voice sounds out as if from a dream, and the taller of the two figures runs toward the wagon.

I stare at her in shock. She is so thin, and her clothes are soaking wet. Her light hair lies flat against her pale face, and her cheekbones are sticking out. An identical but smaller version of her runs toward us, too, and grasps her hand. I take the bottle that is hidden under my coat and put it at the foot of the bench.

"Maria…" I whisper and jump down from the wagon. My former life suddenly bursting into my present one illustrates the horror that has befallen us all the more deeply.

"Miss Ania, I'm so glad you were able to make it to us." Maria embraces me and then grabs my hand and kisses it again and again.

"Don't." I pull my hand back. "Don't kiss my hand," I say, distraught. "I'm the one who should kiss yours." I take her hand and press it to my lips. Her skin is rough and dry. "Maria, I am so ashamed of my despicable behavior." I kiss her hand once more. "Please forgive me."

"Miss Ania, why are you asking me for forgiveness?" She looks at her hand awkwardly. "Your family provided my family with a good living for many years, and none of us could have dreamed that this would be our fate."

"I was very sorry to hear about your brother." I put my hand on my heart. "I know that he was in charge of managing the farm."

Maria bows her head in gratitude and takes a deep breath. "But now he's back." She turns to Anton, who is carrying the sacks off the cart and putting them inside the barn. "Władysław is back to help us on the farm for as long as necessary."

Her sister bursts into tears, and Maria strokes her head.

"Have you heard from your father?" Maria asks apprehensively. "Have you heard anything from Michalina?" This time her question is directed at Anton.

He stops without looking at us and shakes his head no.

"That's good," Maria murmurs in a thoughtful tone. "That means they're far away from here. In America."

A burning feeling jolts my stomach, and I nod.

Ida shields her face with her hand and stands beside me.

"This is my friend, Id…"

"This is Izabella, my brother's wife." Maria approaches her and kisses her on the cheek. "And this is Ludmiła. Luda," says Maria, pointing to her sister.

"Thank you," Ida wails and hugs Maria, then bends down to hug Luda. "I will be forever grateful."

"You're soaking wet." Maria shakes her head from side to side as if she hadn't noticed until this very moment that the rain was also coming down on her and her sister. "Let's go inside, and I'll get you some dry clothes."

Ida runs into the cabin after them, and I look over at Anton unloading the sacks and follow him into the barn. The exhausted horse munches on the hay, and the muscular man puts down one sack and immediately turns around to fetch another.

I can't hold back and run to him, wrapping my arms around his neck and leaning my head on his chest.

"Promise me that we aren't putting these sisters in danger." I stand on my tiptoes and stretch my neck to look into his eyes.

"I cannot promise you such a thing," he says, tenderly stroking my bruised cheek.

I look away for a second and then look at him again. "Then promise me that if the time comes when you have to choose between them and us, you'll choose them."

"Ania, what are you asking me to promise?" He slides his thumb around, tracing my wounded lip.

"Our stay here could be a death sentence for them," I whisper. "They're putting themselves at risk for us, and we'll never be able to repay them. So if the time comes when we're all in danger, I'm asking you to save them first."

His brown eyes cloud over, and he doesn't say a word.

"If you cannot promise me such a thing, I will promise it to myself." I kiss his cheek lightly and feel his shoulder blades tense up. "And now I will allow myself to celebrate this rare moment of freedom." I break away from him and run back to the wagon, grab the bottle, and continue into the cabin.

Ida is sitting on a chair in front of a huge pot that hangs from two iron bars with a black kerosene stove burning under it. She's covered with a blanket, but her teeth are chattering. The aroma of the stew cooking in the pot fills the small space, making my stomach growl.

I quickly examine the ground floor. It seems that Ida is sitting in what is supposed to be the parlor. It's small and clean and very modest. Among the furniture is a long, faded couch, a low table, and a gray armchair positioned under the window. The fireplace in the corner of the room doesn't appear to be in use.

I take off my dripping coat, hang it on the rack next to the door, and peek into the kitchen. An extended counter stretches under the window, but there is no sink; the wooden cabinets are old and rudimentary, and a square dining table is pushed up against the wall.

I hide the bottle in the bottom of the trash bin and leave the kitchen just as Maria and Luda come down the narrow staircase. They look tired but flushed and excited by our presence.

"You can get dressed in private upstairs." Maria hands us a pile of clothes.

Ida stands up and mumbles a few words of thanks. We take the clothes and climb the stairs.

We both study the landing. It's one open space with mattresses placed side by side on the wooden floor. Each mattress is covered with a sheet and a thick woolen blanket folded on top. On one side of the space is a small closet, and on the opposite side are two dressers. A few towels sit on the taller dresser, and a lighted lantern sits on the other. We exchange a look and then drop our new clothes and hug. We sob in each other's arms, and she doesn't have to say a word for me to know that she feels exactly as I do – that we are incredibly fortunate.

We take off our wet clothes and put on the dry garments we accepted from our hosts. Simple, plain brown dresses and pants that tie closed with a string. This is my first-time dressing without an undershirt; even in the ghetto, I made sure to wear pantyhose and garters. I think I insisted on wearing them to maintain something from my former life, but I have a feeling that I won't miss them here. I throw them onto the pile of wet clothes, and with all my heart, I give thanks for what I have been granted. Ida looks at me, giggles, and immediately comes up behind me and braids my hair into a long, tight braid.

I turn around, and she brings her hand to her heart.

"On my life, now you look exactly like..."

"My sister." Pained, I finish her sentence and finger the pendant around my neck. The longing I feel for my better half doesn't leave me alone.

Ida pats my arm in understanding and nervously looks at her prayer book.

"I couldn't leave my prayer book in the ghetto." She opens the book and runs her finger over the black writing on the first page. "It's a dedication from my mother," she explains. "I left my family photo behind in the ghetto, but when I hold this book, I feel that a part of her heart is still with me."

"It's too dangerous," I whisper. "You're not a Jew here."

"I'll wrap it up and bury it in the garden," she says, her voice trembling.

"I have a better idea." I sit down on one of the mattresses and reach for a pillow. I open the buttons and ask her to hand me the book. I push it deep into the soft padding and button up the pillow. "Now it'll be with you when you sleep." I pat the pillow, and seeing her tortured face, I smile reassuringly.

"This cabin gives us an illusion of security," Ida whispers, running her fingers through her hair.

"True. And it's a dangerous illusion." I nod, touching my swollen cheek. "But I don't want to think about what would have happened to us if we'd stayed in the ghetto." I bite my lip and frown in distress. The memory of the harrowing event I experienced still haunts me. "Ida, I'm not sure I made the right decision when I abandoned my children. Who will take care of them now?"

"I think you can trust their family members to take care of them until Anton manages to get them out of there."

"Which family members will take care of them?" I moan. "They can't even take care of themselves. I'm afraid that the children are the ones taking care of their families."

"They'll be fine," Ida says confidently, but I know she's just trying to reassure me.

"They'll be fine," I repeat after her to console myself. But the image of their little faces consumes me. I left them behind, and I have no idea how I'll handle my concern for them until we're finally reunited.

We go down the stairs arm in arm, and Anton comes inside the cabin. He shakes the water from his hat and rubs his eyes. He looks tired, but stands upright and proud.

Maria hands him some dry clothes. He nods in appreciation and raises his eyes toward us. His gaze lands on me, and his mouth falls open in surprise. His eyes are drawn to the intersection between my cheek and my ear. And when I raise my hand and touch the spot devoid of a beauty mark, he hastens to look down. The braid reminds him of her. I decide not to let his reaction upset me, but my selfish heart won't cooperate. In my dreams, he looks at me without searching for her.

Anton passes us by and heads upstairs.

Ida and I sit down on the couch and cover our knees with a blanket. We both stare at the pot of stew but don't say a word. My thoughts send me back to my former life in my luxurious home, and a blush rises on my cheeks as I remember how I relished sneering at our good-hearted maid. I inhale the rich aroma of the stew and shudder with shame. How could I have been so arrogant and stupid?

Maria urges Luda to join her in the kitchen, and they come back together with bowls and spoons in hand. Anton comes downstairs in dry, rustic clothing. Cloth suspenders hold up his pants, and his hair is parted to the side. He sits in the armchair and looks out the window into the darkness.

"Please forgive us. The food we have to offer you is very modest." Maria pours the stew into bowls and serves Anton first. "Since Władysław left us, we have been forced to ration the food that he hoarded." She hands me a bowl, and I bring it to my nose and inhale. My stomach is making loud, embarrassing noises. "We have a few sacks of rice and lentils left, and I managed to get some potatoes as well."

"It looks amazing," Ida says excitedly as Luda hands her a bowl.

"We didn't come empty-handed." Anton stirs the stew but does not taste it. "I stowed several sacks of supplies in the barn. It should be enough for all of us to live comfortably until we receive another shipment."

Maria nods in relief. No one asks where the supplies came from and who exactly is supposed to restock them. Once again, I feel extreme gratitude toward this man.

"Władysław anticipated what was to happen." Maria hands her sister a bowl, and Luda sits down on a cushion beside the low table. "He stockpiled preserved foods and even managed to obtain a pig." She chuckles sadly and pats her sister's head. "He's in the hut out back. But we're not going to hurt him. Luda likes him very much."

I'm waiting impatiently for our hostess to begin eating, but to my dismay, she sets her spoon down in her bowl and runs into the kitchen. She returns with an unlabeled bottle in her hands. "Władysław was obsessed with preserving food. He even made liquor." She waves the bottle with pride. "There's a whole cupboard full of these bottles. Luda and I don't drink alcohol, so if you want, they're yours." She puts the bottle on the table and sits on a pillow next to her sister. "You must be starving, and I can't stop chitchatting." She blushes.

"You've always been chatty," I retort and immediately look down, my cheeks burning with shame. "I can't believe I made fun of you." I shake my head in embarrassment. "Please forgive my audacity. My outburst was shameful."

"Don't apologize, Miss Ani... Katarzyna." She waves her hand, brushing off my discomfort. "That's what sisters do. They tease each other."

Maria puts her spoon in her mouth, and we all immediately follow suit. Luda goes to the kitchen and returns with a jug of water and five cups. She pours the water into the glasses, and when we thank her, she just bows her head.

"Luda doesn't speak." Maria sighs. "The day we received the awful news about Władysław, she stopped talking. I believe that the grief caused her to lose her voice." She strokes her sister's arm, and Luda continues eating as if we aren't talking about her.

"She'll find her voice yet," Ida says with determination. "This damned occupation will end. And when we celebrate the defeat of the Nazis, she'll find her voice."

"I hope so." Maria takes a sip of water.

Anton places his empty bowl on the table. "Have the Germans come through here?" He sneaks another look out the window.

"No." Maria shakes her head vigorously.

His face remains expressionless, but the tremor in his jaw betrays the fact that her answer troubles him.

"But they went through the neighboring village." She adds another serving of stew to her sister's bowl. "When I visited the neighbors to ask if they had any medicine for Luda's cough, they told me that the Germans were looking for Jews in the next village," she whispers. "They discovered a young woman hiding in the chicken coop of one of the houses and took her with them." She falls silent and bites her lip. "They locked the whole family inside the house and set it on fire."

"God save us," Ida whispers, shivering. I suddenly feel nauseated and put my bowl down.

"The neighbor claimed that no one informed the Germans. She said everyone knows SS officers can smell Jews from kilometers away." She snorts contemptuously. "I didn't want to tell her she was a fool. I needed the medicine."

"Maria," Anton says as he stands up. "You won't be able to visit the neighbors. We can't trust anyone in the foreseeable future."

"I know." She smiles at him with confidence. "The man you sent here to ask if I would agree to host you explained everything to me. He was very nice." She furrows her brow and looks at Ida. "He had beautiful green eyes just like yours."

Ida's hand feels for mine, and we interlace our fingers tightly. The knowledge that Leib is alive fuels the treacherous hope within us.

"I'd be happy to wash the dishes." Ida collects the bowls and stands up.

"We'll wash them tomorrow morning," Maria says, taking the bowls from her. "The sink is under the awning outside, and we'd better not go outside in this rain."

Ida nods. "And where is the bathroom?"

Maria bows her head in embarrassment. "We don't have a fancy bathroom inside the house like..." She doesn't say my name but gestures toward me. "We have a toilet outside, in the outhouse, and we wash ourselves under the awning with water that we draw from the well."

"That sounds perfect," Ida replies politely.

"If you need to use the toilet at night, I suggest you use the bucket next to the outer kitchen door. We prefer not to leave the house at night."

We both glance toward the kitchen and nod.

"But we have night clothes for you," Maria says with pride. "They're not fancy, but they're comfortable and warm." She turns to Anton, still sitting in the armchair. "Władysław used to sleep in his clothes."

"That's fine." Anton removes the cloth suspenders and puts them on the table. "You can go upstairs. I'll turn off the kerosene stove and go sleep in the barn."

"In the barn?" Maria opens her eyes wide in astonishment. "Władysław and Izabella always slept upstairs with us. It will look very suspicious if the man and wife don't sleep together."

Anton combs his hair to the side with his fingers and looks like he feels uncomfortable.

"Izabella and my brother only spent time in the barn when they wanted privacy." She hands the bowls to Luda, who carries them into the kitchen. "Do you need privacy?" She turns to look at Ida.

Ida pales and shakes her head no.

"Then we'll all sleep upstairs," Maria resolves, and urges Ida and me to go upstairs with her.

She opens the closet and takes out two white nightgowns made of the same coarse, thick material as the brown dresses we are wearing. In my heart, I thank her for not presenting us with satin nightgowns in the harsh cold that prevails here. I just want to lay my head on a pillow, curl up under the blankets, and drift off into a dreamless sleep.

I choose the last mattress, and Ida leaves a spot for Anton between us. I'm sure she doesn't feel comfortable sleeping next to him and only does so out of respect for our hostesses. The silence that abounds here is different and exciting. I feel as if I've been pulled out of a swarming beehive.

After a few minutes, the light downstairs goes out and Anton climbs the steps. He leaves a dim lantern lit and lies down between us. His body grazes against mine for a second, and I know that there is no way I'll be able to fall asleep.

Ida's faint snoring tells me she's already fast asleep, as does the deep breathing of the sisters. I close my eyes tightly and am careful not to touch him. Being so near to him confuses me. I've never lain beside a man like this, except for Peter. I'm hungry for Anton's comforting and protective touch, but I know it's not my touch that he yearns for. I roll over on my side, turn my back to him, and curl up in the fetal position. I sigh when it becomes evident to me that I need to use the toilet.

I carefully stand up, take the lantern, and cling to the wall that leads to the staircase. On my tiptoes, I walk down step after step and freeze when one of the beams creaks. I steal a breath and continue going down. Next, I head to the bucket by the kitchen door, untie my pants and lift my nightgown. It amazes me how much I took the luxury I had in my former life for granted, and I'm shocked by how grateful I am for the humble shelter I have the privilege of staying in now. I close my eyes and surrender to the silence for a few more seconds. Absolute, true silence without looming peril.

I position the bucket against the door and tie my pants. As I make my way back, I stare at the wooden floorboards and listen to the silence. There are no noises from neighbors' apartments, no sounds of crying and moaning from pain, no screaming from terror, and I don't feel the constant fear over the screech of approaching trucks. I'm not even afraid of hearing footsteps. Hope is dangerous, I scold myself. This sanctuary is a mirage. At any moment, a squadron of Germans could come through here and shake my world again.

I pick up my head, and the lantern almost falls from my hand when I notice the flicker of a lit cigarette. I lift the lantern and see that Anton is sitting on the couch and looking at me.

"I see I'm not the only one who can't sleep," I whisper and smile at him.

"I don't think I've had a good night's sleep since the second I saw your name on the list of the Jews," he replies, but without smiling.

I move toward him and put the lantern on the low table. The light that floods the room is soft and pleasant, but the cold air freezes my bones. I sit down next to Anton, and he spreads the blanket over my legs. I stretch it so that it covers him as well.

"Anton," I whisper and turn to look at him, "How did you manage to organize our escape so quickly? And how did you get all that food and..."

"I've been preparing for several months." He blows out cigarette smoke. "I rented a repository to store the food and maintained contact with members of the Resistance every day. The Germans probably didn't suspect that when terrorized by a common enemy, even Jews and Polacks can cooperate."

I rub my swollen cheek. "Where were you?" Tears fill my eyes. "Considering that I saw your blue uniform every time I looked down the street. How is it possible that specifically when the Germans wanted to... wanted to...?" I can't finish my sentence. "How is it possible that just when I needed you in that damn alley, I didn't see your uniform?"

He blows out smoke once more and then throws the cigarette into a glass of water left on the table.

"What happened to you was my fault." His voice sounds grim. "If I hadn't raised my club at that old Jewish man who stole your bottle of milk, I wouldn't have marked you." He locks his jaws and growls. "He ran off and reported what happened to the Jewish police, and they tipped off the Germans. That same night I was taken in for questioning at the offices of the SS."

I keep staring at his face but don't say anything.

"I had to convince them that I have no connection to you. I claimed that your screaming made me lose concentration, and the Jew had time to run away. I told them that the reason I wanted to hit him was that I didn't think I needed permission to hit a Jew." His jaw quivers. "I thought my explanation had satisfied them, but I didn't consider how sophisticated and brutal they are." He fumbles for my hand and clutches it. "They sent me to the square after they marked you as their target. The soldiers could have dragged you into the alley and put a bullet in your head, and I wouldn't have had any idea."

I consider his words and shiver. "Anton, if they had finished what they started, it would have been as if they'd murdered my spirit. I would have preferred a bullet to the head."

"But they didn't." He still won't look at me.

I bend over toward the liquor bottle and pull out its cork. I pour out two glasses and hand one to Anton.

"I'm glad you weren't there." I sip the strong drink and cough into the sleeve of my dress. "If you had been there, you would have come to my defense, and then I would be hung in the square, and you... you would have been brutally tortured in the Gestapo basements and then hung you beside me."

"But that would have happened only after I put a bullet in each of their heads." He finishes his drink with one long gulp and leans over to refill his glass.

"I was so scared." I take another sip and feel the warmth of the drink coursing through my body. "I was afraid they would rob me of what I'm saving for..." My cheeks turn red, and I sip my drink.

"Saving for whom?" My body is lifted off the couch, and I almost drop my glass as Anton sits me down on his lap with my legs spread wide. My eyes plunge deeply into his sad stare. "For whom?" In a hoarse voice, he repeats his question and leans us forward to put the glasses on the table.

When he looks at me again, the redness in my cheeks spreads down my neck all the way to the top of my nightgown.

"For a man who's not mine." I exhale sharply.

He closes his hands around my waist and pulls me to him. My brain commands me to run outside and cool off my body, but my heart begs me to stay, and the warm sensation spreads to every part of my body. I hold his shoulders, rest my forehead on his and move my pelvis slowly. The air he breathes blows between my lips, and I close my eyes. One hand holds my waist, and the other strokes my back. I feel him harden between my legs, and I rub against him harder.

"I just want to feel you," he growls hoarsely. "I *need* to feel you."

"I need it like the air I breathe." I dig my nails into his shoulders.

His hand grabs my braid, and for a split second, his breathing changes.

The pains in my stomach return, and I thrust myself back and bury my head in my hands with a muted sob.

"Ania..." he pleads in a whisper and caresses my head.

"Did you promise her?" Sniffling, I ask him coldly. "Did you promise her you'd wait for her?"

His silence is deafening.

"It's not your fault." I shake my head and then stand up and turn my back to him. "You long for her so badly you are willing to settle for an imitation of her."

"Ania." He stands up and grabs my arm. "I... I..."

I don't linger around to hear the end of his sentence.

I climb the stairs, lie down on the mattress, and wipe away my tears. Feelings of guilt fill my heart. If he hadn't touched the braid, I wouldn't have found the strength to break away from him. My body wants him, but it's my heart that *needs* him.

I rub my belly and silently ask my sister for forgiveness.

CHAPTER 11

Paradise. There is no more accurate way to describe waking up in our hostess's welcoming abode. I stretch my arms and legs and smile at Ida. Anton and the two sisters have already risen and begun their day and – judging by the light flooding the room – it's clear that we've slept in.

"Can you believe we're not in the ghetto?" Ida whispers and sits up.

I inhale deeply, stand up, and look out the window at the backyard and the green fields that surround it.

"I needed to make sure we weren't dreaming," I say, pressing my hands to the windowpane.

"I find the silence a bit unsettling." Ida stands up and changes out of her nightgown into the brown dress. "I'd gotten used to waking up to the noise of the street. The footsteps, the shouts, the pleas..."

"The screeching of truck wheels," I complete her sentence and take off my nightdress. "The clicking heels of the German's boots and our rapid heartbeats." I put my hand on my heart. "My heart has calmed down." I put on my dress and turn to look out the window again. I see Luda's slender figure. She goes into the hut and brings out the pig. She hugs him affectionately and walks around the barnyard with him. "Ida, I don't feel scared, and that in itself worries me."

Ida stands beside me and taps on the window pane with her nails. "Here it's so easy to imagine that the war is over."

My torso shudders, and I hug myself. "I'm grateful to Maria for her hospitality, but I feel far from perfectly happy. I miss my father and Michalina, and I'm worried about my mother. Unlike us, she isn't staying in the village along with her dearest friends. She must be so lonely." I squeeze Ida's hand. "And I can't stop thinking about my sweet children." Tears collect in the corners of my eyes. "How can I be happy knowing I chose to save myself and leave them behind?"

"Anton will get them out of there," she replies confidently. "It may take a little while, but he'll keep his promise. I have no doubt about it."

I nod and take some comfort in her faith.

"I keep thinking about Peter," Ida chuckles sadly, "Imagining what he would say if he saw us now."

A smile stretches across my lips. "He would look at us with an absolutely appalled expression." I mimic the way he always curls his mustache, and I imitate his voice, "The two fair maidens clad in such rags is positively out of the question." I point at Ida's dress in disgust. "The cursed Germans can rob us of our freedom, our sustenance, and our happiness, but under no circumstances can we allow them to rob us of our sense of fashion."

Ida bursts out laughing, and her eyes fill with tears. "I pray that he is safe and sound."

"He has to be." I bend down and fold my blanket. "He promised that we'd drink the brandy we have left in the bottle together."

"I'm so happy that you're with me here." Ida surprises me with a tight embrace. "I used to think you were arrogant and felt really guilty about having such unkind thoughts," she confesses awkwardly. "Michalina always spoke very highly of you, but it was so hard to win a place in your heart."

"I was proud and stupid." I pat her on the back. "I believed that the sun shone on me alone and that I was the center of the universe."

"You are the center of the universe to me." She breaks away from me and bends down to fold another blanket. "You are the center of the universe for both your children and for Anton."

My heart skips a beat when she mentions his name, and I turn away from her to hide the blush rising on my cheeks.

"You won't be able to fight your feelings forever." Her tone is thoughtful. "You're punishing yourself and him as well."

I gasp. Ida never before asked me about my feelings for Anton.

"The feelings I have towards him are those of gratitude. I mustn't get confused and think that they're some other profound emotion," I say and bite my lip. My lie almost makes sense.

"I understand that you feel tormented by your duty to your sister." She hands me two ends of a blanket, and I have no choice but to turn and face her. "But Michalina isn't here. She left."

"And does that mean I'm allowed to betray her now?" My voice shakes.

"It's not a betrayal," Ida replies adamantly. "If I had a sister, I would want her to be happy. I would hope that despite the madness raging throughout the world, she would have the chance to bring to fruition the special connection she created with a man who sees nothing but her."

"He sees her in me," I insist, and I fold the blanket. "Every time he looks at me, he thinks of her."

Ida rolls her eyes but remains silent.

Footsteps sound on the stairs, and Maria appears before us, her face aglow.

"Breakfast is ready."

Gratitude floods my heart. I drop the blanket, run to her, hold her hands, and press them to my lips.

"Maria, I hope the day will come when I can repay you for all the suffering I have caused you."

"Katarzyna." She says her sister's name and pulls her hands away, "You are not our guests on the farm, and I forbid you to thank me even one more time. We are family now."

I swallow the lump in my throat and nod.

She urges us to walk down the stairs and sit at the table where there are two steaming bowls of porridge. I throw a questioning look at the door.

"Luda and Anton have already eaten," she says, and sits down next to us. "It's still hard for me to get used to the fact that we're not alone," she whispers and smiles. "Working on the farm is so hard. I wish this war would end and I could come back to work for you. Do you think your parents would agree to accept Luda to work for them as well? She is very hard-working, and I won't be able to leave her alone."

My spoon is suspended in front of my lips, and I can't bring myself to take a bite.

"Maria, are you really asking me that question?"

Her expression is one of disbelief

"My parents and I will never be able to repay the debt we owe you." I lean down and squeeze her hand. "We are the ones who will have to work for you and Luda."

"No, no." She waves her hands, and her lips stretch into an awkward smile. "At the end of the war, we'll settle for the opportunity to earn a decent living working for you." She puts a heaping spoon of porridge into her mouth and chuckles with her mouth full.

Ida, who had been listening to our conversation until now, begins to gobble down the contents of her bowl.

We finish eating and take the dishes to the hut in the back. The rain has stopped, and the sun is shining, creating a false sense of warmth.

Maria shows us how to draw water from the well, and Luda approaches and proudly presents the filthy pig to us.

Ida grimaces in disgust, and I giggle but take care not to touch the smelly creature. We wash the dishes and I close my eyes, listening to the sounds of chirping birds. The feeling of freedom is unimaginable.

We can hear footsteps coming from the barn, and Anton nods to us. He swings an ax over a log and splits it into firewood-sized pieces. I wash the breakfast bowls and stare at him. The cloth suspenders press against his shoulder blades, and his muscles expand with each swing of the ax. The sun's rays glimmer playfully on his hair. I remember the events of last night, the explosion of desire that flooded my body in response to his touch. He looks at me, and my cheeks turn scarlet. I hurry to turn my head. Staying here with him is the best thing that has ever happened to me – but also the worst thing. I have no idea how I'll be able to keep my distance from him when he's so close. Every time he looks at me, another crack opens in my heart.

"We should take advantage of the sun to do laundry." Maria interrupts my ruminations. "We'll wash the sheets and towels. We even have scented soap flakes." She picks up two empty buckets and runs into the house.

Luda puts the pig back in its pen, and her feet sink into the mud. She feeds him potato skins and pets him. My heart aches as I remember the soft fur of my cat. Images of the ghetto attack me mercilessly, and I shake my head and command myself to suppress such thoughts. The only thing I should be thinking about is my children. I have no idea when we'll get any news, and my concern for them is driving me insane. I walk over to Anton with determination.

He swings the ax, chops the log, and puts the two halves on the pile.

I cross my arms over my chest and give him a stern look.

"How can I help you?" He gives me a half-smile.

"I need to know when my children will get here."

He swings the ax into the tree trunk and stands up straight.

"You know I still don't have an answer that will please you." His jaw quivers, and he combs his hair back with his fingers.

"So when *will* you have an answer that'll please me?" I wrinkle my nose in frustration.

"We'll patiently wait for word from our contacts in the Resistance."

"But I have no patience." I stomp my feet. "Every day that goes by is a day that one of them may starve to death." I understand that my anger is irrational, but I can't help it. I groan and force myself to turn and walk away into the fields. A few seconds later he catches up with me.

"Ania, I share your concern." He sighs and puts his hat on. "Trust me, if there had been a way to get them out of there with you, I wouldn't have hesitated."

"We could have crowded them into the car with us." Tears flow from my eyes. "We could have hidden them in the trunk. We should have tried," I say, sniveling. "They're so small and fragile."

"No," he replies angrily and seizes my arm. "Any such attempt could have ended in disaster." He cups my chin and forces me to look into his eyes. "We can't risk the lives of five children just because your conscience torments you." He lets go of my chin and strokes my cheek. "Can you imagine what would have happened if they'd caught us with them?"

Goosebumps pop up on my arms.

"And what would happen if they were here and the Germans raided the farm? Where would we hide them?"

I have no answer, so I remain silent.

"Trust me," he pleads. "I know how important they are to you, and therefore they are important to me as well. Let me prove to you that I can keep my promise."

His hand moves away from my cheek, and I grab it and pull it back. I close my eyes and tilt my head toward his palm. "I trust you," I whisper, "The problem is that I don't trust myself to maintain my sanity."

"I'm here with you," he replies tenderly. "And as long as I am breathing, I will do anything to protect you."

I feel activity again in my stomach, and I open my eyes.

"My feelings for you are confusing me." I drop his hand and step back. "Every time you look at me, my heart skips a beat." The bare confession bursts out of me uncontrollably. "Anton, please help me protect my heart."

He approaches me, his eyes shining, and I pull away again.

"When you are this close to me, and you look at me like that, I forget for a moment that you see her in me." I gnaw on my lip in embarrassment.

He opens his mouth to answer me, but I reach out my hand and cover his lips. "Guilt plagues me constantly." Tears fill my eyes. "You promised her you'd wait for her, so I ask that you promise me one more thing." I take a deep breath and sniffle. "Promise me you'll keep your distance from me."

He doesn't say a word.

"Anton." I say his name imploringly.

"I never make a promise I can't keep." He spins around and heads back to the farm.

CHAPTER 12

The wind whips in my face, and the silence thunders in my ears. The silence holds a false promise of security.

I sit on the chair outside the house and look out over the muddy fields. The rain falls sporadically, so whenever I get the chance, I sit outside on the chair and wait for Anton to keep his promise and for my children to join me.

A long time has passed since we arrived at this safe haven. Maria insisted on celebrating my birthday four months ago. Three years have passed since I got to celebrate my birthday with my twin. Almost a year has gone by, but so far 1942 has been confusing and full of extreme changes ranging from hope to unbearable worry. We have had the privilege of enjoying weeks of blazing sun, have been excited by months of bright white snow, and have huddled in a cabin for weeks of heavy rain. The seasons pass, but danger still looms over us. The longing I feel for my family is like a silent companion that's with me from the moment I open my eyes until I fall asleep at night. But it's the concern for my children that intensifies day after day. Nightmares haunt me, and there is a pain in my chest that doesn't subside. Ever. Every time I ask Anton when he'll fulfill his promise, he answers that he's waiting for updates from his contact person.

Every day here is the same as the one before it. Our routine has brought with it a sense of security, and I no longer wait apprehensively for a catastrophe to befall us. Over the past few months, we have managed to revive the farm and are enjoying new crops. We've tended beds of vegetables, tiled the front yard, and ensured that the cabin is always clean and tidy. We try to keep ourselves busy for hours on end, but from time to time we content ourselves with sitting together in the parlor and sewing patchwork quilts. The idle hours don't bother me. I am grateful for every moment that I can inhale fresh air as a free woman. Free for now.

I gaze at the green landscape tinted in murky sepia tones and remind myself that our freedom can be taken from us at any moment. Throughout our stay here, a coachman has arrived twice. Anton sent us all to the cabin and held a long conversation with him in the barn. The news that came from his contact last month shocked us to the core. The goddamned Germans have conquered country after country – with the help of the Italian fascists. They are still fighting against those who were once their allies— the Russian army. Europe is bleeding, and Britain, still waiting for help from the Americans, stands alone on the battlefield. But the most challenging news for me to hear was about the evacuation of the ghetto's inhabitants. Men, women, and children. Anton could not explain why and where so many Jews were being moved to. He didn't know where the children were being sent. After all, there's no way they could be useful in the labor camps. I've implored, begged, and even screamed at him to bring me back my children; every time, he simply repeated his promise that the children would be brought to me but refused to tell me when.

I glance in the direction of the barn and know he's there. From sunrise to sunset, he isolates himself in the work he has taken upon himself. He splits firewood for the fireplace, sands down wooden beams, digs pits and covers them, takes the horse out for its daily walk, and takes care of our daily meal rations.

Anton comes out of the barn carrying firewood toward the house. I stare at his broad shoulders and his immense arms. It seems that since we've been here, his muscles have doubled in size. The unkempt, rustic look flatters him. He gives me a small smile as he walks past me and into the cabin.

I sigh and hug myself. During the day, I valiantly face my nearness to him, but at night, when I lie next to him on the mattress, hearing his breathing and feeling the warmth emanating from his body, my self-restraint threatens to fade, and I agonize over my need to take comfort in his touch. Sometimes I think it is another punishment imposed upon me because of my behavior in my former life. It's a punishment that only gets worse as time goes by.

When he leaves the cabin, I look away from him and rub my belly. During the last few months, the abdominal pains no longer come and go; they're there all the time. I've been trying to understand what it means. Is Michalina plagued by concern for Mother and me? Is she signaling to me that I should be worried about her? I bite my lip and groan softly. Alongside my longing, anger also bubbles up in me. Why won't she leave me alone? Why does she have to add to my concern and distress? After all, she's with Father – and in the safest place in the world.

Suddenly I hear a strange noise. It comes from afar, rising out of the sounds of nature that surround us. I turn toward the noise and squint before a cloud of dust. Anton runs out of the barn, and I cower in the chair.

He stands in front of me with a grim expression. "Katarzyna," he says my fake name harshly, "We've practiced this countless times, and now you must make sure everyone plays their roles."

"The Germans?" I whisper in terror. "Is it the Germans?"

"I find it hard to believe that it's the Swedes." He raises his hand and gestures for me to go inside the cabin.

I leap out of my chair and storm into the cabin. I know what I have to do, but the pressure threatens to paralyze me.

Ida puts her prayer book on her lap and gives me a questioning look.

"The book." I point at it in horror. "Hide the book in the pillow. They are coming."

She turns white and runs upstairs. I head to the kitchen. Maria and Luda aren't there. I go out to the backyard, walk around the well and go into the pig's hut. Maria and Luda are rolling in the mud, covering themselves in muck from head to toe. Maria nods at me to indicate that they already understood the nature of the noise and are preparing themselves for the Germans' visit. I get down on my knees, soil my dress, and then grab a handful of mud from under the pig's feet and rub it on my face. The smell is nauseating.

The noise gets louder, and I exhale apprehensively.

Ida prostrates herself on the mire and smears herself with mud as well. I give her a wry smile and, for just a moment, imagine what Peter would say if he were here with us. He would surely look at us in shock and walk around the hut swinging his hips. *Look at yourselves! Swine excrement won't touch me! I'd rather the Germans hang me from the ceiling of the barn!* I stand up and spread hay around the yard. Then I grab a rake and Ida grabs a pitchfork. Maria and Luda sit cross-legged before the pig and feed it the food waste they save in the bucket. Fear gnaws at my bones.

The ground shakes as the procession of vehicles crosses the path leading to the cabin, and then I hear running footsteps and shouting in German. I try to regulate my breathing and calm myself down.

I sweep hay to the corner of the hut, and Ida piles it up.

The noise coming from the cabin is absolutely dreadful. Doors opening and slamming, furniture breaking, heels clicking, and yelling in German. The ground vibrates as the clangorous footsteps approach us. My breathing is rapid, and I realize that I must regain my composure immediately.

I look cow-eyed at an SS officer accompanied by several soldiers in gray coats. Anton is standing next to them. His cheek is swollen, and his lip is bleeding, but he stands up straight and directs an alert look at us. I don't dare to breathe, and I don't utter a single syllable.

"Heil Hitler!" The SS officer announces, raising his arm in a salute and examining the spectacle in front of him with disgust. "Filthy country Polacks!" are the words that he spits out. "Even their pig is cleaner than them."

None of us says anything.

"Juden!" The officer barks. "We are looking for stinking Jews."

I move my head from side to side to indicate that we cannot understand him.

"Translator!" The officer barks again, and instantly, a young soldier with rosy cheeks and cruel, beady eyes appears at his side.

"The commander wants to know if you are hiding Jews here," he addresses us in Polish. "The commander won't punish you if you hand over the Jews to us right now." He looks me over with distaste, and then his gaze settles on Luda. "If you deny that you are hiding vermin here and we find them, the commander will order us to lock you in the cabin and set it on fire."

My shoulders tremble, and I grip the rake with all my might.

"I showed you our documents. There are no Jews here," Anton answers for us, and the translator turns and punches him forcefully in the face. I purse my lips and stifle a cry of panic. My friends look horrified.

"Come with me." The officer gestures to us with his hand.

"Move it!" The translator barks and holds his nose as we leave the shed.

"I hope the next step will be to eliminate all these stinking Poles as well." The officer grimaces and motions to us to keep our distance from him.

We follow him into the cabin and view the destruction in silence. The officer clicks his boot heels, and the soldiers stand at attention.

"Load the truck with everything you find in the barn and come back here."

The soldiers drag Anton outside and leave the cabin with him. Only the translator lingers, continuing to look at us with disgust.

The four of us stand against the wall with our heads bowed.

The officer takes a step forward and whistles to himself. He folds his arms behind his back and steps on the wooden planks as if taking a leisurely stroll.

"Look at me!" he commands with a shout.

The soldier translates, and we hesitantly raise our heads.

"The Jews aren't human. They're like small, pesky rats."

The soldier translates.

"When I whistle, they get so scared I can hear their panicked breathing." He puts his finger to his lips, signaling to us to keep silent.

He paces back and forth to the kitchen, whistling a chilling melody. Abruptly he pulls out his gun and shoots the couch, which is lying on its side.

The four of us gasp but don't say a word.

He goes back to pacing and whistling and then shoots the floor.

"Too bad..." The officer shrugs. "I was really hoping these stinking Poles were hiding some rats here." He raises his hand to the side, motioning for us to get out of the way, and we move as one. "At least we can enjoy a juicy pork stew." He clicks his heels and leaves the cabin. The translator looks at Luda again, and then follows him.

None of us dares to breathe.

"Don't load the sacks yourselves," I hear him scolding his soldiers, "Let that Polack work a little."

A few minutes later the officer returns, accompanied by his soldiers.

"Kick the whores out. I can't relax in this stink."

None of the soldiers dares to touch us. Instead, they kick our legs so that we understand the order.

"Sit here." The translator points to the outer wall of the hut, and we sit down on the ground.

Anton comes out of the barn. A sack rests on his shoulder, and he looks tormented. He appears to sigh in relief when he spots us. I realize that the shots that sounded from the cabin were much more frightening for him than for us.

He loads the sack onto the truck and then goes back to the barn. Time after time, he carries sacks on his back and loads them onto the truck. I rub my filthy face and examine the German's magnificent procession. A black car is parked in front, and behind it are several motorcycles and two trucks. A shiver runs down my spine. The world is scorching, ravaged by war, yet the Germans are sparing no means to find Jews. I lean against the cabin wall and close my eyes. But a horrible scream makes me open them again.

"It's just the pig," Maria whispers to Luda, "As soon as we have enough money, I'll buy you a new one."

Luda's eyes flood with tears.

The noise of footsteps and the opening and closing of cupboards accompanies us for a long time, until the strong aroma of cooking wafts out of the open door.

The Germans must be sitting down to eat on the couch because their voices keep getting louder and clearer.

"The Polack's wife doesn't look Polish."

Without noticing what I'm doing, I grab Ida's hand.

"We've seen Polish women with dark hair before."

I turn to Ida and tighten the kerchief around her head. She looks terrified.

"If she was a man, we would strip her to make sure."

Thunderous laughter makes me clench my fists.

"Their documents aren't forged," I hear the officer's angry answer. "If I had the slightest doubt, they would have already been slaughtered like their pig."

"Heil Hitler!" The cynical soldier shouts back, and then there is silence.

I look in the direction of the barn. Anton keeps doing what he was told and doesn't look at us. He lifts the sacks without difficulty, and the sun behind him illuminates his silhouette.

Two soldiers come out of the hut with bowls full of stew and stand in front of us.

"Would you fuck these stinking whores?" one of them asks and shoves a fatty piece of meat into his mouth.

"I'd rather fuck the pig," the other one chuckles, "Believe me, even the pig wouldn't have fucked them." He shakes his fork, and the chunk of pork lands in the mud beside Ida's feet. "Eat it, you filthy whore!"

Ida looks away and doesn't respond.

The soldier takes his rifle from his shoulder and uses it to push the meat toward her. "Eat it, or I'll put a bullet in your head." He points to the meat and acts out a chewing motion.

Ida stares at the pork flesh.

The soldier points his weapon at her, and I stick her with my elbow. She grunts, and I reach out to eat the chunk of meat instead of her. She groans softly and then slaps my hand. She picks up the pork and shoves it into her mouth. She chews it quickly and swallows it. Gagging sounds rise in her throat.

"If she throws it up, I'll make her eat her own vomit." The soldier laughs and then kicks her leg, and they go back inside the cabin.

"Don't vomit!" I order her quietly. She looks at me with teary eyes and doesn't have to say a word for me to feel her pain. I know her religion forbids her to eat pork. Even in the ghetto, on the days when Anton's delivery was delayed, she never agreed to taste the dried pork that I saved for a rainy day. It is her unwavering faith that helps her keep her sanity, and now the Germans have robbed yet another piece of her soul. I squeeze her hand and weep with her.

The officer exits the cabin and lights a cigarette. "Do one last inspection of the barn," he orders his soldiers. "And don't hesitate to shoot if you smell rats." He laughs and gets into the black car.

Four soldiers run towards the barn, and the rest carry out the canned food and the bottles of liquor from the kitchen.

The translator comes out of the cabin, rubs his belly with satisfaction, then turns and looks down at us mockingly. "If you weren't so smelly, I would end the meal with dessert." He holds his groin. "But who knows… we're not leaving Poland anytime soon, so maybe we'll meet again." He gets on a motorcycle and puts a helmet on his head.

The last soldiers leave the barn and jump into the back of the truck, and the procession leaves with the squeal of wheels, giving us a shower of mud.

None of us moves until the silence returns.

I'm the first to shake off the shock, and I run to the barn. Anton is standing next to the horse and sweeping the hay into a high heap in the corner.

He turns to me, and his downcast eyes brighten slowly.

"We did it." I put my hands over my mouth. My body is trembling with emotion and tremendous relief.

"For now," he whispers and comes closer to me.

"No, no." I wave my hands in alarm. "Don't come any closer. I'm filthy."

He tilts his head to one side and studies me intently. "Ania, even when you are covered in mud, there is no one as beautiful as you in the entire world."

His compliment warms my heart, but I regain my senses quickly this time. "There is one other person" – I give him a lopsided grin and turn to pet the horse's mane – "my better half."

A powerful clap of thunder shakes the sky and enormous drops of rain land on the ground outside the barn.

"Do you think they'll be back soon?"

"No." He lets out a snort of contempt. "They've moved on to wreak havoc on the home of some other poor villagers."

"Then I'd better go get cleaned up." I sigh. "After that, we'll try to figure out how to survive without food."

"Tonight we'll have a festive supper," he announces, and I spin around and look at him in astonishment. "I prepared for this visit in advance," he says, exposing massive wooden beams concealed beneath the hay.

I tap the beam with my shoe but don't hear any echo beneath it.

"I dug a deep hole." He kneels and knocks on the beam with his knuckles. "I buried sacks of food and covered them with hay and several layers of wood."

"So we won't starve?" I keep staring at the beams.

"Not as long as the Guardian of the Realm is here." He laughs a short, husky laugh.

"Maybe we should clean your face." I point to his bruised countenance.

"It's nothing." He rolls his eyes. "Every man gets punched from time to time. I'd just really love the chance to even the score." He undoes the rope that keeps the horse tied to the beam and leads the animal outside.

* * *

Evening has begun to fall, bringing with it a false sense of peace.

"Why didn't they take the horse too? They took everything else." I ask and lean against the doorframe.

"What would they do with this old horse? He deserves a mercy killing, and they aren't exactly known for their mercy." He pulls on the rope, and the horse follows him out to the back fields.

I watch his broad back disappear into the darkness, and the knowledge that we are all still here in our make-believe safe haven fills my heart with fervent hope. The sense of triumph that envelops me is very powerful. I feel as if we alone defeated the entire German army.

I go back to the cabin and see Maria and Luda standing next to each other at the entrance, trembling and terrified.

"Anton says they won't be back soon." I give them half a smile. "And he even hid food in the barn."

A sigh of relief escapes both of their lips.

"So we can bathe?" Maria says while clutching her sister's arm.

I nod in consent, and they run through the kitchen and out to the shed. I open the door, look into the darkness and finally let my tense shoulders relax a bit.

I join Luda and Maria in the back shed. They are already naked and scrubbing themselves clean. They are soaping themselves under the open sky and letting the rain wash away the grime. I look around for Ida and spot her leaning against the side of the hut, sticking a finger down her throat. She vomits and sobs loudly.

"Ida." I place my hand on her back. "I'm sure your God will forgive you. You had no choice."

"I know." She stands up with difficulty and rubs her soiled face. "I'm not afraid of His wrath. But Ania, what do I have left?" She spreads her arms out to the sides. "My parents aren't with me, my brother is risking his life in the forest, and I'm covered from head to toe in pig shit. What kind of a life is this?"

I've never seen Ida so forlorn, and I don't know how to lift her spirits. "This is life." I shrug. "Just life." I pick up the bucket and splash water on her face.

In shock, she opens her eyes wide, and I wrinkle my nose in a fake apology.

She exhales forcefully and then picks up the other bucket and pours water over me. I shriek and flail my arms, and we both burst into raucous laughter.

Maria giggles with delight and hands Ida the soap. Luda smiles and runs, dripping with water, into the cabin. She returns a few minutes later, clothed in a white nightdress, and puts towels and nightdresses on the chair for us. Her teeth chatter from the biting cold, and she scurries back inside.

I get undressed and soap myself up, spinning around under the pouring rain. Even the intense cold cannot ruin my mood.

The soap falls from my hand when I hear the screeching of the wheels.

CHAPTER 13

I grab the towel from the chair, wipe my face, and put on my nightgown.

"Where's Luda?" I ask with a shout.

Maria points to the cabin, and the blood drains from her face.

"Go to the mud!" I command Ida, who quickly wraps Maria in a nightdress and pulls her to the shed.

I consider joining them for a moment, but I don't want Luda to face the Germans alone. I tiptoe inside, cross the kitchen and gasp.

The soldier who translated for the SS officer is standing at the door of the cabin and studying Luda, who stands in front him with her head bowed. He doesn't notice me.

I gnash my teeth when I see the hat he left on the chair by the door. Our arrogance caused us to lose focus, and we may pay a heavy price.

"Interesting..." the soldier mutters and wrinkles his forehead. "You've undergone quite a transformation since I left."

Luda hugs herself and doesn't answer.

"That white nightgown almost makes you look pretty." He takes one step toward her, and she steps back. "I can imagine what's underneath," he snickers. "Are you trying to seduce me?" He closes the gap between them with two long strides and grabs her arm forcefully.

I close my eyes and try to decide what to do. If I scream, Anton will hear me, but the soldier might draw his pistol and shoot Luda in the head. If I flee, I'll save myself, but at a heavier price than I'm willing to pay.

I walk out of the kitchen and stretch my lips in a naughty smile.

The soldier pierces me with a cold stare and raises an eyebrow in surprise. "So clean and fragrant..." he sniffs. "And so pleasant to the touch." He slides his hand over Luda's arm. "Get out of here," he barks at me.

"She's just a little girl," I say, coming closer to them. "Don't you prefer a woman?" I swallow the lump in my throat and force myself to keep smiling.

"I prefer them young." He presses himself against Luda, and I hear her whimpering in terror.

"She... She doesn't know how to pleasure a strong man like you." I bat my eyelashes. "Leave her alone, and I promise you won't leave here disappointed."

He scrutinizes me with his beady, wicked eyes and then drops her arm and smirks. "I'd better be satisfied, or I'll have your little sister for dessert." He unbuckles his belt and approaches me.

I only look at his face but with my hand motion to Luda to run away. I peek out of the corner of my eye and see that she's doing what I asked. Now I only have myself to worry about.

Before I have time to blink, the soldier lifts me up by the waist and spins me around. He pushes me until my belly is pressed against the kitchen table. "I'm waiting to hear you moan, bitch." He pulls up my dress, and I whimper on the table. He spreads my legs apart and slaps my buttocks. Strangely enough, I no longer feel anxious. This time no one is watching my humiliation. "It will only hurt for a second," I murmur and shut my eyes. "It will only hurt for a second."

"It will hurt him much more than that," I hear a deep angry voice, and the body looming over me is separated from me. I open my eyes at the sound of a loud whack and hurry to stand up and pull down my nightgown. The spectacle unfolding before my eyes can't exactly be called a struggle. There is one figure in a gray coat sprawled on the ground and another figure with sparks of fire shooting from his eyes, relentlessly pummeling the first in the face.

Anton looks as though he's been possessed by a demon. His expression is frozen, and his hands are clenched into fists. He punches the soldier in the face again and again. Each colliding fist is accompanied by the sound of bones cracking. The soldier's horrified eyes are practically popping out of their sockets. Another punch. Blood spurts from his mouth and his teeth fall to the floor. After the next blow, his nose loses shape. A smile stretches across my lips. I taste the sweet flavor of revenge on my tongue. The sound of the soldier's breathing gradually fades.

Ida leaps on Anton's back in an attempt to pull him off. He growls like a wounded animal, shakes her off, and continues clobbering the soldier's limp body with a fury the likes of which I have never before seen.

"He's dead!" Ida shouts and jumps onto Anton's back again. "You killed him. You can stop now."

Anton growls again. His looks from me to the mangled body lying on the floor, and he exhales forcefully.

"What'll we do now?" Ida slides off his back and scratches her forehead. "What'll we do when they come looking for him?"

Maria grabs Luda in alarm, and the smile is wiped off my face. The momentary happiness I felt is replaced by horror.

Anton stands up and massages the back of his head. He fidgets, combing his hair to the side with his fingers and nods decisively. "I'll make him and his motorcycle disappear, and you'll have to convince them that he wasn't here."

"But... But he came back to get his hat," I stammer and point to the hat on the chair. "He must have told one of his friends."

"Then think of some other explanation!" Anton barks at me, and I recoil in alarm. He flings the body over his shoulder, picks up the hat the soldier forgot, and leaves the cabin.

"What'll we do?" Ida paces around in circles. "They'll come back here and presume we hurt him. They... They..."

Thoughts are swirling through my head, but I force myself to keep my composure. I motion for them to follow me and run to the pig's empty shed. We take off our nightgowns, put on our dirty clothes again, and spread mud and grime all over each other. I imagine dozens of possible scenarios. We are brutally murdered in every single one.

When we leave the shed, we see Anton holding a hoe and filling one of the holes that he dug with mud. Until today, I had wondered what he dug all those holes for. For a time I'd feared that he was preparing in case he would have to bury one of us, but now I understand that he must have been preparing for a completely different scenario. He flattens the soil and compresses it, then runs to the front of the cabin and starts the motorcycle's engine.

"First, we must clean up the blood marks. Then we have to look busy," I say as we head back to the cabin. Maria and Luda vigorously scrub the blood stains from the floor, and I take out a hammer and nails from one of the busted cabinets.

I pound the cabinet door with the hammer and find that the hammering calms my nerves a bit.

Bang after bang... time passes... and the Germans do not return.

Anton comes back into the cabin, confirming with a nod of his head that he has successfully completed his mission. When our eyes meet, his jaw trembles, and I understand that he is still angry. He walks into the parlor, lights a fire in the fireplace, and sits down in the armchair by the window.

Maria and Luda continue scouring the cabin, and I stand by the kitchen window and stare into the darkness outside. Maybe there'll be a miracle and we won't merit another visit. Maybe he didn't tell anyone he was coming back here. Maybe his despicable friends thought he was driving off to abuse the occupants of a different farm. And what the hell are we going to do if they come back here?

I detect flickers of light on the horizon and realize no miracle has occurred. The racket of their engines gets louder and louder, and I take a deep breath. Suddenly my mind clears. The idea forming in my brain is so far-fetched, but every other idea has loose ends and concludes with a bullet in each of our skulls.

"Go back to looking busy," I say calmly and also signal to Anton to continue sitting in his place. He keeps looking out the window, and clenching his hands into fists over and over again. He seems to be preparing for one final battle.

I peek out of the kitchen window and see two soldiers getting off their motorcycles. They take their helmets off, put them on their seats, and put on their hats. They look out across the yard, searching for their friend's motorcycle.

Ida hands me a nail with trembling fingers, and I pierce it into the cabinet door and knock on it with my hammer to the rhythm of my breathing.

The door opens with a bang, and the soldiers enter. They look into the kitchen and then at Anton. He stands up and looks at them, his face expressionless.

"Heil Hitler!" they announce, with raised arms and a click of their heels.

None of us responds.

"Where is he?" one of the soldiers barks in German.

Anton moves his head from side to side to indicate to them that he can't understand their question.

"Where is the soldier?" He barks again and points to his uniform.

I approach them tentatively, and they hold their noses grimacing with disgust, gesturing at me to keep my distance.

"Soldier?" I repeat after them in broken German.

"Yes. Yes. Soldier," they reply impatiently.

"Ah..." I nod. "The soldier was here," I say in Polish and point to the floor. "He took his hat," I continue to explain in Polish and point to their hats.

The soldiers exchange glances until one clarifies to the other, "I think she's saying he came back to get his hat."

"So where is he?" barks the taller of the two.

"He drove away." With my hands, I mimic the motions of holding the motorcycle's handlebar. Then, before they can ask any more questions, I point in the direction opposite from the way they came. "He went there," I say in Polish and continue to point.

"What is the whore saying?" The tall soldier scowls in annoyance.

"I think she is saying he went west," answers the short one, frowning.

"What the hell would he be doing there?" The tall one's face broadcasts suspicion. "We didn't receive an order to retreat." Abruptly he opens his eyes wide in shock. "Do you think he deserted?"

"I think if he was stupid enough to do such a thing, he won't have time to visit that whore from Berlin that he's always blabbing about." He adjusts his hat and glances to the sides. "They'll throw him in one of the camps with the stinking Jews and exterminate him along with them."

Did he say exterminate? I purse my lips when I realize that I almost blurted out a question in German that would have sealed our fate.

"I never tolerated him," says the tall one with a venomous smile and then stands at attention and clicks his heels. "But before we tell the commander, we should make sure this pig isn't lying." He turns toward the kitchen and points to Ida. "You! Come with us!"

Ida turns white and puts the nails on the counter.

He motions for her to go up to the second floor, and they both climb the stairs after her. The mattresses and pillows are thrown over the railing, and none of us dares move or make a sound. I can't breathe until Ida finally comes down the stairs with the soldiers at her heels. They proceed into the kitchen and then bark at her to exit the cabin. I hear their roaring in the backyard and then from the barn.

Maria and Luda stand in the kitchen, petrified like two statues, and Anton watches through the window with his fists clenched and his entire body rigid. I close my eyes. The seconds stretch into minutes. This is the first time I am happy that my children are not with me. My concern for their fate would drive me crazy.

I see the soldiers approaching their motorcycles without Ida. They exchange their hats for their helmets and drive off without looking back.

I run outside and breathe a sigh of relief when I see her coming out of the barn. She ties the kerchief around her head and rubs the back of her neck.

"They didn't make me eat hay," she says with a half-smile, "They just kicked me a few times."

I hear Anton's growl behind me and hug her to my heart in a tight embrace. She sobs just once and then sniffles. "They left, and everything is fine now," she reassures him – and herself.

We go into the cabin and close the door behind us – an action so simple and natural that somehow seems incredibly superfluous. The door cannot protect us from the hands of evil men. None of us hurries to wash off the filth, and none of us smiles or celebrates.

I check the two floors over and again to make sure that the soldiers didn't forget anything this time. We try to straighten up the chaos they left behind, and Anton carries the mattresses up to the second floor and then goes out to the barn. A gloomy atmosphere prevails in the cabin.

The hours go by. The house is clean and tidy, and other than the door of the rear shed, it looks like the Germans never visited our cabin. The smell of fear wafts from us, and I know that my friends are also having trouble digesting the recent events.

We sit around the kitchen table. Luda rests her head on her hands and yawns, and Maria closes her eyes, but Ida and I sit upright, tense and watchful.

Anton comes into the cabin and goes up to the second floor. He returns with clean clothes in his hands. "I don't think they'll be back again tonight." He walks through the kitchen to the door to the backyard. "When I'm finished, you can shower and change into your nightclothes." His tone is chilly, and I can tell he is angry, but I can't understand why.

I move to stand in front of the window. The rain has stopped, and I stare out into the darkness. Images of the day's events play out in my head, and my body trembles every time I imagine the lights of the motorcycles on the horizon.

Anton goes into the kitchen. He is wearing clean clothes, and his wet hair is combed to the side. I look at him, but he doesn't return the look.

He motions with his head toward the rear shed, and we go out quietly. We soap ourselves in silence with bowed heads and wash ourselves with water from a bucket. Our sense of security has been shaken to its core, and we don't dare break the silence.

We put on our white nightgowns and go back inside the cabin.

Anton puts the food supplies on the kitchen table, and we stare at it in exhaustion.

"It's so late." I yawn. "I don't think any of us are hungry."

"I said we'd have a celebratory dinner, and that is exactly what we'll do." His tone is angry, and he bangs on the table and leaves the kitchen.

"So, I guess that's what we'll do..." I mumble and look at Ida. She seems too tired to be astonished by Anton's anger.

Maria peels the potatoes, and Luda cuts them. I fill the pot with water, and Ida sets the table. While the stew cooks on the stove, Anton looks out the window and smokes a cigarette, and we sit back down around the kitchen table and take turns yawning.

My eyes open and close involuntarily, and I sigh with relief when Maria announces that the stew is ready.

Anton sits at the head of the table. He waits until we each have a bowl before us and then starts eating. We follow suit, and the silence around the table is deafening.

Suddenly he slams his glass of water on the table and gives me a withering look. "How could you be so stupid?" he roars into my stunned face.

"What... Why would...?" I can't find the words to answer him.

"You heard his motorcycle coming!" He attacks me in a voice dripping with venom, "But instead of fleeing to the shed with them," he points to my friends, "you foolishly decided to greet him in the cabin."

I go pale and swallow the lump in my throat.

"What did you think would be the result of your encounter?" He spits out the words. "What did you expect? Did you think he would tell you that you're beautiful and promise to return for another visit after the war?"

I bite my tongue at the insult.

Luda sits up straight and waves her arms, trying to get his attention. Anton continues glaring at me angrily and then slowly turns to look at her. Luda frowns sadly and then points at me and shakes her head. She motions toward the door and then points at herself, and her eyes fill with tears.

Anton grumbles impatiently.

She points to the door once more, then hugs herself and bows her head in embarrassment.

Maria pats her back and stands up straight. "She's trying to say that the soldier tried to touch her."

"And why didn't she run to the shed?" Anton pounds his fist on the table.

Luda points to the upper floor and then to the exit door to the shed.

"She says she didn't have time to escape to the shed," Maria translates her sister's hand gestures.

Luda points at me, and then she stands up and hugs me. She bows her head in thanks and then goes back and sits next to Maria.

"Ania offered herself to the soldier so that he would leave Luda alone," says Maria with a trembling voice. "I'm her older sister. I should have been the one to do so, but I hid in the shed, and my fear paralyzed me."

I'm having a hard time joining the conversation and defending myself.

"And Ania said that..." Maria juts out her chin, "She said you assured her that the Germans wouldn't be coming back anytime soon."

Instead of apologizing to me, Anton stands up abruptly and his chair flies backward. He snarls loudly and leaves the cabin, slamming the door behind him.

"He didn't mean to attack you like that." Ida puts her hand over mine. "He's not mad at you. He's mad at himself. He told us to get cleaned up, and the guilt is driving him crazy. He wasn't there when you needed him in the ghetto, and he almost arrived too late today."

I let my shoulders sag and I sigh. My head tells me to focus on how he insulted me, but my heart tells me that Ida is right. I've seen him angry before, but I never thought I'd witness him lose control. I put my bowl on the counter and realize that he needs me to comfort him.

I wrap myself in the blanket from the couch and go out to the barn.

The cold penetrates my bones. I stand in front of the closed door and take a deep breath.

I know with every fiber of my being that I will only leave this barn after I've given him my heart.

CHAPTER 14

I close the barn door behind me and wrap my body in the blanket. Anton is standing with his back to me and sweeping the piles of hay.

He doesn't turn around to face me. "Go back to the cabin. There's nothing for you here," he commands coldly.

I put the blanket down on the pile of hay, pet the horse, and approach Anton.

"What do you want?" He stands up straight and makes a fist.

My teeth chatter from the cold, but I keep going forward and stand behind him.

"What do you want?"

"You," I whisper, putting my hands on his back.

His shoulder blades tremble, and suddenly he turns around and wraps his arms around my waist. He swings me into the air, and I wrap my legs around him and stare into his feverish eyes.

"I don't need you to comfort me," he whispers angrily.

He still looks so enraged, but nothing he can say or do will make me leave the barn now.

"Yes, you do." I graze his wounded lip with my fingers. "And I need you too."

He groans softly and walks ahead, still carrying me, until my back bumps into the barn wall. His eyes ravage my face with forbidden longing. He pushes his pelvis towards me, then releases my hips and cups my cheeks. He lets out another groan and tucks my hair behind my ears.

I close my eyes to avoid seeing the disappointment on his face. I won't let his longing for her break my heart.

"Open your eyes," he whispers hoarsely.

I shut them tighter and shake my head no.

"Open your eyes so you can finally understand that I'm not searching for her." He runs his thumb over my upper cheek. "So you can finally understand that I'm making sure it's *you*."

I open my eyes in surprise.

"I can't remember the exact moment that I realized I was crazy about you." He presses his thumb against my bottom lip. "So crazy about you that I'm on the brink of losing control." His eyes dart across my lips, and my heart pounds. His words materialize as if from a dream, and I don't want to wake up.

"Anton," I whisper, trembling. "The first time you walked me home, you were right."

He continues to touch my lips and shakes his head in incomprehension.

"You were right when you said no one has kissed these lips." I lick the lip he is stroking. "I should have given you my first kiss then, too."

He looks up at me and then cups my cheek and tilts my head to the side. "Ania, I'm going to take it right now." His eyes are filled with passion. "I'll take your first kiss and settle for that alone." His lips are close to mine, almost touching, teasing me, testing my incredible need for him, but before I can protest, he moans softly and bombards my mouth. His lips collide with mine, biting, sucking, devouring, and I try to accommodate his longing. His tongue penetrates my mouth, and the kiss becomes fierce and urgent. I am incapable of thinking about anything other than his tongue flirting in a seductive dance with mine. After a moment, I feel him not only in my mouth but in all the organs of my body. I slide my hands up his back and then grab the back of his neck and run my fingers through his hair. My touch arouses him, and he moans into my mouth and grips my buttocks. His pelvis plunges into mine, and his kiss ignites me like oil poured on a fire. His lips separate from mine for a split second, and I gasp for air and lunge at him again. This time I'm the one devouring his mouth with intense hunger. His hips thrust towards me again and again, and the burning warmth between my legs spreads down to my thighs and, from there, to my calves. I steal another breath, and he buries his head in my neck. His lips flutter over my skin and journey down to my collarbone. I dig my nails into his shoulders and rest my head against the wall behind me. A louder moan escapes my lips. His shoulders tense up, and his chest heaves as he pulls away. I feel his stiffness harden between my legs, and I don't understand why he has stopped kissing me.

"If I continue, I won't want to stop." He strokes my cheek and then bows his head and puts me down. "The restraint I'm so proud of melts away when I'm around you." He turns his back to me and runs his fingers through his hair.

My body is on fire and mourns the distance between us. I bite my lip, trying to think what I can say to bring him back to me, but my mind won't cooperate. My heart urges me to demand his touch. And this time, I won't settle for just a kiss.

I open my mouth and close it, open it again, but the words won't come out. I approach him cautiously and put my hand on his back. He turns to face me but doesn't look at me.

"I'm not leaving the barn," I whisper determinedly. "I'm not leaving." I push his chest with both hands.

"Ania..."

"I'm not leaving." I push him harder. His legs fold under him, and he tumbles onto the haystack behind him. I don't wait for him to regain his balance and sit on him with my legs spread wide. "I need you like the air that I breathe." I slide my hands over his chest and push my pelvis into his. "I thought I was choosing to give you my body, but the truth is that it's no longer a choice" – I wrap his hands around my hips – "It's a need I have no control over."

He lifts a pair of dark eyes to meet mine, and I know he shares my passionate desire. His hands move up to my waist, pulling my nightgown up above my buttocks. His chest rises and falls heavily.

"I've imagined this so many times." I open the top button of his shirt and continue to move my pelvis over his. "But my body never burned so hot in my imagination." The material of his trousers that rubs against the sensitive area between my legs makes me feel drunk. I open another button and another and almost rip off the rest. I remove his shirt and raise my arms so that he can take off my nightgown. It falls to the floor, and his eyes fly over my bare body, igniting like two open flames.

I press my chest to his and pant in relief. My body is on fire, and every part of me demands his attention. I pull his hands to me and place them on my breasts. My nipples tingle, and I moan into his ear. My moaning ignites a fire in him, and within less than a second, he seizes control of my body. He cups my breasts and buries his head in my neck. His tongue slides over my skin and then travels toward my bosom. He presses my breasts together and exhales into the crevice between them. His fingers play with my nipples, and I dig my nails into his shoulders and tilt my head back. A louder moan erupts from my throat as his teeth bite into my tender nipple, and he gently begins to suck on it. He proceeds to the other nipple and intense waves of pleasure flow down my spine. The friction between my legs becomes unbearable, and I rock on top of him and moan with pleasure. I fumble for the top button of his trousers and yank it open. My fingers collide with my burning center of pleasure, and my entire body arches backward.

Anton looks at me with a half-smile and then grabs my waist, lifts me into the air, and lays me down on the blanket. I try to rise and grab the buttons of his trousers with my fingers, but he clasps my elbows and pins them to the hay above my head.

"But... But I want more," I stutter, blushing red.

"You will get everything you want." The smile is gone from his face, and his dark eyes consume my naked body. Suddenly I am overly aware of my body exposed before him, and I squeeze my legs together and shut my eyes. "You aren't the only one who fantasized about this," he whispers hoarsely and spreads my legs apart, "But I had no doubt that the fantasy would pale compared to reality." He positions himself between my legs, but I still do not dare open my eyes. His lips press against my neck and then sprinkle kisses down my body. His tongue doesn't miss any part of my sensitive skin, and when he sucks on my nipples, I forget my embarrassment and start to moan. His tongue slides over my belly as heavy raindrops shake the ceiling of the barn, creating dramatic background music for the fire that burns in my veins. Anton's hands release my elbows, and his body glides down my body. He spreads my legs wider, and my mouth flies open with a loud cry as his lips press against my core. I open my eyes in wonder as he kisses the most private area of my body. The fire inside me grows stronger as he pleasures me there.

The horse rears in the corner of the barn, and I mutter muffled sounds and clutch the blanket's edges with all my might. My upper body jerks from side to side, and my hips quiver in anticipation. I feel so very close to the pinnacle of bliss. My moaning grows louder, and I raise my pelvis higher toward him. His lips journey up my abdomen again. He kneels between my legs, and the animalistic desire I see in his eyes makes my heart flutter.

He unbuttons his trousers without taking his eyes off me and then grabs my waist and sits me down in front of him. I pant in tense anticipation. He takes my hand and pulls it closer to his loins. He wraps it around and slides it down his manhood and then closes his eyes and moans in satisfaction. I look at his face twitching in restraint and continue to slide my hand up and down his member. He clenches his jaw, and I'm afraid my touch is hurting him, but he clamps my hand around his manhood, cups my cheeks, and moans into my mouth. He lowers me onto my back and extracts himself from his trousers.

"I'll be gentle," he says huskily, leaning over and kissing me tenderly. He picks himself up a bit and rests on his elbows, and I beam with relief when I feel the titillating rubbing between my legs again. The smile is wiped from my face as a feeling of severe pressure causes my arms and legs to tense up violently. I look at his face, which is strained in concentration. The pressure intensifies, and I cry out and bite my lip. He moves his pelvis, and the sensation between my legs grows stronger. His pelvis stops moving momentarily, and his shoulders shake with effort. He leans down, kisses my lips, and I attempt to relax my body, but to no avail. He closes his eyes and proceeds to grind his pelvis into mine. I cry out in pain as he penetrates, stiff and deep inside me. I cover my mouth in mortification and look away from him as he impales me once more. The pressure makes me forget the pleasure I was so looking forward to, and I gasp again and again as he moves inside me.

Little by little, the pain becomes bearable, and when he grabs my chin and wordlessly implores me to look at him, I dive deep into the brown eyes that envelop me with walls of protection. I position my hands on his chest and exhale sharply with each thrust. The friction with the center of my pleasure ignites waves of heat inside me, but I cannot relax and enjoy it.

"You're so beautiful..." He places his hands on my shoulders, then lifts his head and quickens the pace of his penetration. His thrusts grow stronger and more intense, and the blanket under my buttocks sinks into the hay. He supports himself with one hand, and with the other, he grips my buttocks and draws me to him, piercing me wildly over and over, but now, his every thrust is accompanied by loud moans. I see his arm muscles stretch and tighten and watch as his chest convulses. He thrusts into me once more, more forcefully than ever, and then lets out a deafening moan, pulls out of me, and empties himself on my abdomen.

His strong face looks so calm. The constant worry line on his forehead has disappeared, and with excitement, I realize that this tranquility is thanks to me alone.

He pants like he's just completed a long sprint and then bends down and kisses me softly. "Thank you," he whispers into my mouth. "Thank you for this rare gift." He kisses me again and then collapses beside me on the blanket and exhales sharply.

I press my legs together and rub my thighs. Raindrops hit the roof to the rhythm of my heartbeat, and I try to take in the experience.

Anton pulls my hand to his face and presses it to his lips. He kisses my hand tenderly and then rolls over onto his side and strokes my hair.

I look at the ceiling, unable to say a word.

"You're so beautiful..." Anton whispers, pressing my hand to his chest. "I'm crazy about you."

His last sentence brings tears to my eyes, and the intense heat that encircled me dissipates. I shiver from the frigid cold of the barn. I gave myself to him, and I have no idea what will happen next.

"Am... Am I supposed to leave now?" I turn to him with an awkward look. "Maybe I should go wash up."

"Leave?" Anton looks puzzled. "Do you actually think I would let you leave here right now?"

I open my mouth but don't know what to say. What do people customarily do after such an exhilarating physical unification?

"Don't move," he commands quietly, standing up and pulling on his pants. He runs out of the barn, and I fumble around for another blanket to calm my shivering body. I yank on the blanket's edges, stare at the ceiling, and listen to the raindrops. The old horse is chewing the hay intently and I ponder the supreme pleasure I felt up until Anton penetrated me. I smile to myself when I remember the expression on his face when he reached his climax and wonder if women's bodies are just a tool for men's satisfaction and whether we are supposed to enjoy their pleasure. Exhaustion overtakes me without warning, and I close my eyes, shaking with fatigue.

My eyes open with the barn door, and Anton steps inside, dripping with water. He is carrying several blankets on his back and holding a pot and a towel in his hand.

"Stay where you are," he says with a little smile and then sits on his knees at the foot of my makeshift bed of hay and dips the towel into the pot. He slides the towel over my belly, and I gasp with pleasure as I feel the warm water. He dips the towel in the pot once more and then slips it between my legs. I cover my face with my hands and sigh with pleasure. He continues to gently bathe me for several minutes before finally covering me with two blankets.

He lies down next to me and folds me in his arms. We gaze at each other. His brown eyes sparkle, revealing his heart to me. I hope my eyes are revealing the exact same thing to him.

"Do you want to tell me how you feel?" He asks as he caresses my hips.

I frown, trying to think what a real woman would answer. I look at his serene face and slide my finger over his forehead to the junction between his eyebrows. The worry line hasn't returned yet. I desperately want to satisfy him and decide that my answer doesn't have to be the absolute truth.

I bat my eyelashes and smile. "I really enjoyed it. It was quite an exper…"

"Ania," he interrupts me, irritated, "Don't flutter your lashes and fake smiles at me. I'm not another one of your suitors. I'm your only man."

His answer stuns me. My heart pulsates, and my feelings for him intensify so much that it hurts.

I bite my lip and look down. "The truth is, it was different than I had imagined." I cough awkwardly. "Every time you touch me, I feel drunk with pleasure, but this time when... when you entered me, my pleasure stopped. But..." I pause, afraid that I'm upsetting him. "But I'm not complaining. Seeing you experience such pleasure because of me made me feel the greatest possible joy. I promise you that even if I had suffered, I would still be happy, and I'm prepared to surrender my body every day anew if that's what you would like."

I don't hear a response from him, and the fear that I made him sad overshadows my embarrassment. I look up at him cautiously.

Anton looks at me silently, and suddenly his chest quakes. He throws his head back and bursts into laughter.

I open my eyes in astonishment. I don't understand what I said to make him laugh, but it's such an uplifting and rare phenomenon.

"Ania." He cups my cheeks and continues to laugh. "Do you really think that your first time indicates anything about your future satisfaction with your man?"

Now that I know that he's laughing at me, I'm no longer so touched by his laughter. I bare my teeth and beat his chest. His laughter dies down as quickly as it began.

"Don't you ever talk to me again! Not ever!" I growl into his face and pull off the blankets to escape from this barn and from him. Before I can even lower my legs, he has already grabbed hold of my waist and pulled me to lie down with my back to him. He wraps his arms around me and holds me down.

"I'm sorry, my Ania." He showers my neck with kisses. "Please forgive me."

"Get away from me!" I tell him as I try to shake him off my shoulders.

"Don't be mad." He continues to sprinkle kisses on my neck. "My reaction was vile." He nibbles on my earlobe. "I was sure you already knew that I would dedicate my life to pleasuring you." His fingers extend across my belly, and I try my best to keep being annoyed with him. "I assumed that your mother explained to you about the first time."

"Mother never used foul language!" I exclaim. "She said we're not common riffraff who talk about what goes on in the bedroom."

"Now I feel even worse. I beg you to forgive me." He kisses my shoulder, and I close my eyes and beg my body not to give in to him. "I promise you that the next time will be much more enjoyable." His hand slides up my abdomen and cups my breast.

"I'm not interested in finding out," I lie, while inadvertently moving my backside nearer to him. His moaning makes my eardrums feel like they're being perforated, and I have difficulty remembering why I'm mad at him.

"Let me make it up to you," he whispers hoarsely, and I stifle a moan. "Let me prove to you that my pleasure depends on your pleasure." I feel his pelvis move as he unbuttons his pants again.

"Now you're the one who's lying," I groan as he cups my bottom, and his erection rubs against me. "Your pleasure does not depend on my pleasure."

"I've never lied to you, and I don't plan on starting now." He traces a path around my lips with his fingers. "My pleasure depends on your pleasure, and your pleasure depends on mine." He sticks a finger in my mouth, and I ponder his words and suck on it. "A man who wants release goes to a whore. A man who wants pleasure spends time in bed with a woman who makes him worship her and be enraged by her in the same breath." He pulls his wet finger from my mouth and places it on the hot spot between my legs. The sudden heat that circulates through my body astounds me. I rest my head on his shoulder, and his lips press against my forehead. I moan softly, twisting as the ripples of heat intensify. His rigid manhood rubs against my sensitive area, and I flinch. "If you let me go on, I will prove to you that you can experience enjoyment far greater than you have ever imagined." His raspy whisper caresses my heart, and I take a deep breath and let my body relax.

Slowly my buttocks rise, and I allow him to push his stiffness up against me. I take another breath as he begins to gently penetrate and pleasure me. He clasps my waist and pulls me to him. The pressure wanes, and I breathe deeply as he pushes his pelvis and thrusts himself deep inside me. He doesn't move, but just keeps fondling me. He then lifts his free hand to touch my breasts, and the pleasant warmth quickly kindles flames. I long to hear him moan. I carefully move my pelvis, and he groans into my ear. I move it again, and his pelvis begins to move along with mine. My back is pressed to his chest, and his tender caresses slowly become more determined. Another touch, another caress, another kiss, and I cry out as the waves of pleasure turn into a burning fire. My body contorts uncontrollably, and his thrusts become wild and powerful. I cry out once more as I share his pleasure, and he moans loudly and empties himself on my back.

I collapse onto my belly and close my eyes. The waves of pleasure still shake my limbs, but most of all they shake my heart. It's clear to me that I will never want any man other than him.

CHAPTER 15

The barn is still bathed in darkness, and I'm cocooned in Anton's arms. I don't know how long I was asleep, but it was a deep and potent slumber. I know by Anton's slow breathing that he needs this respite just as much as I do. He rubs his nose in my hair, and I close my eyes again and pray that this magical night will never end.

Michalina's soft voice calls my name, and I quickly look left and right. The trees around me are very dense, and I have no idea which way to turn.

"Anushka." *I hear her whisper again, and I begin running towards her voice.* "Anushka, come to me." *This time the hushed voice comes from behind me, and I turn around and keep running.*

"Where are you?" *I'm spinning in circles around myself.* "Michalina, where are you?"

"I'm right here." *Her voice sounds like a whisper in my ear. I look around sharply and suddenly see her leaning against a tree trunk. She is wearing a tailored gray dress, her hair is in a tight braid, and a peaceful smile is spread across her face.*

"What are you doing here?" *I whisper with concern and try to walk in her direction. My feet are planted deep in the forest floor.*

"I missed you, silly." *She giggles.*

"But it's dangerous here." I look around, afraid the Germans will return and see my delicate, good-hearted sister. "You have to go back to America," I scold her.

"America?" She repeats after me and raises an eyebrow in wonder.

I hear the rumble of an engine, and I stop breathing. The worry I feel for my sister hits me like a punch in the guts.

"Michalina, run!" I wave her away with my hands.

"But I need you so much." Her expression turns sorrowful. "And I need him." She sighs. "I shouldn't have left him. I miss him so much that I cannot breathe."

"Anton?" I swallow the lump in my throat.

"You're watching over him, aren't you?" She smiles as if she were confiding a secret to me, "You're watching over him for me."

I avoid looking at her and rub my belly. The pains make me gasp out loud.

"Anushka, answer me!"

I sit up, panting in panic. The pain in my stomach is unbearable, and my eyes fill with tears. Severe guilt attacks my conscience. What have I done?

The sun's rays penetrate the narrow cracks between the barn's wooden beams, and I see that Anton is gone. A brown dress and clean pants are on top of a haystack, and the horse is no longer tied to the post. They probably went out for a morning walk together.

I stand up with difficulty and massage my thighs. The sensual intoxication that overcame me during the night has dissipated, and reality slaps me across the face. I betrayed my sister, and I will never be able to forgive myself. The pain is burning in my heart now as well, and I wipe away my tears and get dressed.

Ida is sitting by the window in the cabin and reading her prayer book. She's immersed in prayer and doesn't lift her head. I want to scold her for being irresponsible and tear the book from her hand, but she seems so engrossed in pleading to her god that I don't dare disturb her. The sisters are sitting at the kitchen table, and when Maria sees me, she pours porridge into another bowl and motions for me to join them.

"The sun is out," says Maria, looking at me for a few moments. "Maybe the weather will finally take a turn for the better."

I murmur in agreement and taste the porridge. It's clear as day that Maria is chitchatting to dispel the embarrassment. They know that Anton and I didn't sleep with them last night.

"I wonder what the weather's like in America," Maria says thoughtfully.

The burning pierces my stomach again, and I set the bowl on the counter and go outside to sit on the chair in front of the cabin.

Anton's tall and brawny figure walks from the field toward me. He's wearing his country clothes with the suspenders that hold up his pants. His half-open shirt accentuates his impressive chest muscles and broad shoulders. His hat is tilted to the side, and he's pulling on the horse's bridle and ambling leisurely. Images from last night cross my mind one after another, and shivers of excitement vibrate in my chest. His beautiful words and exhilarating touch made me forget the nightmare I am living in for one night, one incredible night that allowed me to escape to a parallel universe that belonged to him and me alone.

He comes closer and gives me a meaningful look. I want to run to him, leap into his arms, and beg him to choose me. The pains in my stomach make me shudder, and I hug myself in misery.

"Ania." He drops the bridle and rushes over, kneeling before me on one knee, the worry line deepening on his forehead. "Don't you feel well?"

His concern and the way he looks at me make my heart tremble, but the guilt still pounds away at me. "I've never felt so good." My eyes tear up, and I grab his hand and press it to my lips. "The night you gave me was the best night of my life." I kiss his fingers but find it hard to look at him. "I want you to know that I gave you not only my body but my heart as well." My tears wet his fingers, and he leans forward and rests his forehead on mine. I sense that he shares my tumultuous feelings. "But such an encounter between us can never happen again," I whisper and straighten up until I'm staring straight into his wild eyes. "I took advantage of your need for consolation." I wipe my tears with the sleeve of my dress. "I took advantage of your longing for my better half and seduced you deviously."

Anton's jaw quivers, and his eyes seem to darken. "We both know that's not what happened."

"That's exactly what happened." I stick out my chin. "From the moment I saw that your heart belonged to her, I swore I would get you for myself. I didn't hesitate for a second. I wanted to steal what belonged to my sister just to prove to myself that I could." I smile contrarily. "I took advantage of your hunger for her. I used my appearance to confuse you. I spun a web and trapped you in it. It wasn't your fault."

"Ania..." he says my name in a menacing tone.

"I'm the one who betrayed her. Not you," I interrupt. "You were wrong when you said I was back to my old self. I never changed. This abhorrent behavior is part of me, and I'll never be able to change."

"What are you doing?" Anton shakes his head from side to side to show a lack of understanding. "Why are you telling yourself lies?"

"Everything I've said is true." My throat chokes up with tears. "If it wasn't, my punishment wouldn't be so severe." I whimper and hug myself. "You promised her that you would wait for her, and that's exactly what you'll do. I must believe you keep your promises because you still haven't fulfilled your promise to bring my children back to me." I steal a breath and exhale forcefully. "I'm leaving my heart with my better half's man," I whisper, then turn and run back inside the cabin.

I sit on the couch, cover myself with the blanket and stare at Ida, who is swaying back and forth in prayer. My heart is in agony, and the burning in my stomach is only getting worse. I want to stop her and ask her to pray for my tortured soul as well, but I know all too well that prayers don't come true in our dark world.

* * *

Ida is standing in front of the fireplace, lighting candles, and I realize that I've been sitting on the sofa for hours. I've been staring at the same spot on the wall from the moment she kissed her prayer book and pressed it to her heart. She hasn't asked me anything, and I thank her silently for letting me sink into my grief in peace.

Ida covers her eyes with her hands, whispers a prayer, then presses them together and scrunches up her face in silent entreaty. When she's finished, she lets out a deep sigh and sits down beside me.

"Haven't you had enough?" I ask and lean my head on the back of the couch. "Aren't you sick and tired of praying only to find that your prayers have remained unanswered?"

"Who said that they haven't been answered?"

"The Germans are still here," I reply angrily, "You have yet to be reunited with your family. We are captives in a perilous state of perceived freedom that could implode at any second."

"But yesterday we defeated the forces of evil twice," she says proudly, "and I believe Leib is surviving in the forest, and that if I continue to pray, I will be reunited with him and the rest of my family."

"But why do you light candles?" I wrinkle my forehead. "Will your god not hear your prayers if you don't light them?"

Ida doesn't answer right away. She ponders my question and finally pulls my hand towards her and holds it in her lap. "I think that up until we were dragged into this nightmare, I lit Sabbath candles because it was part of the tradition that I love so much.

A set table, a made bed, and Sabbath candles," she recites. "That's how I used to bring in this holy day. But from the moment they forced us into the ghetto, I felt something else." She squeezes my hand. "I feel that the Germans are trying to extinguish the light that shines within us." Her chest trembles. "If they rob us of our freedom, our food, and our self-respect — and shatter our faith — all they need to do to destroy us is to extinguish our light."

My eyes are on the candle's flame, and I stare into the rich hues coming from the miniature fire.

"When I light these candles, it's a way of reminding myself that there is a small light inside each of us, and that when these atrocities will have passed, our job will be to combine all of our tiny lights into one big light that will brighten up the world and banish the darkness that the Germans have created."

"Ida, I feel like my candle has gone out." My voice is shaky, and tears fill my eyes. "I feel like I put it out myself when I abandoned my children and when I betrayed…"

Before I can finish my sentence, I straighten up in a panic. The horse's neighing outside is different than usual and is accompanied by the crunch of wheels rolling over the ground. Ida stands up, moves the candles away from each other, and walks to the window. I wipe away my tears and join her.

Anton is leading a cart carrying an unfamiliar man toward the barn. We both sigh in relief. It's probably his contact.

"Maybe he has good news about Leib," Ida murmurs excitedly, placing her hand on her heart, "And maybe happy news about your children."

I bite my lip and stare at the two men speaking in hushed tones outside the barn. Even from here, I can see that Anton's expression is troubled, and as the man goes on talking, Anton buries his head in his hands and then rubs them forcefully over his face.

"It's not good news," I whisper in trepidation.

Anton glances towards the cabin, and when he sees that we are looking at him, he hurriedly turns back to the man. But it's too late. I've witnessed the anguish in his eyes, and now I can barely breathe.

The man hands Anton a package wrapped in paper and pats him on the shoulder sympathetically. Anton goes into the barn, and the man lights a cigarette and looks out at the fields surrounding us. Anton comes outside again, carrying small velvet boxes in his hands. Jewelry? Why is he giving this man my mother's jewelry?

The man peeks at the contents of the boxes and then bows his head in approval and goes on his way.

Ida grabs my hand, and we run outside to Anton and look at him anxiously.

His face is stern, and a deep worry line is etched between his eyebrows. He lights a cigarette, and his shoulders sag. It seems that the news he's received is weighing on him.

"There isn't any news about Leib," he addresses Ida. "And when there's no news, it's good news," he reassures her, but sighs with difficulty.

Ida nods and continues to look at him. We both understand that that's not what is plaguing him.

"Ania, no one can find your children in the ghetto." He bows his head and blows out white smoke. "They moved almost all the residents of the ghetto to the labor camps, but your children never arrived there."

"What... What do you mean?" I stutter.

"They've disappeared as if they were swallowed up by the earth." He pushes his hair to the side and locks his jaw.

I gape at him with my mouth open.

"I will do everything to find them." He avoids looking directly at me. "There are still members of the Resistance in the ghetto, and they've rallied to help us."

I want to scream or cry, but fear has paralyzed me. He made a promise, after all.

"I have another update." He inhales hard on his cigarette and flings it to the ground. "Your sister is... she's..."

"In America." I blurt out as a terrible sensation of dizziness overwhelms me. "She's in America with Father taking care of her."

"They never made it to America," he expels the words. "It appears that she's been imprisoned in the labor camp that the residents of the ghetto were moved to for quite some time."

My knees buckle, but his strong arms catch me and keep me from falling.

"We'll get her out of there." He kisses my head, and I hear Ida's sobs from behind me.

I can hear him talking but can't understand what he's saying. A black screen has come down over my eyes, and I can only wail in agony.

"Ania." Anton steadies me and tightly cups my chin. "The Polish Resistance will help us get her out of there. I gave my contact expensive jewelry to bribe the Ukrainian guards. Tomorrow evening I will leave to go bring her here."

I open my mouth, but the air refuses to fill my lungs. I inhale again and again, but his horrifying announcement seems to have caused the oxygen around me to evaporate.

"But... But..." I stammer, "But Michalina is so delicate and sensitive. What on earth can they use her for in a labor camp?"

"Ania, I promise I'll bring her here," Anton states determinedly.

"Then why wait until tomorrow?" I blink repeatedly, hoping to wake up from this nightmare. "Why tomorrow?" I hear myself shouting, "What good are your promises if you don't hurry to keep them?" I burst into tears and shake off his hug. "I refuse to see you or speak to you until you prove to me that you're not lying." I pummel his chest and run inside the cabin. My anger consumes me.

My sister. My better half. She's in dire peril.

* * *

I stand by the window and watch the setting sun. The beautiful orange colors are likely the universe's way of mocking us. It's as if a higher power has painted the grayness that reigns in this country in order to ignite a dangerous hope within us. Anton has respected my request and hasn't come inside the cabin since yesterday, and I've only plunged deeper into despair. I was unable to close my eyes all night, and monstrous scenarios flooded my mind continuously. I rub my stomach, which burns with unrelenting pain. Has she been trying to communicate her distress to me all this time? How did I not understand?

The barn door opens, and I stand up alertly. Anton leads the horse out and ties him to the cart. Ida, Maria, and Luda stand in front of him and bid him farewell with emotional embraces.

I stand up and walk outside to them.

Anton approaches me, and I step back. He bows his head and sighs.

"I'm coming with you."

Four awestruck faces gawk at me in silence.

"I'm coming with you," I repeat.

Anton studies me and frowns. After a few seconds, he shakes his head. "The journey is too long and dangerous," he states firmly. "I don't intend to stop and rest, and I don't intend to put you in unnecessary danger."

"I'm coming with you." I defiantly fold my arms over my chest.

"Ania..." Ida puts her hand on my shoulder. "The roads are overrun with Nazis. It would be better if Anton went without..."

"Don't butt in." I shush her and climb up onto the cart. "I'm going with him even if I have to follow him on foot."

Anton walks up to me with brisk strides, his eyes flashing with rage. "This is not the time to act like a child."

"Okay." I step down from the cart and smile at him insolently.

He snarls softly and leaps onto the bench, clicking his tongue and shaking the reins. The cart starts moving forward, and I follow behind.

"Ania, don't do this," Ida pleads, grabbing my arm.

I shake her off and keep marching forward. I hear her crying softly, but she doesn't follow me. The wheels of the cart creak over the path, and I quicken my pace.

Just before the bend in the road, the horse rears, and the cart comes to a halt. Anton jumps down and I approach the cart but keep my distance from him.

"You're so stubborn," he snaps angrily, motioning to the cart with his head.

I let out a sigh of relief and run to him. He grasps my waist and lifts me onto the bench, then climbs up and sits beside me without saying another word.

I find no comfort in my nearness to him. The fear surrounding me stabs me in my heart. I touch my triangle pendant and swear to myself that she is the one who will sit next to him and comfort him as we make our way back.

CHAPTER 16

I yawn loudly under the rising sun in all its glory. Sitting for so long on the bench – combined with the fatigue of a sleepless night – is beginning to show on my body. I sway from side to side on the seat, and my head keeps hitting Anton's shoulder. He's respected my request and hasn't said a word throughout the many hours of our journey together. Awful thoughts plague me, and the searing pain in my stomach torments me. Why didn't Michalina get to America? Where has she been all this time? Did they hurt her? And where is Father? He was supposed to protect her. I massage my temples and imagine Sarah's wise, black, doe eyes. Where are my children? Did they keep their promise and stick together? Did they reach the labor camp without anyone noticing? I have so many questions – and no answers.

"We still have a long way to go." His deep voice sounds like something out of a dream to me. "Go lie down in the back."

I shake my head no and press against him. All my senses tell me that when we are reunited with Michalina, my separation from him will be final, and my heart aches.

Anton wraps his arm around me and kisses my forehead. I can feel his pain.

My eyes close, and I permit myself to find comfort in him just one last time. "Anton," I whisper, "When did you realize you no longer despised me?"

"Despised?" He sounds surprised. "I never despised you." He kisses my forehead again. "I admit there was a time when you were impossible – so arrogant and proud." He emits a short, melancholy laugh. "Your refusal to acknowledge our new reality drove me crazy, but I think deep down I was hoping that your childlike optimism would triumph over my – and everyone else's – pessimism."

"My optimism suffered a crushing defeat." I sigh. "When I think of how I acted in my former life, I'm ashamed. The ridiculous pursuit of entertainment and suitors, the ease with which I ignored the plights of others, my ignorance, and my tendency to look down on those who didn't have lives as abundant as mine. How could I think I was better than people like Ida and Leib or Bruno...?" I bite my lip in shame. "People who are much more moral than I." One tear runs down my cheek. "How could I sympathize with the hatred towards the Jews? And why? Because they warily guard their faith? After all, if the war hadn't broken out and I hadn't been imprisoned in the ghetto, I wouldn't have met my children." My chest quivers in intense pain. "I wouldn't have known that my real treasures weren't fancy dresses and expensive jewelry, and I wouldn't have gotten to feel the power of such pure, unadulterated love."

Anton caresses my arm sympathetically and remains silent.

"Were there moments when you regretted promising Michalina that you would look after me?" I ask, burying my face in his neck and inhaling his scent.

"There were so many moments like that." He sighs, and my heart sinks. "Every time you put yourself in danger, I wanted to shake you and instill some sense into your pretty little head." He jiggles the reigns, spurring the horse to go faster. "But it was actually on that first night when I went to the restaurant just with you that I discovered you wouldn't hesitate to get your claws out to defend the people you love against anyone trying to hurt them."

I furrow my brow and look at him questioningly.

"You were besieged by so many hostile looks," he explains. "Even your girlfriends sneered at you, yet you managed to remain composed until one of them made a nasty comment about your sister."

I remember Paulina's hateful comment, and I clench my hands into fists.

"You charged at her with claws drawn." His chest heaves as he laughs softly. "Maybe I shouldn't have stopped you."

I feel the beginning of a smile spread across my lips.

"But there is one defining moment etched in my mind." His lips brush my forehead. "When the Germans broke into your house when you were there alone. Without your father and mother and your sister to support you, I was supposed to calm you down and make you feel safe, but when I came into the apartment, I was so terrified for your fate that I couldn't breathe." He sprinkles kisses over my forehead and lifts his head. "But you stood before them upright and fearless. You were so focused on being angry with me that you didn't blink – even when the commander held a gun to your head."

"I was stupid," I say as I rub my eyes and sit up straight.

Anton nods slowly and then sneaks a smile at me. "You were foolish and childish and proud, but when you stormed at the place the gun was hidden, I realized just how strong your fighting spirit is."

"They managed to drain me of it." I shrug. "I matured, wised up, and learned an essential lesson in humility. I no longer want to be the center of the universe. I just don't want anyone to notice me."

"It's too late." The smile disappears from Anton's face. "I notice you all the time. And whenever you're out of my sight, even for a minute, I can't breathe until I see you again."

His declaration excites me tremendously, but the burning in my guts intensifies, and I grimace and whimper.

"Ask me when I realized I was head over heels in love with you."

"In love?" I open my eyes wider in astonishment. "You're confused. You're not in love with me. It's true, we needed each other, but now that M…"

"Ania." He takes his arm off my shoulder and grabs my hand. "For such a long time, I convinced myself that I was just looking out for you. I thought that once you were safe and I could stop feeling responsible for your well-being, I would no longer be driven mad by the unshakable feeling that we belong together."

I stare at his enormous hand holding mine, and my heart beats wildly.

"The first time that little girl sat down in front of you, and you welcomed her with open arms, I knew my heart belonged to you."

I gasp, and he takes my hand and presses it to his lips.

"But… But you promised her." I pull my hand away and bury it between my thighs. "You promised her you'd wait for her, and I promised her I'd take care of you for her."

"And now we're going to bring her back." He grabs my hand again and presses it to his chest. "Ania, it's been a long time, and Michalina is not a foolish girl. I'm sure she'll understand that we didn't plan for this to happen and will give us her blessing."

I look at his strong profile and ponder his words. It really has been a long time. Maybe she left him with me knowing that this would happen. Maybe she left knowing that if she – the wiser of the two of us – fell in love with him, it would happen to me too? And maybe she met another man who makes her heart skip a beat since we last saw each other?

I rest my head on his shoulder and close my eyes. My thoughts are so selfish. My guilty conscience comes back to torment me. The unadorned truth is that my sister is imprisoned in a labor camp, and I stole her man.

I open my eyes when the wagon comes to a stop. Fatigue overwhelmed me, and I must have fallen asleep.

The horse is tied to a tree, and Anton is kneeling beside it and studying a map spread out in front of him.

I get down from the wagon and stretch my limbs.

"From here we'll have to continue by foot." Anton points towards the forest. "We should be at the camp in a few hours."

I nod and tighten the belt of my coat. Anton folds the map and puts it in a sack that he slings over his shoulder. He takes my hand and leads me into the forest.

We walk in silence over the muddy ground, and every time we hear an unusual noise, we stop and hide behind a tree trunk. The walk is slow and excruciating. I reluctantly bite into the cold baked potato he hands me and continue to tread carefully in his wake.

The darkness is closing in on us, and the cold chills me to the bone. Anton takes a flashlight out of the sack and continues to lead us onward with confident steps.

The burning in my stomach is getting worse. I hear Michalina's voice whispering my name. I look left and right but see nothing except thick trees and a train track. Why would a train pass through this godforsaken place? And where would it go?

A strange, sharp, and unfamiliar smell infiltrates my nose. A smell like I've never smelled before. I wrinkle my nose in disgust. The terrible smell gets stronger with every step we take.

"We're here," Anton whispers, pulling me behind a tree trunk to hide with him.

"We're here?" I reply in a whisper and peek out from behind the tree. A tall, never-ending fence stretches out in front of me, surrounded by a wide trench. The heavy darkness is disturbed by flashes of light from watchtowers. "What is this place?" I swallow in apprehension. "How are we supposed to get in?"

"We're not," Anton whispers and motions for me to sit down. "We paid enough to have her brought to us."

I sit down with my back to the tree, bend my knees and hug them. Every time I hear a branch snap, I tense up, and fear gnaws at me. Anton is standing beside me, and all I can hear is his breathing. From time to time, I hear a dog barking, but apart from them, there is total silence here. Is it possible that we were wrong, and this camp has been abandoned? And where is that horrible smell coming from?

Suddenly a noise comes from the direction of the camp. Creaking sounds and heavy footsteps move toward us. The noise is accompanied by voices speaking a language I've heard before. I close my eyes tightly and remember hearing it when two Ukrainian women visited Mother's boutique.

"Don't move," Anton commands almost soundlessly and then stands on the other side of the tree.

I cannot breathe.

The steps stop, and with them, the creaking noises.

"Where is she?" Anton asks in Polish, and I can't restrain myself any longer and peek out from my hiding place. The blood drains from my face when I see that he is standing in front of two tall soldiers in black uniforms. One of them is holding the handles of a large wheelbarrow, and my eyes open wide when I see what's inside: motionless, naked bodies.

I cover my mouth with my hands, and my upper body shakes uncontrollably.

The soldiers throw the bodies into the trench and then pull a hunched over, trembling body in dirty, ragged clothes from the wheelbarrow and throw it into Anton's arms. The scarf falls from her head, revealing short, blonde hair, and it's clear to me that this frail body belongs to my sister.

"Michalina," I whisper noiselessly and get to my feet.

The guards chuckle and turn towards the trench, and Anton clutches the limp body in his arms. He walks towards me and carefully strokes her head.

"Michalina." I pounce on him and caress her pale face. Her blue eyes are wide, and she blinks slowly and stares at me like she's in a dream. I block the sobs emanating from my mouth with my hands. She looks like a skeleton. Fear clouds my senses. I try to recognize my sister in her gaunt face, try to recognize myself. But her eyes look haunted, and although she stares at me, she looks right through me.

Anton sits behind the tree and cradles her in his arms like a baby. His eyes are downcast, and his silence is solemn.

I fall on my knees in front of her and sprinkle kisses over her face. My tears run down her soiled cheeks, and she raises her hand, touches her cheek, and then stares at her moist fingers.

"Michalina," I say, whimpering in despair. "It's me. Your sister. Your twin."

"Anushka?" she whispers, bringing her fingers nearer to my face. "My Anushka, am I dreaming, or am I in heaven?"

"You're not dreaming." I sniffle and bury my head in her chest. "You're not dreaming. We've come to get you."

I glance in horror toward the guards standing with their backs to us. They light cigarettes and throw their used matches on the dead bodies lying at their feet.

"This isn't a dream?" She blinks a few times and then turns to look at Anton. Her hand slides over his jaw, and his cheek quivers. "Anton..." Michalina whispers his name and exhales, "Did you come to get me?"

He nods and purses his lips in anguish.

"I dreamt about you every night." Her fingers flutter over his cheek, and her sleeve slips, revealing an emaciated arm. "I dreamt every night that you came to me and saved me from this hell."

He gives her a tormented smile and clasps her to him. She is still shivering, and I take off my coat and drape it over her.

"I knew you would keep your promise and care for Anushka." Tears flood her eyes, and she gropes for my hand. "Knowing that you were taking care of each other for me has helped me survive this inferno." She squeezes my hand.

I lower my eyes. My wise and beautiful sister… What have they done to you? The watchtower lights flicker, and I sneak another peek at the guards, afraid they might turn around and demand we give her back at any moment.

"Where is Father?"

"They separated us in Czechoslovakia. I was imprisoned in labor camps until they brought me here and forced me to work in a fake infirmary." Her eyes flash in terror. "Anushka, every time a train came from Warsaw, I thought I would see you." She wipes her eyes and wriggles, freeing herself from Anton's embrace. He helps her sit, but his arms continue to surround her like a protective bulwark. "I cried with relief every time you didn't step off the train."

My chest trembles as I try to hold back my tears. She looks broken and tortured, but I know Anton won't let anyone hurt her anymore. My dark thoughts wander to the children I left behind. "Michalina, on the trains that came from Warsaw…" I whisper and sneak a look at the guards. One of them is clutching his genitals and emptying himself over the bodies while his friend laughs. "Michalina." I squeeze her hand, and I look back at the barbed wire fences. "Did children arrive on those trains as well?"

She coughs, stifling her sobs. "Many children came to hell on the trains."

I pull my hand away and rub my face with force.

"Did any… Did any of the children recognize you?" I stammer.

"No, Anushka." She puts her hands on Anton's arms and frowns. "Why would they recognize me?"

Too many questions flood my mind, and I know my time is running out. "Where are the children?" I look toward the fence.

"They arrive at the camp but… but they don't stay. They are the first to be taken."

My chest rises and falls heavily. I want to ask where they are taken and what the terrible smell is. I want to beg her to give me more precise answers, but Anton clears his throat, and his eyes seem restless.

"Are there no children left in the camp at all?" I strain to breathe.

Michalina's eyes dart in terror to the guards, and then she whispers almost soundlessly, "Maybe... Maybe there are a few left but they're in hiding."

I stand up and pace back and forth.

"We need to leave right now." Anton pulls Michalina to her feet and continues to support her.

"But... But if they find out I ran away, they'll kill all the women in my cabin." Michalina shakes her head and hugs herself. "I'll miss the count." She scratches her arms in dread. "I want to come with you, but maybe I'm only dreaming..." She wobbles on her feet and looks so confused.

"You're not dreaming, and they won't find out," Anton replies determinedly. "The Nazis will think you're lying here in the ditch with the other bodies."

She continues to wobble restlessly back and forth.

I look at the fence once more, and my eyes lock on the light shining out from the watchtower. Suddenly my mind clears, and my paralyzing fear dissipates.

I touch my triangle pendant and lean forward to touch Michalina's neck.

"They took our pendant," says Michalina bitterly, placing her hand on mine. "I begged them to let me keep it. I wanted to believe that this moment would come, and you and I would connect our triangles into a whole star." She brushes her fingers over her chapped lips and sighs. "Now my job is to sort through the jewelry of the unfortunate souls who went into the showers."

I don't have time to try and interpret her words. I remove my necklace and put it around her neck. She touches it in confusion but doesn't say a word.

"Take off your clothes," I command quietly.

"What are you doing?" Anton's eyes open wider in horror.

"Michalina, give me your clothes," I repeat the order and remove my dress.

She hesitates for a moment, but it appears that she has become used to following orders without questioning them, and she unties the knot holding up her pants, and takes off her shirt. We stand naked in front of each other. She shivers with cold, but I feel a comforting, warm tickling in my stomach.

"Ania, what are you doing?" Anton snarls and grabs my arm tightly.

"I'm doing what needs to be done," I reply calmly and put on her filthy clothes. "I'm going to find my children."

"No, you are not!" He glares at me, crazed with fear. "I promised you I would bring them to you. I just need a little more time."

"I'm afraid that time has run out." I put my dress on my sister's emaciated body and then wrap my coat around her.

"You have children?" She stares at me like she's sleepwalking.

"You're not thinking rationally." Anton supports Michalina with one hand and grabs my arm with the other. "Meeting with your sister has shocked you. We'll return to the village, and I'll make sure to bring them to you."

"I've never been more clear-headed." I smile at him and, out of the corner of my eye, see the guards pushing the wheelbarrow toward the camp. "I'm going to the camp to look for my children, and I'm leaving you with my better half."

"Where is Anushka going?" Michalina thrusts her hand forward to grab me.

I kiss her and then pull away.

Anton howls in terror. He shakes his head from side to side and rushes towards me. Michalina falls to her knees, and he turns around in confusion and lifts her up.

I don't wait for another second and run to the guards. I pick up the kerchief that fell from my sister's head on the way and jump into the wheelbarrow.

Two shocked faces stare at me from above, but a second later, they continue onwards. I wrap the kerchief around my head and fold my knees to my chest.

"Ania!" Anton's whisper echoes in my ears like a scream, and I close my eyes and rub my belly. For the first time in a long time, it doesn't burn in pain.

Soon I'll be reunited with my children.

CHAPTER 17

H ell.
I drag my feet and stare at my bare toes. One step after another, and I wonder how many more times I'll stare at my swollen toes, trying to hold onto the cracked sole of my shoe. How many more times will I manage to command my legs to move onward before my knees buckle under me and I fall forward onto my face? I take in some air and try to raise my head. Hollow eyes flash past me, and then I hear a thump. Another body has collapsed. Another soul is finally at rest. I don't remember when I arrived at this hell or how long it's been since I was thrown from the wheelbarrow. Time has no meaning here.

The sun's rays are blinding, and I bow my head and continue to drag my feet. I blink and remember that I used to love watching the sunset. In hell, the sunset heralds the arrival of another excruciating night.

A rock pierces through the crack in my shoes and cuts my skin, but I feel no pain.

Shots echo in the yard, and I count them. One, two, three, four… four more souls are at rest.

"You!" A shout rings out near my ears, and I order myself to continue shuffling my feet forward. "You!" My back wobbles under a forceful blow, and my knees again threaten to buckle under me. I blink and straighten them with my last drop of strength. "Move the bodies!" The command comes from above my head, and I turn and drag my legs in the direction the finger of the black uniform is pointing at. In this hell, there isn't just one devil; there are many, many of them.

I stand before the body of someone who was once a woman and grab her legs. Across from me, a pair of sunken eyes glances at me indifferently, and together we throw the body into the massive pit at the center of the camp. We continue moving the other bodies, then turn and go our separate ways.

I lie down on the bunk in my cabin, reminiscing vaguely about my first days in the camp when I still thought there were days and nights in hell. I huddled next to the hollow figures and whispered the story of my magical kingdom. Someone snarled in annoyance and told me to shut up, but another woman scolded her, saying that I'd lost my mind and must be whispering to my children. Since then, no one has shushed me. Now there is practically no one left to do so.

I purse my lips and whisper. I whisper the children's names over and over again. Sarah, Bella, Misza, Oleg, Gershon. Then I tell my magical story over and over again. My throat is so dry, but I can't stop whispering. I think of my desperate searches right after I arrived in hell. I wandered around every corner and whispered, begging them to show themselves. Every now and then I encountered youthful eyes that looked at me in bewilderment, but none of them belonged to my children. I whispered my story to them, too, calmly and peacefully, until they vanished. Perhaps I only imagined them.

I close my eyes and pray for a dreamless night. The most dreadful thing in this place is my dreams. In my dreams, I'm not a lost soul waiting for my end. In my dreams, my name is Ania, and I am surrounded by family and friends. My children run around me laughing, and one man looks at me with longing. In my dreams, I have feelings. Damn feelings. Feelings that fill my heart with intense pain every time I open my eyes and remember where I am.

I put my hand in my pants pocket and feel the piece of black bread I saved just in case I encounter a hungry child. I do this every time I get my meager ration at daybreak. There was a time when I refused to eat the bread and left it on my bunk. The bread was always gone when I returned after sunset, giving me hope. But hunger gnawed at my limbs mercilessly, and my hope vanished with it. I nibble the bread carefully. I lick the crumbs from my lips and rub my abdomen.

The night I decided to starve myself is still etched in my mind. I closed my eyes, convinced that the hell awaiting me beyond the grave must be better than the one I am in. But that night, I dreamt a different dream. This time I wasn't free and surrounded by love. I was here, on this bunk, and on a chair in front of me, Yózef, my mother's brother, was seated. He gave me a comforting, fatherly smile and then stood up. I wondered how it could be that he had regained the use of his legs in hell, of all places. "Your candle is still burning," he said, stroking my head. "Fight for your light and remember that you must not extinguish it yourself."

I blinked hard, but when I opened my eyes, he still stood over me, wearing a pressed black suit and a white shirt. In his hands, he held Mother's prayer book. I tried to grab his hand so that he would continue stroking my hair, but his image faded away, and I just stared into the darkness.

It could be that his visit was simply another punishment inflicted upon me because, at that very moment, I took the slice of bread out of my pocket and broke my fast. Since then, I just keep looking at my swollen toes as I drag my feet over the bloody ground, inhaling air into my lungs, and wondering when I will steal my last breath.

I chew the last scrap of bread and lick my chapped lips. Screams sound from outside, and I cannot understand which lost soul found her voice to scream.

Grunting emanates from the body lying on the bunk above me, and I know it won't be long before I don't hear it any longer. The darkness in the cabin slowly envelops me, and I surrender to the fog of sleep.

I close the barn door behind me and pull the blanket tightly around my body. Anton is standing with his back to me and sweeping the piles of hay.

"Go back to the cabin. There's nothing for you here," he commands coldly, without turning to face me.

I put the blanket on a haystack and approach him.

"What do you want?" He stands up straight and makes a fist.

My teeth chatter from the cold, but I keep walking forward and stand behind him.

"What the hell do you want?"

"You," I whisper, and I put my hands on his back.

His shoulder blades tremble, and abruptly he turns around and wraps his arms around my waist. He swings me into the air, and I wrap my legs around him and stare into his wild eyes.

"I don't need you to comfort me," he whispers angrily.

He looks so mad, but there's nothing he can say or do to make me leave the barn now.

"Yes, you do." I slide my fingers, circling the wound on his lip. "And I need you too."

He groans softly and then walks forward, still carrying me, until my back hits the barn wall. His eyes ravage my face with forbidden longing. He pushes his pelvis against mine, then releases my hips and cups my cheeks. Letting out another groan, he tucks my hair behind my ears.

I close my eyes and feel the cold penetrating my bones. I can no longer feel his electrifying touch.

"Where are you?" I grope about for his body. "Anton?"

I sit up in alarm, and my head hits the bunk above mine. I hear myself moan in pain and run my hands over my face. "Damn dreams!" I whisper in exhaustion and lie back down. The grunting sounds above me have died down.

* * *

I drag my feet over the ground and stare at my bare toes. The sun's rays whip my eyes, and my head wobbles from side to side. If I close my eyes and allow my knees to crumple, I can rest. The thought of lying limp on the ground is so appealing that I try to command my legs to stop moving. They refuse and continue dragging themselves over the dirt.

The train wheels screech on the rails, and the carriages stop.

Don't look at them, I tell myself. Keep walking and don't look at them.

The doors open, and I look up. A groan of horror erupts from my throat when I see the figures bursting out of the cars. Exhausted, hungry, and thirsty. They can still feel the agonies of the body. They still believe that this hell is a labor camp. And they feel lucky to have survived this far.

The black-uniformed men push them into the yard. Then come the screams. Women to one side and men to the other. The women are torn from the men's arms with chilling cries. They still don't understand that this is the beginning of the end. I quickly lower my eyes at the sight of the children clinging to the men and women. I no longer look for my children there. The trains from Warsaw have stopped coming, and the unfortunate souls arriving now are from other cities.

I drag my feet and lean against the wall of a building. No one notices me. The forces of evil are focused on the new shipment that has been delivered.

The orchestra members take their places in the center of the yard and begin playing lively music. I will never again be able to hear a woodwind instrument without feeling dread in my bones.

I know what's going to happen now, and I turn on my heels. I go into the laundry and start to fold the sheets. Time has no meaning in hell.

CHAPTER 18

Darkness has fallen in hell, and I drag my feet to my cabin. There are no people in the front yard anymore. The dance of the demons is over. Now there are only tall piles of clothing, shoes, and luggage. The horrible smell no longer makes me nauseous. I don't remember an existence without the smell of death in my nostrils.

Those wearing the blue ribbons unload the last of the bodies from the train carriages, and those wearing the red ribbons sort the property in the suitcases. They seem to be new workers. Their eyes are still haunted; soon they will become hollow and empty.

I go into the cabin, lie down on the bunk, and close my eyes. I hug my bony body and think that if I were given one last request before I took my final breath, I would ask to meet with Ida's god. I would ask him only one question: "What sin did the children commit?"

I touch the piece of bread in my pocket, then take it out and shove it in my mouth. My gums hurt, and I cannot chew. I swallow the piece whole and shudder as it shocks my stomach.

I purse my lips and whisper the story of my magical kingdom. My voice slowly fades out, and I fall into a troubled sleep.

"*You look like a princess.*"

I grunt, hoping she'll understand that she's bothering me and leave me alone.

"Are you really a princess?" She kneels down and pets the cat's fur. Her body is tiny, and her clothes are filthy. Her black hair is wild, and her skin pale. Her eyes are fixed on the bowl of milk, and her mouth is watering.

My chest tightens, and Dziecko moves back as if sensing her desperation.

It's not your problem, I scold myself. This girl has nothing to do with you.

Wise and beautiful doe-like eyes beam up at me. I am her captive.

"Sarah." I whisper her name and try to stroke her cheek. "Where are you?"

"You're a funny princess." She smiles at me and walks away. "We're waiting for you to come and take us to your kingdom."

I sit up in a panic and shield my head with my hands. My breathing is labored, and I rub my chest in distress. Goddamned dreams!

The cabin door opens with the whack of a club. Single-file, we walk out to the yard.

The count is short. There are only three of us left.

Each of us grabs the meager ration served to her, and I shove the soft pulp into my mouth and bury the piece of bread in my pocket. My gaze roams to the yard. The piles are gone. The yard is ready for the next shipment.

I turn around and drag my feet, staring at my swollen toes and counting my steps.

"You!" A shout sounds out, and I stop and blink. A black uniform is blocking the sun's rays. I blink again, faster this time, and see the butt of a rifle coming toward me.

The butt of the rifle lands on the back of my neck, and my knees buckle, sending me onto the hard ground. My eyes close, and I savor the warmth climbing up my cheek. I didn't blow out my own candle. They extinguished it for me.

* * *

I hear faint breathing noises close to my ears. I'm surrounded by total darkness and peace, and a small smile stretches across my lips. My light finally went out. I've left hell, and now I'm finally entitled to eternal rest. Suddenly a sharp pain shoots down my neck, and the smile is wiped off my face.

I close my eyes tightly and try to focus. My chest trembles in alarm at the sound of wheels screeching on the ground. I try to wave my arms, but they're pressed close to my body, and I seem to be wrapped in some coarse material from head to toe. Is it possible that I'm still in hell?

I scream a muted cry and wriggle my body. The cloth wrapped around me loosens; I look down and stare in horror at my naked body. Am I on my way to the ditch of death? Are they going to bury me alive?

I wave my arms in panic and accidentally hit the sacks next to me. Sacks? Why do I have burlap sacks next to me?

The cart screeches to a halt, and I gasp at the sound of a horse neighing. I crouch down and listen apprehensively to the sound of footsteps moving near me. My heart flutters with fear – an old emotion I didn't think I'd feel on the verge of my long-awaited death.

I steal a breath and remind myself that I've been waiting for this, waiting to breathe my last breath.

A large figure looms over me, but I ignore its presence. I will not reveal my distress to the Angel of Death. Out of the corner of my eye, I notice that he isn't wearing a uniform but gray pants and a brown shirt. Don't let his attire confuse you, I command myself. The devil has many faces; if he decides to amuse himself, the joke will always be on you.

"Ania..." The deep whisper penetrates my ears.

An illusion. The devil is tricking me, and I'm hallucinating.

"Ania, please look at me."

The voice is so familiar. It's a voice that warms my heart. I'm dreaming. I'm in my dark cabin, and this is just another cruel dream. I shut my eyes tightly and vigilantly await my rude awakening.

"I'm dreaming..." I hear my own raspy voice. "I'm dream..."

"My Ania, you're not dreaming. Please. Look at me."

I open my eyes to a narrow slit and groan. Damn dream. I carefully look toward the voice, and my chest trembles, ignited by a bygone emotion. Wide-eyed, I stare at the face of the man who dominates my dreams.

"Dear God, Ania!" The man moves his hand forward and tries to touch my face. I draw back in alarm and clutch the blanket forcefully. I am on my deathbed. I am scared because this is my final dream. This is my last dream, flooding me with old, forgotten feelings just before I leave hell. The man keeps his hand close to my face but doesn't touch me. "I thought I was bringing home a corpse." His deep voice sounds tormented, and his brown eyes are wet.

The sharp pain pierces the back of my neck again. In my dreams, this man never cries. He always looks at me the way a man looks at a woman, and I'm never embarrassed by my naked body in his presence. He floods me with repressed passions that make me want to harm myself when I wake up in hell.

"Ania," the deep voice repeats my name. "I can't believe you're here with me." He buries his face in his hands and sighs heavily.

"Wake up," I whisper hoarsely. "Wake up from this weird dream." I blink again and again. Darkness surrounds me on all sides, and I can only see the shadows of thick trees. "Damn dream..."

"You're awake, and you're not in Treblinka anymore." The man peers over his shoulder and then looks back at me with a somber expression. "I also need time to take in this meeting," he says apologetically, "but we don't have time, and you must get dressed." He pulls a brown dress from one of the sacks and brings it to me.

I grimace and try to move away from him. I don't like this dream. This man looks so disappointed in me. I inhale. The pungent smell of death penetrates my nostrils, confusing me. In dreams, there are no odors.

"Get dressed!"

A command. My brain reacts instantly. I must follow orders. I drop the blanket and raise my arms. I haven't performed this action in such a long time, and as this man slides the dress over my arms, a groan of pain escapes my mouth.

"I'm sorry," he whispers, and I stare in terror at the palm of his hand moving towards my cheek.

"It's just a dream," I mutter hoarsely and close my eyes. In dreams, you can't feel physical contact. His palm brushes my cheek, and I feel it. I feel it on my body but mostly in my heart, like a caress rousing me from a prolonged slumber. My eyes open, and I stare at him in wonder. Intense emotions flood me like a raging river, threatening to drown me.

My throat burns, and my chest is on fire. "Anton?" I whisper and tilt my cheek toward his hand.

"I've missed you so much." His voice quakes as he pulls me to him and folds me in his arms. My upper body shivers with the vague memory of a sense of safety. I breathe into his chest and clutch his shirt. "We'll have time to hug." It sounds as if he's trying to reassure himself. "But for that to happen, first we have to get out of this stinking forest." He carries me in his arms and sits me on the bench. His body separates from mine, and the biting chill envelops me.

"This is not a dream," I murmur. "This is not a dream." I'm cold, and I'm scared. Terrified.

He hurries to sit beside me, and I hug myself and wonder when he'll hug me again. Suddenly time has meaning.

He takes a red apple and a pocketknife out of his pocket and cuts the apple in half. My eyes fixate on the juice left on the blade, and saliva floods my mouth. He gives me half, and I lick my lips but don't dare lift my hand to take the piece. Images of guards in black uniforms whiz through my head. The guards offer me a juicy slice of apple. I take it excitedly. A forceful blow lands on my neck. The apple falls to the ground, and a whistle sounds. Skeletal bodies of people who were once women storm at the apple…

"Take it!" commands the deep voice.

A command. I understand commands.

I grab the apple, hold it to my chest, and close my eyes.

Three… two… one… The blow doesn't come, and I cautiously open my eyes.

Distressed brown eyes look at me. "It's yours," he says softly. "Eat."

I bring the apple to my lips and try to bite into it. My face is contorted as fire torches my gums. I don't look, and I lick the sweet liquid from my lips. The taste is heavenly. I lick the apple and hum with pleasure.

The cart starts moving, but my body is too weak to sit steadily on the bench. I hug the apple as I swing every which way. A strong arm hugs my shoulders, and Anton pulls me close to him.

"Anton…" I mumble almost soundlessly, bringing my nose close to his neck and sniffing him. He is real. This is the aroma of the man who stole my heart and rocked my world.

"Your name is Katarzyna." He strokes my arm. "And my name is Władysław. We are siblings."

His assertion isn't unfamiliar to me. I remember hearing it in the past when I was a woman, and I also recall his reasons for saying it.

"We are traveling to other villages to trade goods."

I nod in agreement.

"I can't believe you're here with me." His voice sounds tortured. "I had so much time to plan what I would say to you when I got you out of that hellhole, but I can't remember what I wanted to say." He shakes the reins and sighs. "Don't ever do anything like that again!" His tone becomes harsh. "Don't you dare do anything like that to me ever again!"

The pain emanating from his words awakens something in me, and my own pain erupts inside me. It is not the pain of hunger or a limb that has suffered a blow. It's a pain that squeezes my heart suddenly and forcefully, sending sparks of fire that sear my chest. The understanding that I am sitting on this cart, outside of hell, hits me like a bolt of lightning. I slide down on the bench, lie with the apple pressed to my chest, curl up like a ball, and rest my head on Anton's lap. "Anton..." I whisper his name again and force my eyes to stay open. I'm afraid if I close them, I'll wake up on the bloodstained ground again. "I didn't find my children," I whisper and hug myself. "I didn't stop whispering for them, but they didn't hear my whispers."

He rubs my back over and over, attempting to calm the tremors shaking my body, and my eyelids begin to feel heavy.

My back is jolted by a brusque motion, and I open my eyes and sit up. I repeatedly blink to adjust my eyes to the darkness of the cabin but realize that it's light around me. Where am I? A thump sounds out near my feet, and I scurry, panicked, to pick up the apple that evaded me. I clutch it close to my chest and rub my eyes. Where am I?

I'm sitting on the wagon's bench, and enormous green fields surround me. I look straight ahead and see the man who has taken over my dreams. The understanding that he has taken me out of hell is beginning to sink in. Anton is standing in front of the horse and feeding it hay. He looks at me and smiles slightly. I manage to stretch my lips a little, but a sharp pain pierces the back of my neck, and I quickly look down. His smile reminds me of the dream about the barn. It's the smile of a man looking at a woman who fills him with secret passions. How can he smile at me when I am just a shadow of the woman I used to be?

"Soon we'll reach the cottage of a friend," says Anton, walking back to the wagon.

I nod and avoid his gaze, so he won't detect my embarrassment. He hands me a flask of water; I put the apple on my lap and take a long gulp. He doesn't try to take the flask away from me or insist that I hurry. I drink until I feel like if I take another sip, my stomach will explode. I peek in his direction distrustfully and then put the flask on my lap, too.

The wagon starts to move, and I look at the horse and frown. "That's not our horse." *Our?* Did I just use that word? Nothing in this world belongs to me, after all.

"Our horse got too old, and I had to replace him." His protecting arm wraps around me. "He would never have survived all my travels."

I want to ask him what travels he's talking about, but it feels like there are so many other questions I should ask first. The burden overwhelms me, and I just keep quiet.

The greenery that surrounds us is spectacular in its beauty. I feel as if I've been pulled out of a painting of the underworld, painted in shades of black and gray, and flung into a painting of my magical kingdom. I glance behind me, expecting to see a black tidal wave flooding the foliage and dragging me back into the darkness. But the green hue remains potent, and the orange sun shines in all its glory.

I sigh and press the apple to my lips. I gnaw on its succulent skin and lick the sweet juice.

The sun is slowly setting, and I notice a little cottage on the horizon. As the wagon rolls forward, the cottage gets bigger, and when Anton pulls the reins, I study the farm. It seems like the land here is blessed. Around the cabin are colorful beds of vegetables, a chicken coop, and a big barn.

A heavy-set woman walks out of the cabin and claps her hands in excitement. She's wearing a long floral dress, and a matching kerchief covers her head. Her eyes are light blue, her cheeks are rosy and round, and strands of fine, blond hair rest on her cheeks. Her broad smile reveals a row of pearly white teeth.

"You found her!" she exclaims and claps her hands. "I can't believe you found her!" She runs to the wagon and stands in front of me. "And he's smiling," she addresses me with tears in her eyes and points to Anton. "This is the first time I've seen this man smile." She holds out her hand to me, and I shrink back.

"I'll help her down," Anton says, squeezing my arm in understanding. He jumps to the ground and circles the wagon. The woman hugs him as if he were a family member, and he affectionately pats her on the back.

I hurry to drink the water remaining in the flask and tighten my fingers around the apple.

He turns to me with a smile and gently carries me off the bench. The woman examines me from head to toe, and an angry snarl escapes her throat.

"Animals. That's what they are." She shakes her head. "Despicable Nazis." She spits on the ground. "What kind of person could possibly believe that such a delicate creature is a threat to them?" She brings her hand up to my head, and I flinch again. "You need to clean their filth off of you," she says in a maternal tone. "And let me take care of your wounds." She points to my bare feet.

My good sense refuses to accept her kindness. Is she planning to lure me to the showers? I must not go into the showers!

I step back and hide behind Anton's back.

"I'll do it." Anton reaches back and grabs my hand.

"Absolutely not," the woman shrieks. "According to your papers, you are siblings. What if Germans or nosy neighbors pass by and discover that a brother is bathing his sister?" She walks toward us and extends her hand to me. "Girl, if your man trusts me, you can trust me too."

I cling to Anton's back.

"She's right," Anton says and turns to me. He picks up my filthy hand and kisses it. "I'll watch your apple while Inga takes care of you."

"But... the showers," I whisper and shiver. "I mustn't go into the showers."

"Don't worry." The woman waves her hand in dismissal. "There is no shower here. I'll draw you a pampering, perfumed bath."

My mouth drops open in astonishment, and she grabs my arm and carefully pulls me out of my hiding place. I send Anton a pleading look, but he just smiles reassuringly and takes the apple from me.

The woman leads me to the cottage, and I continue to stare at Anton forlornly. My eyes are fixed on the apple, and I wail soundlessly. He nods approvingly, then unties the horse from the wagon and leads it to the barn.

"This used to be a thriving roadhouse," the woman says with pride, and I focus and look around at the large room. A long bar stretches out before me, and behind it are empty shelves. Tables and chairs are spread out in front of the bar, and beyond them are a reception area and a square dining table. "They took all the liquor, but we hid the best bottles." She urges me forward. I drag my feet and stare at my swollen toes. "My Klaus uses them to barter with the neighbors."

Inga and Klaus. I memorize their names and then tense up suddenly.

"Yes, we are German," she says as if reading my thoughts, "but we are not Nazis." She spits the word out angrily. "When the Führer, may he rot in hell, seized power, we knew we had to leave our home as soon as possible." She tugs my hand, and I follow her down a narrow hall. "We left our farm in Germany and set up our roadhouse here in Poland." She opens a door, and I see a ceramic bathtub with iron claw feet. The bathtub in the luxurious apartment from my past life appears before my eyes, and I blink in confusion. "And then those dogs came all the way here." She lets go of my hand and pours a bucket of water into the bath. "I admit there is a certain advantage to being part of the Aryan race," she says, scoffingly stressing the last two words. "They allowed us to keep the roadhouse and didn't seize our farm. But I can't stand by while they continue to destroy the rest of the world." She leaves the room, and I stay frozen in place, not daring to move. A few minutes later, she returns holding a huge steaming pot and pours its contents into the bath.

"Take off your clothes."

A command. I must obey orders.

I wriggle out of the dress with the rest of my strength, and it falls off my body.

"Skin and bones." The woman sighs and ushers me to the bath. She holds my arm as I dip one foot in the water. A cry erupts from my lips. I cover my mouth with my hands and hear rapid footsteps in the hall. The door handle moves downwards, and I gasp and dive into the tub.

The door flies open. "What happened?" Anton asks, his expression terrified.

Blushing, I attempt to cover my nakedness.

"It was merely a cry of pleasure." The woman chuckles. "Now get out of here."

He stares at me for an instant and closes the door behind him.

"What you put that man through!" The woman rolls her eyes and hands me a bar of soap.

I hold it with both hands and relish its smooth texture. I hold it up to my nose and sniff. In dreams there are no smells, I remind myself.

"I'll never forget the day he arrived here with your sister."

My sister? I look up at her wide-eyed and suddenly feel a violent shaking in my chest. Michalina. My twin sister.

"She left here in much better shape than when she arrived," the woman continues with pride, "And I'll make sure you do as well." She dips a cup in the bath water, leans towards me, and gently wets my hair. "He left her here and went back to the camp. For four days and four nights, he hid there in the ridiculous hope that someone would realize you didn't belong and bring you out to him."

I murmur softly, remembering the night I abandoned him and entered hell willingly.

"When he came back here, I saw what a man whose entire world has fallen apart looks like." She takes the soap from me, lathers it, and soaps my hair. My scalp burns, but I dare not protest. "I thought he understood that you were lost for good, but ever since then, he's stopped here every month on his way back to the camp. The Resistance forces are too absorbed in the war against the Germans, and none of them could make time to help him liberate you." She gives me back the soap and pours water on my hair. "Soap yourself."

A command.

I soap my shins and hips, bend down to reach my feet, and soap between my toes. My skin burns and tingles and the bath water turns murky.

"When his contacts finally realized how determined he was regarding you, they tried to contact the Ukrainian guards at the camp. I heard they are the most brutal and corrupt guards there."

I take a deep breath and command myself to banish the images of figures in black uniforms, but I cannot. Images of the cruel guards siccing bloodthirsty dogs on poor, unfortunate souls give me no rest.

"For a long time, they refused to jeopardize themselves even in exchange for the hefty bribe that was being offered to them." The woman wraps a towel around my head. "Who would have thought that even the cruelest men are actually just cowardly mice?"

I grab onto the sides of the tub and stand up, exhausted.

"But the winds of war changed direction." She helps me out of the bathtub and wraps another towel around my body. "America finally realized that if they didn't join the fight against the Nazis, the whole world would be painted black. Even the Russians have now succeeded in angering the Führer." She snorts mockingly. "Soon they'll squash him like a cockroach." She mimics squashing a bug with her fist on the dresser, and I gasp. "So, I guess you got lucky because the Ukrainians realized they had better start worrying about their future and were finally willing to accept the bribe." She dries me thoroughly and examines my body. "You don't have any serious wounds. That's good." The woman nods. "You'll be able to convince yourself that you were never there."

My eyes inspect my wounded skin and then move back to her rosy cheeks.

"No one could forget being imprisoned in hell." My voice sounds so unfamiliar to my ears. "And what about the scar in my heart? Will that ever heal?"

The woman's eyes fill with tears, and she pouts in shame. "Forgive me. Maybe I said what's in my own heart. Maybe I'm praying that the day will come when I will be able to convince myself that you and many others like you weren't there."

I feel sorry for the woman's sorrow and try to think of a way to console her. I remain silent.

She sighs and helps me into a brown dress, then motions for me to sit on the chair and takes a rectangular box out of the dresser drawer. She applies a tingling ointment to the back of my neck and bandages it on top. The pain is a comfort to me because it assures me that I am not dreaming. She gets down on her knees and rubs the ointment on my feet. She blows on them as if I were a little girl who got hurt while playing and then bandages them. "Now you're almost mended." She groans as she pushes herself up. "I'll make you a meal fit for royalty, and we'll celebrate your safe return to your gentleman's arms."

I tense up as an old pain reappears in my stomach.

"Inga." My voice sounds rusty. "Anton isn't my man. He's my sister's."

A short laugh causes her bosom to shake, and she strokes my hair. "You're still confused, dear. Even my Klaus, who clearly worships me, wouldn't endanger himself for six months if he was told I was already a ghost."

"What month is it?" I ask, emitting a loud yawn.

"If I'm not mistaken, we're nearing the end of April 1943."

"April..." I repeat after her. Six months? I spent six months in hell. How am I supposed to come back to life now?

* * *

I sit in the chair next to Anton at the dining table and look at the plate set out in front of me. My serving is more modest than theirs but looks like overabundance to me. The aroma of the stew is so pungent that it makes my head spin. Inga loads a heaping amount of rice onto her fork. Anton follows suit. I keep staring at the plate put in front of me.

"Eat." Inga points her fork at my plate.

A command.

I lunge at the rice with my bare hands and shove it into my mouth. The mound is too big, and I gag and spit it back onto the plate.

"Oh, my goodness..." she mutters. "They turn them into starving animals over there."

I shake the rice off my hands and bow my head in humiliation.

"Ania, everything is fine," Anton says soothingly and hands me a fork. "You can choose whether to use this or to continue eating with your hands."

I take the fork from him without meeting his eyes. I manage to scoop up some rice, put the utensil into my mouth, chew slowly and with concentration, and finally successfully swallow without choking. I do so again, this time with a small piece of chicken, and my gums burn and tingle. The taste is so rich. I eat faster and faster and pant with excitement. Abruptly, I feel Anton's hand on my back, and I understand that he is signaling me to stop.

"You mustn't eat too much," he explains slowly, as if speaking to a small child. "It will take time for your body to get used to food again."

I want to scratch his face. I can't believe my plate is full, and he's preventing me from finishing it. I feel around for my dress's pockets, desperately searching for places to save the remaining food.

"Inga will store the food in the box for you," Anton says, moving my plate away from me. "She'll keep everything that is left over for us." He pushes his plate next to mine.

I scowl but dare not protest.

"I set up two bedrooms for you." Inga says as she picks up the plates and puts them on the counter on the other side of the room. My eyes follow the plates. "Before the damn war broke out, you couldn't find even one empty room here, but now there are plenty of them." She turns down the hall, and Anton stands up and clasps my hand. I drag my feet and stare at my bandaged toes.

Inga points to one of the rooms and another across from it.

"We'll only use one room." Anton opens the door of the room on the left.

"No, no." Inga waves her hands in protest. "What if we get an unexpected visit from..."

"I'll sleep on the floor," he interjects. "Ania will sleep on the bed, and I'll sleep on the floor. If anyone seems suspicious, just say that the siblings couldn't afford to pay for two rooms."

Inga furrows her brow but finally nods in agreement.

Anton closes the door and heads to the closet. He takes out a pillow and blanket and puts them at the foot of the bed. I step back and lean against the door. The double bed is big and wide, and the down blanket looks so soft. I linger nervously, expecting to hear additional footsteps and the creak of the opening door. After all, there is no way this big bed is meant for me alone.

"Ania, you can have the bed," says Anton tenderly. He lies down on the blanket and arranges the pillow under his head.

I drag my feet and stare at my bandaged toes. My hips collide with the wooden bedframe, and I carefully climb up. The sheets are as smooth as silk, and the pillow is fluffy. I rest my head on it and moan from the pain in the back of my neck.

Anton turns off the lantern, and the room goes dark.

I turn cautiously from side to side and groan. The mattress is too soft. I try to curl up like I did on my bunk, but my aching muscles refuse to obey. I blink and remind myself that this darkness is natural. A forgotten fear seeps in slowly; it is a paralyzing fear that emerges when there is something to lose. I hear Anton's breathing become heavy, and I shudder.

"My apple?" I whisper, saying the only thing that comes to mind.

"Wrapped in a handkerchief in my pocket," he replies, yawning.

I tighten my lips and struggle to breathe. Anton's breathing sounds peaceful, and I imitate the rhythm of his breaths and feel the fog of sleep pulling me under.

The darkness penetrates the cracks between the wooden beams. My eyes are open, and I'm staring at the black swarm making its way toward me. The phantom lying on the bunk above me rasps in distress, and I know the darkness has come to take me along with it. I'm struck by an irrational fear, and I wave my hands and try to push it away. It swirls around me, closing in on me.

I sit up in a panic, shielding my head.

"I'm here beside you, and you are safe." Anton's deep voice envelops me and soothes me. "You can go back to sleep." He caresses me tenderly and goes back to his blanket.

I can't relax my body. My fear is too powerful. I swing my legs off the bed and lie down on the blanket beside him. His body tenses up, and he doesn't touch me.

"Ania, do you want me to sit beside you on the bed until you fall asleep?"

"The bed isn't comfortable for me," I whisper. "It's too soft."

"Do you want the pillow?"

"No. I don't need anything else."

He puts his arm under my head and holds me close. His familiar smell overwhelms me, and I sniff his neck.

"Anton," I whisper. "I'm scared."

"You're with me now, and I promise I'll take care of you." He kisses my head.

"I'm afraid they'll come to get me," I wail. "I can't go back to hell after you brought me out of it."

"You'll never go back there." His tone is firm.

"So... So, you promise that if they come to capture me, you'll prevent it at any cost? Even..."

"Ania, they won't be able to catch you as long as I breathe. I promise."

One single word echoes in my head and I close my eyes and take a deep breath.

CHAPTER 19

A few bites of creamy, delicious porridge remain in my bowl, but Anton motions to me to put my spoon down. I scowl in annoyance. This morning he let me to eat two additional spoonsful. I should be grateful. I bend my head toward the bowl and then peek at him. His eyes are fixed on me alone, studying and scrutinizing me as he has done since the minute we arrived here. He is consistently in my line of vision.

"You should stay here one more week," Inga scolds him. "Look how much her physical condition has improved under my care. I don't think she's strong enough to spend an entire day on your wagon."

"She needs to get back to her home," Anton replies calmly.

I look up at him.

"I meant our house in the village," he explains apologetically. "You should be with Michalina and Ida and Maria and Luda. They deserve to know I was able to get you out of there."

I ponder each of the names he says, and I feel my heart expanding. Aside from having my biological sister, I now have additional sisters, and they have become an indispensable part of my family. I stand up immediately. My need to see them is so strong.

"Inga," Anton addresses her and pulls her into a hug. "I wish I knew some way to thank you. If I owned any property, I would entrust it all to you." He clasps her hands and kisses them both.

Inga's eyes tear up, and she waves her hands in dismissal. She chokes up and cannot speak.

I approach her and look into her rosy face. In the two weeks since I arrived at her safe haven, she has taken care of me like a mother tending to a toddler taking their very first steps. She caressed, scolded, bathed, and fed me as if I were a member of her own family. Little by little, I stopped fearing her touch, and now it's hard for me to imagine how I'll cope without her.

"Inga, I... I..." Words of gratitude yearn to burst forth from my mouth, but what can I possibly say that will truly explain the deep feelings I have for her?

"You are a hero." She draws me to her and crushes me in a tight embrace. "You mustn't thank me. I did what any person with even a drop of humanity left should be doing."

"But..." With difficulty, I break away from her embrace and caress her face like a blind man attempting to engrave the features of a loved one in his memory. "But you're not like everyone else," I tell her, managing to complete my sentence. "You're an angel who lost her way to heaven and found herself dangerously close to hell."

Inga bursts into tears, and I'm sorry that I upset her.

She sniffles and dabs her eyes on the sleeve of her dress. She wrinkles her face in feigned outrage and smiles ruefully. "There is no debt between us." She picks up a basket full of food and gives it to Anton. "But if you want Aunt Inga to be pleased, you must make your man happy."

I feel my face turn red and bow my head.

"When my Klaus returns from his long journey, he'll get a ringing slap from me," she chuckles. "Then I'll explain to him how a man who worships his wife should behave."

I turn my back to her in embarrassment.

"I wish you a safe trip," she says, her voice cracking. Then she disappears into the kitchen.

Anton positions his hand on the small of my back and leads me outside. He pads the wagon's bench with a blanket and hoists me up. The understanding that I will see my family at the end of this trip moves me to tears. I swing my legs impatiently and nod with vigor when Anton asks if I'm ready to set off.

For hours on end, the green landscape surrounds us like an enchanting tapestry. I envision my children running through the fields and giggling. My thoughts wander to my time in the ghetto and to each of the beautiful moments I had the privilege of spending with them. I look admiringly into Sarah's black, doe-like eyes, lovingly stroke Bella's golden hair, wink at Misza's innocent smile, pinch Gershon's cheek, and kiss Oleg's forehead. My pure, good-hearted children have disappeared, and my excitement and anticipation to finally see them again has faded.

Anton squeezes my hand as if he senses my pain, and I realize that I'm being ungrateful.

I bite my lip and take a deep breath. "Please forgive me for not saying thank..."

"Don't insult me with declarations of gratitude." He exhales sharply. "I'll let you tell me you missed me, and I'd love it if you would say you had no doubt that I would never give up on you. But I refuse to let you thank me for getting you out of hell after six goddamned months of losing my mind." He pushes his hair to the side and his jaw trembles. "I demand that you promise me you will never do such a thing to me again. Ever."

The unmistakable pent-up rage in his words unnerves me. "I... I..."

"Promise me!"

A command.

"I promise."

"No. Not like that." His manner softens. "I am not ordering you to perform a goddamn task like the beasts of prey who imprisoned you in that camp of horrors. I'm demanding that you promise me that you will never again put yourself in danger. Because I cannot lose you again." He goes silent for a moment and then adds, "Ania, I know I cannot compare the suffering I felt while you were gone to the suffering you experienced in there, but I swear to you that every time I dared close my eyes, I heard you whispering for me to help you. The first time I was able to sleep for more than a few minutes at a time was the night when you lay down next to me on the blanket. It wasn't until I heard your breathing that I felt I could allow myself to breathe."

I put my hand in his. I had descended so deep into the dark abyss that I couldn't see his pain. Now I understand that my hell was also his hell. A twinge in my stomach reminds me of my circumstances, and I pull back my hands and bury them between my knees. I have been punished for betraying my sister, and I won't dare come between them again. He promised to wait for her, and she clung to that promise.

I move to the other side of the bench, being careful that my body doesn't rub against his, and sip from the water flask he put in my lap. The wagon continues moving forward into familiar fields. Their sight fills me with great joy mixed with bottomless fear. I take a deep breath and feel for his hand. I'll take comfort in his strength just one more time, and that will be it.

The small cabin gets closer, and I huff and puff sharply. I shudder with every screech of wheels on the cobblestones, and I put my hand on my heart when four corporeal figures burst out in cries of happiness.

"I brought you a surprise." Anton wraps his arm over my shoulders, and his voice sounds excited. "I didn't want to say anything because every time I left this house, I wasn't sure that when I returned, I would find what I left behind."

"A surprise?" I mumble in confusion and gawk at my sister, who is running towards the wagon.

"You'll see in a minute." He waves his arm, and Ida pivots and runs over to the barn. The wagon stops, and Michalina pulls me off the bench. She clutches me tightly and sprinkles kisses all over my face. Her cries are so loud, but my cries are locked in my heart.

"Anushka, my Anushka! I knew Anton would bring you back to me." She kisses my nose and my forehead, and my hair. I sway on my feet. "I can't believe you're here." She continues showering me with kisses, and her tears wet my cheeks.

Maria pushes forward and touches me tenderly. She whimpers and mumbles indistinctly. I try to smile at her, but my face is frozen. Luda walks around them and hugs me from behind. She sobs softly, and I remember that she lost her voice.

I find it hard to breathe amid all their hugs and kisses and grope behind my back in a desperate attempt to grab Anton's hand. His fingers intertwine with mine, and I can breathe again.

I hear the sound of running feet hitting the ground from another direction, and I close my eyes. My extreme excitement is causing me to imagine the sound of my children's laughter, and I swallow the lump of despair obstructing my throat.

"Princess Ania!" The cry drives me to open my eyes, and the circle that has closed around me draws back.

Over and over, I blink in stupefaction. Seeing my sisters has caused me to lose my mind. I see my children running toward me and I clutch my chest and gasp in anguish.

"I'm hallucinating... I'm hallucinating..."

"Princess Ania." Black doe-like eyes beam at me with excitement.

"I'm hallucinating... I'm hallucinating..." My heart is pounding, and I can't breathe.

"We need to bow down to her." I hear a gentle voice and stare into Misza's playful smile. His two front teeth are missing. I step back in bewilderment. How could I possibly be imagining him so different from what he looked like when I left him?

Five small figures bow clumsily.

"Ania, you're not hallucinating," Anton's deep voice whispers in my ears, "Your children are here."

Five small figures charge at me, and a deafening cry erupts from my throat. I fall to my knees and put my arms out. More anguished cries burst forth from me, and the dam holding back my tears collapses. I laugh and cry at the same time.

"Be careful. You're hurting her!" I hear Michalina's plea.

My back hits the ground, and I'm covered with little bodies, kissing me and hugging me and laughing.

"You're hurting her," she tells them again.

"Don't interfere," Anton orders. "They can't hurt her while they're giving her back her heart."

I manage to kneel and gasp for air. "Am I dreaming?" I cup Sarah's cheeks and draw a circle around her eyes. "My God, if this is a dream, I beg you never to wake me up again." I slide my hands over Bella's hair. Someone pinches my arm, and I turn to look at Misza's illuminated figure.

"You felt my pinch, Princess Ania." He chuckles and runs back to escape Oleg's wallop.

"You're not allowed to pinch our princess!" Gershon scolds him and approaches me hesitantly. He looks taller than the other children, but his face is pale, and his cheekbones stick out just like theirs. He smiles awkwardly and tilts his head to the side as he studies me. "Did the Nazis catch you?" he asks, coasting his finger over my face. "Did they catch you because we weren't here to watch over you?"

I pull him to me and scatter kisses all over his face and head. "The Nazis caught me, but I came back to you, and now you can watch over me so they don't catch me again." The extreme happiness that is flooding me makes me dizzy, and I allow Gershon to break free of my clumsy grip. Pushing myself up with my hands, I stand and turn in a flurry of emotions to face the man standing behind me.

"I love you so much." I bombard him with an embrace. "I love you so much right now." I plant a forceful kiss upon his lips.

The smile that lights up his face is the most beautiful smile I have ever seen in my life. I grope for his hand and bump into a delicate hand instead. My eyes travel down his arm, and I see that Michalina is holding his hand. My heart flutters in distress.

"I love him now too." She laughs and wipes away her tears. "He kept his promise and brought my sister back to me."

I nod, and when I look back at Anton, the beautiful smile isn't lighting up his face anymore, and his expression is one of agony.

"Ania." I hear Ida's velvety voice behind me, and excitement grips me again. I turn to her and look at her smiling face and green eyes that glisten with tears.

"Ida." I clutch my chest and tumble forward. Her embrace encircles me in a wall of love, and I sob and let my head fall on her shoulder. "I couldn't be happier," I whisper, exhausted. "I'm overwhelmed with such extreme happiness."

"Me too." She hugs me tighter and cries. "When you didn't come back..." she coughs as tears flood her throat. "When you didn't come back with them, I sat in your chair day after day and waited for you."

"Now I'm here, and so are you." I moan softly and force myself to stand up straight. "And no one can take this precious moment away from us." I turn around to look at my children and hug myself.

"Princess Ania." Sarah comes up to me and takes my hand. "Now that you're here, maybe you'll agree to tell us the story of your kingdom again?"

"Ania has had a long trip," Michalina says carefully and takes my arm, "She'll tell you a story after she gets some rest."

Sarah's disappointment is evident, and I squeeze her hand and let her support me as I take a seat on the ground.

"What are you doing?" Michalina tries to pull me up.

I shake her off and signal to my children to sit down in front of me. "Nothing in this world will stop me from telling my children my story." I lean forward, and they follow suit. Their sweet breaths tickle my face, and I take a deep breath. "So, what do you say...? Do you want to hear the story about the magical kingdom?" I whisper and laugh hoarsely as five small, innocent figures clap their hands in delight.

CHAPTER 20

I lie on the couch and can't stop staring at my children. They're sitting by the fireplace and playing with pebbles. They look like they belong here; as if they have always been here. It's almost as if my memory of losing them was just some fleeting madness. Sarah has grown taller, and her jet-black eyes look wiser and more mature. Bella's golden hair is longer and now flows down her shoulders. Misza is concentrating on throwing a pebble, and his tongue slides over the gap left by the two baby teeth that fell out. Gershon twirls his sidelocks around his fingers and blinks over and over again with hunched-over shoulders. And Oleg keeps peeking at the bubbling pot that's filling the cabin with mouth-watering smells. My heart skips a beat when I realize that what has changed most about them is how thin and pale they are.

The cushion next to me sinks down. "They were in much worse shape when they were brought to us," Ida whispers. "They looked like they'd been pulled out of a pig pen."

"The table is set, and the food is ready." Maria approaches us enthusiastically. "Ania, there is a seat of honor at the table intended for you alone." She points to the table, which Anton has positioned at the cabin's entrance. Michalina begs him to sit down and immediately sits next to him. Her eyes beaming, she motions to the empty chair on her other side.

My gaze flits to Anton's brown eyes, and I quickly look at my children again. "I'd rather eat here with them."

"But Anushka," Michalina exclaims. "We set the table in your honor."

"Leave her alone," Anton commands quietly, and she doesn't say another word.

Maria and Luda dish the stew into bowls and serve me first. The children sit in a row at the parlor table and wait for me to begin eating. I fill my spoon with stew and nod my head in permission. Silence falls as they devour their food.

I put the spoon in my mouth, gasp with pleasure and chew the soft vegetables gradually. Anton watches me attentively, monitoring the number of spoonfuls that enter my mouth.

"We waited a long time for you," Misza grumbles, licking his lips. "Your boyfriend said we needed to understand that you might not be able to return."

"Boyfriend?" I raise an eyebrow.

"Your boyfriend." Sarah laughs, but the laughter doesn't reach her eyes. "When they came to take Grandpa to the camp to treat him at the special clinic," she explains quickly, and I bite my lip. I have pains in my chest, and I rub it softly, "he told me I should gather my friends and hide until you came to get us. I wanted to go with Grandpa," she pouts, "but he said that if I wanted him to get the treatment, I couldn't come because children aren't allowed there."

My breath gets caught in my chest.

"I listened to him because I wanted Grandpa to be cared for, so I got all my friends together." She points to the other children. "Gershon's mother begged him to stay with her." Sarah stuffs a full spoon of food into her mouth. "But they came to take her, too, so we ran away together."

Gershon blinks hard, and I try to smile at him, but my lips refuse to stretch.

"Grandpa told me that after he left for the clinic, they would try to take all the Jews to labor camps." She wrinkles her forehead.

"And he said that they would take us to an orphanage but that it wouldn't be like Mr. Korczak's and we wouldn't have any fun there."

I hear Michalina's faint cry and cannot comprehend why she is revealing her distress in front of the children.

"So what did you do?" I cough and try to put my spoon into my mouth. My hand is shaking, and the stew spills back into the bowl.

"I suggested we hide in a bombed-out building," Bella blurts out. "I saw that they took everyone who lived there away in the trucks."

"It was a bad idea," Oleg scolds her. "Your friend found us there after just a few days."

I have no idea which friend they are talking about.

"He told us that if he found us, the Germans would, too," Gershon explains, peeking towards the pot.

Maria comes over to us and gives each of the children a second portion.

"He suggested we hide down below." Oleg nods.

"Where down below?" I'm trying to understand the logic of their story.

"Down under," Misza whispers. "Where there is a river of garbage and the smell..." He pinches his nose and giggles.

"In the sewers?" I open my eyes wide in horror.

"Yes." Misza nods. "But it's not that bad once you get used to it."

"We weren't there the whole time," Sarah nudges him. "Whenever your friend came to see us, we knew we could come out for a few minutes."

I swirl the spoon around in my bowl. It's hard for me to imagine my pure, innocent children living underground like rats.

"Misza and Oleg were the real heroes." Sarah softens her voice, and the boy's mouths stretch into proud smiles. "Since they are the smallest, they were able to escape through the holes in the wall and steal food for all of us. We even gave a loaf of bread to your boyfriend."

"Please explain to me which friend you're talking about," I ask.

"The one who brings us candy," Gershon replies.

"Bruno?" I cover my mouth with my hands and sneak a look at Anton. He's listening to the story intently as if he's hearing it for the very first time. "Is he still in the ghetto?"

"Of course not," Sarah shouts. "He brought us out of the sewers when they came to take us to you. He looked so different." She giggles. "We almost threw rocks at him."

"Yeah." Bella nods energetically. "He had no hat and no beard."

"And no sidelocks!" Gershon tucks *his* behind his ears.

"He said he'd been waiting for them to come and pick us up so he could go out into the woods," Sarah says, and I let out a sigh of relief. "But he asked us to tell the princess that after he defeats the Germans, he'll come looking for her and that he'd ask for our permission to court her."

"Anushka has always had many suitors," says Michalina with pride.

"I told him he could come and visit but that we wouldn't let him court you." Sarah sticks out her chin in defiance. "He didn't understand that the princess must marry the Guardian of the Realm."

I blush.

"Who's the Guardian of the Realm?" Michalina laughs.

Sarah opens her mouth, and I open my eyes wider in a silent warning. She nods her head and remains silent.

I dare not look at Anton, but I can feel his eyes caressing my heart.

"And... And how did you get here?" I change the subject.

"In potato sacks," the five of them holler together, clapping their hands in delight. "We were told that we weren't allowed to talk or move and that if anyone kicked our sack, we weren't even allowed to whimper quietly."

"Someone kicked my sack." Misza says while bobbing his head.

"Mine too." Oleg smiles mischievously. "But we bit our tongues really hard and held our breath."

"You are such courageous children." I sigh and force myself to put the spoon into my mouth. "But what will happen if...?" I shrink back and give Anton a frightened look.

"Oh..." Sarah stands up. "If we hear a noise from the fields, we have to run and hide. Come on, Princess Ania, we'll show you our hiding place." She tugs my hand.

I hurriedly swallow two more spoonsful and put my bowl back on the table.

The children stand around me and insist that I join them. Their enthusiasm is contagious, and I try to walk quickly after them. Sarah grabs one of my hands and Bella the other. The boys run towards the barn.

I lean on the frame of the barn's door and look at the haystacks. Images of the intimate, exciting evening I spent right here flash through my mind, and I close my eyes and admonish myself. I've committed the sin of thinking forbidden thoughts again.

"Look! Look!" the children shout, and I open my eyes and see them bending over the hay. They toss the haystacks aside and pull screws out of the wooden beam at Sarah's orders. Misza puts the screws in his pants pocket, and they take another bale of hay out of the space beneath. They pull out more screws, and after lifting up the beam, they scamper to jump into the hole they've opened in the ground. They move the hay and hide the beam, and after a few seconds, I can't hear a thing. A deafening silence pulsates in my heart. Panting nervously, I approach the hay.

"They're perfectly fine," Anton whispers behind my back and rubs my arms, "Watch." He gets down on his knees, moves the hay aside, and taps on the beam three times. A few seconds later, I hear movement under the wood and the turning of screws. The upper beam is hoisted up, and five amused faces look up at me.

"Get out of there." I rub the back of my neck restlessly. "Please don't go into that pit if you don't have to."

"We have food and water down there." Gershon jumps out first. "And we sleep here." He points to the pile of folded blankets on top of a tall haystack.

"And we also have a prayer book to keep us safe." Sarah waves the book that once belonged to my mother.

"Hide it!" I tell him, alarmed, my eyes filling with tears.

"Michalina will sleep here with you tonight," says Anton, turning to the barn door. Only now do I notice that everyone is standing there. Michalina nods in consent and then steps forward and takes his hand. His touch seems to reassure her. "You'll have to hide in the pit with them if any unwanted guests arrive," he explains to her calmly. She looks at the hole the kids have already covered and nods, her face downcast. "Our papers cannot account for the presence of the two of you." He pats her arm in an attempt to cheer her up.

The need to feel his touch makes me involuntarily pat my own arm but I quickly regain my composure. I shake my head.

"I'll sleep here with them and hide with them if need be." I stifle a yawn and spread a blanket out on the hay. "I won't be able to sleep in the cabin knowing they're out here."

"I think you'd better sleep in the cabin for the next few nights," Anton says cautiously. "Michalina will take care of them until you get stronger."

She nods in agreement, but I detect the concern in her eyes. She needs Anton by her side.

"The moment you gave me this gift, you strengthened me in a way that I cannot explain in words." I smile at him and lie down on the blanket. "When my kids fall asleep beside me, I'll get another boost of strength."

They jump up and down enthusiastically on the haystacks and then cuddle up next to me.

"I'll bring you some more blankets." Anton nods his head in understanding, and when he leaves the barn, the women follow him.

Sarah rests her head on my arm, and Misza's leg rubs against mine. I close my eyes and take a few deep breaths. This is the warmest blanket I've ever been wrapped in.

"Misza almost got confused and thought Michalina was our princess," Sarah whispers reproachfully.

"I was only confused for a second," he grumbles. "When I ran to her and hugged her, she flinched."

"And she didn't whisper either," Bella adds. "I knew right away that she wasn't our princess."

I giggle softly and bask in the delightful warmth that envelops me.

"Princess Ania, tell us the story of the magical kingdom. Please!"

I stifle a yawn and nod. My lips tighten, and I whisper the story of my magical kingdom over and over again until their breathing deepens. I'm not afraid to let go and fall into the fogs of sleep. When I open my eyes, I will be delighted again when I realize that my dreams have become my reality.

"I'm ashamed that I didn't insist on switching with her," I hear Michalina whisper. "Maybe you should pick her up and take her inside the cabin, and I'll stay here instead."

"There's no need," Anton replies in a whisper, and I feel the warmth of the blankets he is arranging over us. "She's right where she belongs."

"But look at her. She's so weak," Michalina whispers sadly.

"I'm looking," he exhales loudly in aggravation, "and there's nothing weak about your sister."

Their footsteps recede, and the barn door closes. I turn to lie on my side, and the children's little arms and legs move with me. I smile slightly and remind myself of the reality of our relationship.

I hear the barn door open again and open my eyes a crack. Anton's broad shoulders block the moonlight, and he crosses his arms over his chest and looks at me apprehensively. The darkness hides the fact that I'm staring at him. I have no idea how long he stands and stares at me because my eyelids close, and I resolutely fight to drive away the darkness that's trying to seep in and paralyze me.

CHAPTER 21

I position my chair in the middle of the field, as has been my habit straight after breakfast for the past few weeks. I watch the children running around in delight and bite into the slice of apple that Anton gave me. My gums no longer burn when I chew solid food, and Anton has stopped obsessively monitoring every morsel that I put into my mouth. I feel that my body is getting stronger, and a few days ago I was even able to look at myself without feeling embarrassed. I'm no longer a shadow of a woman, and my heart expands every time I hear the children's laughter. I cannot rest for fear that the Nazis will come to the farm; even though the children have proven to me countless times that they can identify suspicious noises, my apprehension refuses to abate. Fear has become an inseparable part of me.

I quickly glance toward the barn. Anton leads the horse out for a walk, and the children run to him in excitement. He picks up Sarah and Bella, puts them on the saddle, and Misza leaps onto Anton's back. He guides the horse slowly and carefully, and Gershon and Oleg run alongside them, mimicking the horse's trotting.

I lick the apple's juice from my lips and smile. When my children are with Anton, I know I can let myself breathe freely. After a few minutes, Michalina comes out of the cabin and runs towards them.

Her hair is in a tight braid, and the beauty mark on her cheek shines. She takes Anton's hand, and he smiles at her. I stretch my lips into a dutiful smile and remind myself that when they are together, I must be happy. He promised to wait for her, and she came back to him.

I hear a chair being dragged over the ground, and Ida sits down next to me. She follows my gaze and takes my hand in hers.

"He knows she needs him now," Ida says as if I posed a question. "She's incapable of closing her eyes when he's not around her."

I continue to watch the two of them walking harmoniously, hand in hand, and I don't say a word.

"When he brought her here, her condition was almost as bad as yours." Ida keeps answering questions I didn't ask. "Michalina wouldn't eat, sleep, or bathe when he wasn't in her line of vision."

I bite my lip and sigh.

"It's a different kind of love," says Ida in her tender voice. "He understands that he is the stable rock in her life and must make her feel safe."

I bring the apple to my mouth but cannot bring myself to take a bite. Conflicting emotions stir inside me.

"Promises made before the war lost their right to be actualized as soon as the Nazis invaded our country." She presses the palm of my hand to her heart. "Neither you nor Michalina should punish him or yourselves by keeping obsolete promises."

I swallow and put the apple on my lap. I've lost my appetite.

"She needs him now." Ida emphasizes the final word. "But in time, she'll heal, and she'll understand that that man cannot live without you."

I want to say that I have no idea how I'll manage to live without him, but instead I just look down and don't say anything. I stole my sister's man once, and I'll never do it again. Ida will learn to understand that their union is essential to set our horrible, twisted world right.

I turn and kiss her cheek; then, clutching the apple to my chest, stand up and walk to the barn. I need some time alone to let my heart mend.

I sit on a bale of hay, swinging my legs and thinking about Mother and Father and about Michalina's heartbreaking narrative. Shame engulfs me when I remember how much I despised her when I thought she was rejoicing on a ship on her way to America. The realization that the burning in my stomach was due to her genuine distress shakes me to my core every time I think about her story. With haunted eyes, she told me how they realized they wouldn't be able to leave Czechoslovakia. The borders were closed, and they were staying at the home of some of Father's acquaintances. She didn't elaborate on when and how she was torn from Father's arms. Her decision to study nursing is what saved her. She became the right-hand woman of a Jewish doctor and therefore was able to cope with camp life relatively endurably. Until… I sigh when I remember her harsh words: until the Nazis no longer needed the fake clinic. A clinic that never actually treated any patients and was just a stop on the way to the pit of death.

I tense up as the barn door opens, and Anton leads the horse inside. Michalina is still holding his hand. His eyes meet mine, my heart quakes, and I quickly turn aside.

"So, this is where you're hiding." Michalina giggles. "Your children think you're playing hide and seek with them in the grove."

I stand up in alarm. "Alone? Are they alone in the grove?"

"I'll go get them," Anton responds calmly and ties the horse to the beam. Michalina smiles at me and follows him out of the barn.

I approach the horse and pet his coat. Images from my night of lovemaking with Anton flit through my mind like a film and flashing memories of a sublime and addictive feeling of peace tug at my heart. I continue to pet the horse and hear sounds of laughter outside the barn that bring a tiny smile to my lips.

I hear familiar steps behind me and jump. His large body moves close to me, almost brushing against me, but I cannot turn to him.

"Every time I walk into the barn, I imagine you lying on the hay and looking at me." Anton's breath tickles my ears. "You're here with me, but I miss you so much."

I shudder as the horse shakes his neck and realize I pulled too hard on his mane.

Anton's hand slides along my arm. "Ania, I miss you."

Light steps trample over the hay, and my shoulders tense up.

"Anushka, do you feel okay?" Michalina's gentle voice sounds worried, and a twinge of guilt burns in my stomach.

"Don't call me Anushka!" I snarl and turn around. "I don't deserve your affectionate nickname for me." Her hand is in Anton's hand, and he gives me a fiery look.

Michalina's face turns to stone, and she puts her head down in humiliation.

I rub my face vigorously. My feelings of shame are unbearable. I am ashamed of my betrayal and am taking my anger out on her.

"Forgive me, sister," I whisper without looking at her. "Forgive me for my shameful behavior." I leave the barn and walk determinedly to the chair in the middle of the field. Only the sight of my children can comfort me now.

* * *

The intense hues of the sunset paint the fields with mesmerizing brushstrokes, and I chase away my gloomy thoughts. I hear Maria begging the children to bathe, and I shiver. Every evening I remind myself that I'm not in hell and that the word "shower" isn't a synonym for "death."

I pick up my chair and go into the cabin. My eyes open wide in surprise when I see that Michalina is standing beside Ida in front of four burning candles. They're covering their eyes and murmuring a prayer. They look so engrossed; I put the chair down and sit quietly on the couch.

"Anushka, do you want to light Sabbath candles?" Michalina smiles when she notices me.

I shake my head. Ida continues to rock her body back and forth, her face twisted in supplication.

"This is my first time," Michalina whispers and sits next to me.

Ida stands up straight and raises her face in some sort of final prayer and then turns and sits on my other side.

"You should try." Michalina takes my hand. "Ida explained to me that first I must thank God for all the gifts he has given me, and then I can ask him for more gifts."

"Look, Ania." Ida points to the candles. "Michalina added two candles, and after the German bastards get out of Poland, we'll give the world its light back."

"I already have five candles." I turn towards the laughter of the children who are showering in the shed. "They light up my world."

"They are big, luminous lights." Michalina squeezes my hand. "I prayed that someday I, too, will be rewarded such a light."

I don't understand her desire to bring a child into this dark world, but I don't dare upset her again. I still haven't told her about our connection to Sarah. Deep down, I believe that Mother should know first.

"I also prayed that..." she glances towards the door and blushes. "I prayed that Anton would be able to look at me the way he looked at me before I left with Father."

I can't look her in the eyes.

"I thank God that he's here with me," she quickly explains. "I thank God that he carried me out of hell and that he kept his promise and waited for me, but..." she glances towards the door again and whispers, "but it seems as if his concern for me won't allow him to look at me the way he did before."

Ida tightens her grip on my hand and doesn't say a word.

"I can't stop thinking about the first time we met." I can hear Michalina smiling. "I went to Peter's café on our nineteenth birthday. I'd had a hard day at school, and I knew Peter would cheer me up."

I grin wryly when Peter's name comes up.

"I got there early, and the place wasn't full yet. Peter invited me for a drink and entertained me with amusing stories about his customers."

This time it's me who squeezes Ida's hand.

"He didn't stop gabbing until the door of the café opened, and a policeman in a blue uniform walked in. For a minute it seemed to me that the café had emptied completely and that this impressive man was the only person there with me." She giggles in embarrassment. "I had never seen a man who radiates such power."

I close my eyes and imagine myself sitting there instead of her.

"Peter introduced us and invited him to join us. From the second Anton sat down in front of me, I couldn't stop talking. I talked about my studies and our family. I talked about culture and even about the geopolitical situation in Europe. I was amazed to find that he didn't find it off-putting, and he even showed interest." She giggles again. "He offered to escort me home, and I agreed. Anushka, can you believe it?" She whispers in amusement. "That I would agree to let a strange man walk me home?"

I open my eyes to assure her that I'm listening.

"When we got to our building, he kissed my hand and asked if he could invite me to a restaurant." She sighs. "My heart screamed for me to answer yes, but my head reminded me that Mother and Father would never approve of him as a suitor." She bites her lip over and over. "I replied that I couldn't join him alone, but I suggested that he accompany us together instead. Me and you." Her tone becomes sad. "He indeed came to accompany us, and after that he came again every time I asked. Every day my feelings for him intensified until I couldn't imagine myself without him. I suppose it was convenient for Father and Mother to accept my explanation that he was just a dear friend, and I couldn't find the courage to correct their impression." Her voice sounds somber. "Since then, Anton never hinted at his intentions towards me again, but I knew he was waiting for a sign from me. I gave him that sign too late – only when I said goodbye to him at the train station and made him promise to wait for me." Her eyes are brimming with tears. "I shouldn't have left him. I shouldn't have left you." She squeezes my hand again. "If I had stayed with you, he would have taken care of me as he took care of you, and I would have been able to show him my love and..." She blushes and pauses. "Maybe he's waiting for another sign?" She straightens up, alert. "Maybe he's waiting for me to offer myself to him?"

"No!" I hear Ida's adamant answer and throw her a stunned look. "I mean..." she stutters and pales. "I mean, I meant to say that... you should wait a little longer. This horrible war isn't over yet, and I think Anton might be waiting until he can give you a better life. A truly safe life." She avoids looking at me and frowns in distress. Ida never lies, and I realize that now she must be repenting for her sin.

"But who knows when the war will end?" Michalina stares at the candles. "For so long, I didn't feel like a woman. I felt like a broken and abandoned soul. But when I'm with him, I feel whole again. I feel prepared to love him like a woman should. Anushka," she addresses me, and a spasm of guilt jolts my stomach, "you understand men. You always had suitors. What do you suggest I do?"

I leap off the couch. "I don't know anything about men. I never did. I was just a stupid little girl who thought the whole world revolved around her. I'm the last person you should ask for advice." I walk, exhausted, to the kitchen and lean on the counter. The pain in my soul torments me, and I can barely breathe.

The children burst into the kitchen to the sound of Maria's protests. Their wet hair drips on the floor, and she and Luda chase after them with towels. I stare at them, hypnotized, and then stand up straight and inhale deeply. I remind myself that they are lighting the right path for me. I'll never stray from my course, and I'll never betray my sister again.

Anton comes into the cabin, and as soon as our eyes meet, my selfish heart skips a beat. He looks toward the couch, and then he looks at me again. His brown eyes glow with determination, and he takes two steps toward me. I wave my hand, signaling him to stop. He pushes his hair to the side, and his jaw quivers.

Michalina gets up from the couch and goes to him. She puts her hand on his back and smiles at me. "Anton, you can go bathe and get some rest. We'll make sure you have a hot meal waiting for you."

He continues to look at me meaningfully, and I bow my head and moan softly. My heart chafes against the inside of my chest.

He passes by me and leaves the cabin, and I remind myself that he has won my better half.

CHAPTER 22

The sun beats down on my head, so I tie on my kerchief and make little holes in the new garden bed. The children are kneeling beside me and digging in the dirt with great delight. I stand up straight and study them, as is my daily ritual. They've grown taller and stronger, and it seems as if they were born for the country life. I proudly look out over our little piece of paradise. The cabin is surrounded by colorful vegetable beds, a swinging bench has replaced the chair I used to sit on, and the flowers that we planted near the barn fill the air with their sweet perfume.

I shield my eyes and look out toward the horizon. It's been so long since I came back here from hell – almost a year and a half. The summer of 1944 has been sweltering, and if it weren't for Inga and Klaus coming to visit, I would have believed the war was over. But according to them, the Nazis are still on Polish soil, and my children aren't safe. My fear that those vicious beasts want to hunt down my pure, innocent youngsters gnaws at me constantly.

I gaze out across the fields and I see Anton's strapping figure leading the horse back toward us. His hat is carelessly positioned on his head, and his cloth suspenders are stretched over his broad shoulders. His hair has gotten lighter from the sun, accentuating his tan skin. My heart trembles, and I exhale in anguish.

"The Guardian of the Realm looks at you like that when you can't see, too." Bella giggles.

I blush and go back to digging in the soil.

"He looks at you like that when we're asleep in the barn." Sarah chortles. "He doesn't know that sometimes I can't fall asleep because I'm thinking about Grandpa."

I give her a rueful smile.

"He's guarding her," Misza admonishes Sarah. "How can he keep her safe if he doesn't look at her?"

"Get back to work," I scold them affectionately.

"Maybe he's with Michalina all the time because he gets confused and thinks she's the princess." Gershon sprinkles seeds in the holes.

"They don't look at all alike," Sarah rebuts him. "He only looks at Princess Ania that way."

The cabin door opens, and Michalina comes out. She leans down, ruffles Oleg's hair, and then runs to Anton.

"Get back to work!" I command them quietly.

Suddenly the children perk up and, as one, look north. I follow their gaze and concentrate. In the distance, I hear the sound of wagon wheels.

"To the barn!" I jump to my feet and see Anton tugging hard on the reins and pulling the horse toward the barn.

The children run, and I follow them. Michalina dashes inside the cabin.

In no time, the children and I have plunged into the darkness of the pit, with the wooden beams blocking any sounds from outside. I grope around with my hands to make sure the five of them are with me, and then grab the prayer book and hold it close – Mother's prayer book that Sarah brought with her.

I don't have to ask the children to keep quiet. None of them utters a sound, and I can barely hear their breathing. The apprehension is making me woozy, and I feel Sarah's arms tighten around me. She's trying to reassure me when I should be the one reassuring her.

The minutes tick by, and it seems like an eternity has passed before we hear three knocks above our heads. I still find it hard to breathe.

"We can get out," Sarah announces, and the children move around me like a miniature, well-trained army. Everyone knows their role.

The beam above us is raised, and Anton looks down at me with a calm expression and reaches out to me.

"You can get out of the pit," he addresses the children, "but don't leave the barn."

I nod vigorously along with the children.

He goes back outside, and the children sit down on the bales of hay. I carefully tiptoe to the door and peek through the cracks.

Anton is standing next to an unfamiliar man and talking with him. I cannot hear their exchange, but Anton is listening to the man, and from time to time, he nods his head in agreement. I remember a similar meeting that took place long ago and ended in a major crisis when I learned that my sister was in peril. I grit my teeth and force myself to maintain restraint.

The man is gesturing exaggeratedly with his hands to illustrate his point, and I massage the back of my neck and pray for him to leave already. A simple little prayer that we can just go back to digging holes in the ground.

The man jumps back on his wagon and whips his horse. Anton watches him until the wagon disappears on the horizon. He takes his hat off and combs his hair to the side with his fingers. I can see that he's upset, and my heart sinks.

I open the barn door, motion to the children to stay where they are and walk over to him. Four filthy figures run towards us from the cabin. Michalina is cleaning her face with a wet rag, and Ida, Maria, and Luda look at Anton questioningly.

"You can get cleaned up," says Anton in a pensive tone, still looking out at the horizon.

"But what about the news?" Ida bursts out. "Did you hear anything about the Resistance? About Leib?"

He blinks twice, and then fixes his posture and looks at us. "The Home Army, the Armia Krajowa, has declared 'Operation Tempest.' They are openly fighting the Germans to liberate Warsaw." He combs his hair to the side again and puts his hat back on. "Our Armia and the independent Resistance forces are fighting the Germans. This will be the war that will force them to leave."

"That's good news." Michalina nods energetically. "That's good news, isn't it?"

His jaw trembles and my breathing stops.

"It's good news," he replies thoughtfully, "but I cannot simply sit here and walk the horse while my brothers fight for us."

My heart sinks.

"I have to join the Resistance."

I hear Michalina's heartbroken cry and stare at Ida's terrified face. I turn to look at the barn where my five little treasures are gathered and then stare again at Anton's powerful features. Our eyes meet, and I bow my head in concession. He needs to do this, but he will return to us. I have never been as sure of anything as I am of this. I turn towards the barn, and tears run down my cheeks.

***

We stand near the horse and watch Anton as he arranges the rope, suspending the two sacks he is taking with him over the saddle. Michalina weeps quietly, and the children take turns hugging him goodbye.

"Take care of your princess," Anton commands sternly, "and guard the other princesses as well."

The children nod vigorously. Although they are rehearsed in goodbyes, the pain of this farewell is evident in their eyes.

Luda and Maria each hug Anton in turn, and Ida stands in front of him and wipes away her tears. "If you see Leib, tell him that I'm waiting for him." She sniffles. "Tell him that I never lost hope."

He nods in consent and hugs her.

Michalina charges at him. She cups his cheeks in her hands and showers kisses on his face. Her sobs intensify, and she grabs his hands and holds them to her heart.

"You can't leave," she wails, moving her head from side to side. "You'll just be another soldier in the army, and here you're our only protector."

He tightens his lips, and his face shows the anguish that he's feeling.

"You promised to take care of me." Her voice sounds angry. "You promised to take care of Anushka. And now you're leaving us."

"I'm leaving to fight so that you won't require my protection anymore." He yanks his hand away and strokes her hair. "I'm leaving so that you can win back your freedom."

"But we need you," she shouts.

"Michalina..." he speaks her name tenderly. "Please understand that..."

"That you need to do this," I complete his sentence in a soft but firm tone. All eyes turn to me. "You have to do this." I give him a little smile. "No man in the world deserves to join the final battle more than you." I force myself to move nearer to him. "You deserve the opportunity to unleash your fury on the cruel beasts who painted our world so black and dark. You deserve to strike down every goddamn Nazi that made our land bleed." I grit my teeth. "And if I could leave my children, I would join you and fight them myself with my own two hands." I emphasize my words with my fingers.

Anton laughs a short, resounding laugh, then grabs my hands and presses them to his lips.

"I have no doubt that you would triumph." His eyes blaze at me with such intense love that, for a moment, I forget that it isn't just the two of us.

"Promise you'll come back." Michalina hugs the side of his body and bursts into tears.

"Promise," I repeat after her in a whisper.

"I promise that as long as I can breathe, I'll come back here, even if I have to crawl here on my knees." His eyes are fixed on me alone.

His promise is all I need to hear. I bite my lip and close my eyes in acceptance.

Anton turns toward the horse and then pulls a metal object out of one of the sacks. My eyes open wide in astonishment when he hands it to me—Father's gun.

"This is a last resort," he says sternly, closing my hands around the gun. "Use it only as a last resort." He emphasizes every word.

I nod my head in agreement.

"This time, the bullets are already inside." He winks at me, and I swallow the lump in my throat just as my tears threaten to burst forth.

Michalina continues hugging him and sobbing, and he pulls her into an embrace.

"I'll be back," he whispers and caresses her head.

"And I'll wait for you here." She presses her head to his chest and then forces herself to let go of him.

He looks at me imploringly, and I bow my head in consent.

He doesn't have to ask, and I don't have to say anything. I'll wait until the end of time for him to return, knowing that I am doing so to allow the world to finish repairing itself. When he returns, I'll be calm, knowing I am leaving my two great loves together and can depart and find a place for myself in this world.

CHAPTER 23

The war is over. I've engraved the new date that represents the rebirth of the world in my mind. On May 8, 1945, the Nazis surrendered. Nine months have passed since Anton left us.

I cross my legs on the swinging bench and remind myself yet again that the war is over. Two weeks have passed since Inga and Klaus's urgent visit. They came to see us again, expressly to give us the incredible news, causing us all to erupt in shouts of joy. But as the days pass, the excitement fades, and the fresh air of the country feels thick in my lungs. I look at Michalina. She is weeding the garden beds in the rain, and her hunched shoulders betray her emotions. The war has ended, but Anton hasn't come back to us. From the minute he left, she has looked extinguished and exhausted. She doesn't complain or cry, but her silence weighs on me. I want to yell at her not to lose faith. He promised he would come back, and I have no doubt that he'll keep his promise.

The rain comes down harder, and I buckle the belt of my coat and feel for the gun in my pocket. The war is over, but my fear for the fate of my loved ones still keeps me awake at night.

My children are playing near the barn. The rain doesn't bother them. On the contrary, it unlocks a whole new world of possible games, and now they are skipping rocks in the puddles. From time to time, one of them looks up toward the horizon. They don't talk about it, but I know they're waiting. Waiting for their loved ones to return to them.

I sigh and walk towards the cabin. Ida bumps into me at the door and stretches her lips into a smile that doesn't reach her worried eyes. She is waiting, too. She offered to return to Warsaw to begin searching for our loved ones, but Klaus and Inga insisted that she remain. They made it unequivocally clear to us that many Poles have taken to abusing any Jews who try to return to their homes and that the roads are no less dangerous. All we can do is wait.

We both tense up when a noise sounds from the north. I turn towards the children in alarm, but she grabs my arm and stops me. "Ania, the war is over," she whispers firmly.

I grumble and feel for the gun.

The children huddle together, and Michalina runs over to stand beside us. The loud growl of an engine overpowers the noise of the raindrops pattering on the ground, and Maria and Luda leave the cabin. We stand as one, and I feel the anticipation penetrating my bones.

The vehicle that emerges from the fields looks old and dusty, and its tires crush the thorny bushes along the trail. Michalina is holding my hand and panting loudly, or perhaps it's me. The car's tires turn toward the path leading to the cabin, and I squint and tightly grip the handle of the gun. Suddenly a loud cry bursts from Ida's lips, and she runs forward, waving her arms. I want to run after her and protect her, but my feet are rooted in the ground. She doesn't look scared – she looks happy.

With a splash of mud, the car comes to a stop, and Ida continues to shriek like a crazy person. The driver's door opens, and the man who comes out of the vehicle bursts into tears and pulls her into a hug. He spins her in the air and kisses her over and over.

I drop the gun and cover my mouth in astonishment. Leib.

None of us dares interrupt their emotional reunion. They hug, kiss, and cry, touching each other to make sure they're not dreaming. He studies her face and hands as if looking for a sign that he hasn't missed anything, and finally, Ida hangs on his arm and leads him toward us.

Leib wipes away his tears and examines the entourage standing at the cabin's threshold. He looks from me to Michalina and back.

"Good God..." he mumbles. "The beautiful sisters of the Orzeszkowa family." He quickly takes Michalina's hand and kisses it. "It's as if God realized he had created a masterpiece and decided to duplicate it." He smiles. "If I didn't know about the beauty mark He gave you, I'd be positive I was seeing double."

Michalina gives him an embarrassed smile. His eyes encounter the scar on the back of her hand, and he lets out a long, deep sigh. "I know where you've been, and I'm sorry. I'm so sorry." He kisses her hand again and turns to look at me. He pulls me to him in a close embrace. "Thank God you didn't have to go through that," he whispers in my ear. "Thank God that hell passed over you and Ida."

My eyes fill with tears, and I close my mouth and don't say a word.

"Beautiful Ania." He kisses my cheek. "You are breathtaking!"

I blink to banish my tears and kiss him back.

"And who are these little heroes?" He curiously scrutinizes the children who stand beside me and stare at him in suspicion.

"These are Ania's children." Ida giggles and clings to his arm.

"Ania's children?" He widens his eyes in surprise. "They are so big and strong..." He looks from Sarah to Bella and his eyes lock in on Gershon's sidelocks. He bites his lip and shudders. "I deny any relation." He shakes his head and chuckles. "I wasn't here to take part in their creation."

Ida smacks his shoulder and bursts out laughing, and I manage a slight chuckle. Even Michalina grins.

"Your parents?" I ask, "And Yakub, your brother?"

"I haven't been able to get any information yet," he replies gloomily. "But I promised Ida that we'll do everything possible to track them down." He smiles lovingly at his sister.

225

"Of course we'll find them." Ida smiles nervously. "And you look tired and starving." She nudges him to go into the cabin. "We'll spoil you, and then you'll tell us about all that you've been through since you left us."

He nods to Maria and Luda and follows his sister inside.

His presence in our humble cabin warms our hearts. Everyone suddenly seems full of vitality and vigor. We heat pots of water for bathing, peel potatoes, and boil a giant stew of lentils and peas. Ida hovers over him constantly.

But when Leib sits down at the table, clean and smiling, I see that his amused eyes have been tarnished by somber shadows.

Maria serves him a bowl full of aromatic stew, and we all watch him as he eats. None of us touches the bowls that Maria served us.

Leib eats quickly, murmuring with pleasure. Suddenly he frowns and looks toward the door. "Where is Anton?"

A thunderous sigh emanates from us in unison.

Leib lowers his eyes and shoves a heaping spoonful into his mouth. The worry lines deepen on his forehead.

"Anton joined the Resistance forces in Warsaw," Ida states hesitantly. "Didn't you fight in that operation?"

"I did," Leib doesn't look up from his bowl, "Everyone who fought in the woods joined the final battles."

"And… And you didn't see him?" Michalina asks, choking up.

"It was an impossible battle." He puts the spoon down and wipes his lips. "We thought the Russians would help us, but they believed it should be our war. We fought the damn German tanks and cannons with our bare hands. We fought for 63 days, but ultimately, the commander of the Armia surrendered, and those who didn't escape back into the woods were captured as prisoners of war or sent to labor camps." He wipes his brow. "We suffered serious losses."

Michalina breaks out in involuntary sobs, and I take a deep breath and straighten up.

"He'll be back," I reply confidently. "Just as you managed to return to us, so will he."

Leib opens his mouth to answer me but immediately closes it and nods in support. A sad smile stretches over his lips. "Beautiful Ania, if I made it here and discovered that you now have five Jewish children, I can believe that more thrilling surprises await me."

I give him a small smile and lean toward Michalina. I pat her shoulder reassuringly and say, "He'll come back. I have no doubt that he'll come back to you."

Michalina nods, but her expression reveals profound grief.

I clench my teeth and back away from her. Her despair makes me angry. She mustn't mourn him. She mustn't lose hope.

* * *

Leib and Ida stand beside the automobile, and I force myself not to cry. During the week he was here with us, I felt as if a spark from my former life had lit up my soul, and now that he's leaving and taking Ida with him, the spark is slowly fading.

"Ania." Leib comes toward me. "Please consider joining us one more time. We can take you and Michalina to France. The Jewish organizations there have begun gathering information, and they can help you find your parents."

Michalina sneaks a tortured look at me.

"We have to wait for Anton," I give him the same answer that I have given him countless times and cross my arms over my chest.

He nods in understanding and sighs. "I've written down your children's names. I'll pass them on and pray that someone comes forward to claim them."

"They won't be left alone." I look at the children who are sitting in the vehicle and jumping around enthusiastically. "I'll never leave them."

Leib's smile broadens, and his eyes twinkle mischievously. "Who would have thought that when the war ended, I would meet a completely transformed Ania?" He furrows his brow and contemplates silently for a few beats. "When I left you, you were a proud and arrogant girl, and now you are an inspiring woman."

His compliment makes a blush rise on my cheeks.

"Just don't tell me you've suddenly started believing in the God of the Jews." He feigns a horrified expression and laughs.

My chest shakes from the abrupt laugh that erupts from my throat.

"I believe. I don't know what exactly I believe in, but my faith is strong."

"I hope we'll meet again in America." He winks at me. "The idea of surprising Ida with a journey to the Holy Land crossed my mind, but I decided that allowing her to nurse her wounds under more comfortable conditions would be better."

I turn to Ida. She's leaning against the car door, and her torso is wracked with sobs. Parting from her is unbearable, and I pick up the bottle of brandy that I put on the chair and hold it out to her again. "We'll drink from it together when we are reunited," I say with exaggerated joy. "Pray for it to happen soon."

She clutches her prayer book to her chest and nods.

Leib and Ida get into the car and start driving, and the children run after the moving vehicle.

"He'll come back to us, too," I murmur, squeezing Michalina's hand. "Anton will come back to us. I'm sure of it."

Michalina weeps softly and doesn't say a word.

CHAPTER 24

Relentless rain makes the cabin's roof vibrate, and we nuzzle up under blankets in the parlor. Morning has broken, but none of us is keen to begin our chores. Even the children sit on the floor by the fireplace, warming themselves in the light of the last of the firewood we have left.

I stare at each of them in turn, absorbing the changes they've undergone, and am filled with immense pride. I still sleep out in the barn with them. The fear of an unexpected visit haunts me constantly and being near our hiding place comforts me. I convince myself that my fear is the only reason, but deep down, I know that in the barn, I feel close to him. Close to the man who still hasn't kept his promise.

The sound of automobile tires makes us all perk up. I feel for the gun in my coat pocket and breathe rapidly. The war is over, I remind myself again and again, but fear courses through my veins.

We hear two knocks on the door, and I throw a terrified look at the children and stand up.

"That's not German knocking," I hear myself muttering. "That's not the way that Germans knock."

Michalina stares at the door like she's trapped in a nightmare.

"I'll open it," Maria says apprehensively and motions for Luda to sit with the children.

The door opens, and my heart practically bursts at the sight of the figure on the threshold.

"Father?" Michalina shouts. "Father!" She screams with excitement and runs to the man in the black suit.

I blink again and again to make sure that I'm not hallucinating. The man in the black suit takes his hat off and extends his arms out to his sides. Michalina storms at him, crying uncontrollably.

I'm struck by terrible vertigo, and I fumble with my hands, searching for something to grab hold of.

"My daughter!" Father kisses Michalina's head and sobs "My daughter, I was so worried about you."

"Father..." I hear myself whisper but cannot seem to push my legs forward.

He looks at me, and his eyes open wide in astonishment.

"Ania?" He cries out in agony. "Ania!" He says my name over and over, and his gaze shifts rapidly back and forth between the two of us. "Oh my god! I thought I was hugging you." He breaks away from Michalina's embrace and touches her face in amazement. His finger slides over her beauty mark, and his whole body shakes with sobs. "My Michalina, I thought I'd lost you. I didn't know you had escaped that cursed camp." He strokes her cheek and then her hair. He turns to me, and his eyes fill with tears. "You were saved, Ania." He pants as if he has just run a race. "You weren't forced to visit that hell."

"Father, Anushka also..."

"Yes." I nod energetically, and tears run down my face. "You don't have to worry about me. I was safe here."

Michalina glances at me, and I give her a little smile.

Father pulls me to him and wraps his arms around the two of us. He laughs and cries, and I bury my head in his shoulder. My father is here! He is thinner, many wrinkles are engraved on his handsome face, his once abundant hair looks sparse, and his blue eyes are very weary, but he is here.

"Mother," I gasp. "Mother is in the village. Forgive me, Father, for not being able to care for her." I bury my face in my hands. "She was so sick and…"

"Your mother is fine."

A loud cry erupts from my mouth, and I fall to my knees.

"Ania." He pulls me up and clutches me. "Mother survived. She is waiting for me to bring her beautiful daughters to her."

"Where is she? Where is Mother?" Michalina looks from one side to the other as if expecting Mother to suddenly enter the room.

"Mother is in France." He pats her head. "As soon as the war ended, she left Poland. You know your mother." He laughs, weeping. "She's invincible."

I kiss Father's cheeks again and again with intense emotion.

"I so long to see Mother." Michalina tugs on his arm. "When can I see her?"

"We'll leave today." He nods.

I quickly break out of his embrace, and the blood drains from my face.

"We… We can't leave." I squeeze Michalina's arm. "Tell Father we have to stay here and wait."

Michalina nuzzles her face in his chest and cries softly.

I tell myself that she just needs a few moments to contain her excitement, and then she'll come to her senses.

"Wait for whom?" Father sighs and sits down on the couch. He notices the children and, for a long minute, peers at the little faces studying him with curiosity.

"He must be the king," Oleg whispers. "Look at what a nice suit he has."

"Shh…" Sarah shushes him, a troubled look in her black doe-eyes.

"Whose adorable children are these?" He grins at them wearily.

"Mine, Father." I sit down on the floor beside them. "They are my children."

Father wrinkles his forehead once more and then lets out a short laugh. "Ania, I'm pleased to discover that the war hasn't robbed you of your sense of humor."

I groan in frustration, and his eyes settle on Maria. The smile vanishes from his face, and he puts his hand on his heart.

"Dearest Maria, I will never be able to thank you enough for what you have done for my girls."

She smiles awkwardly.

"I promise you that I will make it up to you." He corrects his posture. "I was shrewd enough to smuggle my property out of the country. I am still a man of means, and I assure you that from now on and for the rest of your life, you will lack for nothing."

"Mr. Henryk." Maria shakes her head. "I didn't care for your daughters to receive compensation. I did it wholeheartedly, and for Luda and me, they've become like…"

"Family," I finish her sentence with pride.

"Of course. Of course." He blinks and kisses Michalina's head. "I don't want you to stay here alone. As soon as we settle in America, I'll obtain entry visas for you, and you can come to work for us again. Your sister will be welcome with us as well."

Maria nods with a smile, and I scowl in shock.

"Father." I stand up and take her hand. "Maria will never work for us. Maybe we'll work for her." I press her hand to my lips and kiss it.

Mortified, she pulls her hand away and bows her head.

"I'll take care of her, Ania." Father bows his head. "We'll reunite with Mother, and then I'll make sure to compensate everyone who helped you."

The extreme excitement of his visit fades as I begin to understand the significance of his plans.

"I'll rest a bit, and we'll soon be on our way." He rests his head on the couch, and Michalina snuggles up in his lap. His eyes close, and I sit next to him and rest my head on his shoulder. Michalina and I deserve to enjoy a rare moment of tenderness before our inevitable parting from him.

***

Father sits up, and I kiss his shoulder and get up off the couch with effort. The children, Luda, and Maria are sitting on the floor and watching us in silence. Michalina cries out in her sleep, and Father pats her hair. Suddenly she sits up, shielding her head with her hands.

"It's just a bad dream." He strokes her face. "You're with me, and you're safe."

She clutches his arm and takes a deep breath.

I go to the kitchen, bring him a bowl of porridge left over from breakfast, and sit by his side as he eats.

"You look good." He smiles lovingly at me. "Country life has done wonders for you."

I respond with a lopsided smile.

"From the minute the goddamn Nazis discovered Michalina's identity and tore her away from me, my world fell apart." He sighs and strokes her hair. "My bribe saved me, but not my beautiful, gentle daughter." His eyes fill with tears. "I managed to escape to Belgium and stay with some good friends. I tried to create contacts, I turned to every person I ever met, but Europe's very soil was bleeding and no one was able to help me." He sighs and rubs his face. "I've been looking for information about your hiding place for so long. I had almost given up hope when I heard about a young Polish woman named Maria who had agreed to help Michalina's friend, the police officer. It was a gamble, but I would have traveled to the ends of the earth to find you."

Michalina sits up and blinks, as if the mention of Anton's existence has brought her back to life.

"Father, Anton is the one who got me out of Treblinka." She shudders. "He hid us here and kept us safe."

"And where is he now?" Father looks around toward the door.

"He... he decided to join the armed forces in Warsaw," Michalina stammers.

"I'm sorry to hear that." Father sighs. "We lost so many good people in this damn war."

"We haven't lost Anton," I reply confidently and walk over to the fireplace. "He's been delayed, but he'll return to us. It's only a matter of time. Tell him." I address Michalina.

"Yes, yes." She nods, pouting helplessly.

"I hope Mr. Mrożek does come back." Father puts the empty bowl down on the table. "When that happens, you can be sure that I will give him the world. He can have our apartments in Warsaw. I'll send him a monthly stipend and guarantee that he can enjoy a life of abundance."

I look at Michalina and expect to hear her indignation. After all, it is she who is waiting for him.

Michalina lowers her eyes and goes back to nuzzling Father's arm. I understand that she needs my tenacity now.

"Father." I tilt my head to the side and give him a pained smile. "Michalina and I cannot go with you. We must wait here for Anton, but as soon as he returns…"

"Out of the question!" Father waves his hand dismissively. "My daughters are returning to their mother with me."

Michalina starts sobbing, and I bite my lip and command myself to be strong for both of us.

"We promised him we would wait for him," I jerk my chin. "After all he's done for us, we cannot break our promise. You and Mother can immigrate to America, and as soon as he returns, we'll join you. All of us." I point to the children.

Gershon slides his sidelocks behind his ears, and Father studies him inquisitively. "Ania… you're confused." He rubs the back of his neck. "I would have expected you to be less selfish. Your sister has been through hell." He looks at me again. "These children do not belong to you. I am proud that you were so courageous and that you hid them and watched over them until the war was over, but now they are no longer your problem."

My jaw drops at his choice of words. *Problem?* Did he just call my children a *problem?*

"Ania." He gives me a conciliatory smile. "When we get to Paris, we'll make sure that the Jewish organizations know where they are. They've been caring for children who survived this hell from all over Europe."

He stands up and smooths out his jacket. Michalina leaps off the couch and grabs his hand.

"I understand that you have a sense of obligation toward the policeman who protected you, but that obligation is over. I'm responsible for you now, and if he returns, I'll pay him back accordingly." His voice gets softer. "Mother went through some difficult years in the village. The war didn't pass her by. If she had been able to handle my travels in search of you, she would have joined me. She is waiting breathlessly for her daughters, and I won't let her down."

My longing for Mother tugs at my heart, but my conviction doesn't waver. Now I need my sister's support.

"Michalina," I implore, "tell Father how you feel. Tell Father how long you've waited to confess your love for..."

"Ania," she shouts my name and bursts into tears. "I need Mother and Father. I need to pick up my pieces, put myself back together, and let them take care of me."

"But..." My face pales. "But..."

"I wish I shared your strong belief that he'll definitely return." She sniffles. "Maybe if I was as sure as you, I would muster up the courage to wait, but it's been so long and I cannot stay here alone."

"You're not alone." I swallow the lump in my throat. "I'm here with you, and so are Maria and Luda and my children."

"Forgive me, Anushka." She shakes her head. "I don't have the strength left to be brave. I need my father. I need my mother. I cannot let Father leave without me."

"Ania, stop talking nonsense," Father scolds me. "You and Michalina are coming with me, and it's not up for debate."

The harshness of his tone makes my children jump up and stand in front of me like a small, angry army.

"I'm sorry, Father." I caress Sarah's head. "This war has taught me that a promise isn't open to interpretation. I promised to wait for him, and I will stay here until he returns."

"You are an annoying king," Misza shouts. "Everyone knows the princess has to wait for the Guardian of the Realm."

Michalina opens her eyes wide in surprise, covers her mouth with her hands, and collapses onto the sofa.

My guilt torments me, and I break through the barrier of my children and fall to my knees before her.

"Michalina, I'll go." I clutch her knees imploringly. "Please, Michalina, I'll take the children with Father and go. When Anton returns, you two can bring Luda and Maria and join us. Please Michalina. You have to wait for him." I burst into tears.

"Anushka," she whispers my name in anguish. "I knew. I knew in my heart that he didn't need me. I saw how he looked at you, and I saw that you were consumed by guilt." She strokes my head. "If I had received any of your courage, I would have given you my blessing the moment I realized you had feelings for each other. But I am a coward. I always have been and probably always will be."

"No, no." I sniffle and stare at her with red, teary eyes. "I confused him. I seduced him," I whisper in humiliation. "He was waiting for you. Every time he looked at me, he saw you."

"You're wrong." She rubs her eyes. "Every time he touched my face, and his finger slid over my beauty mark, I saw the way his expression changed. An expression of longing for my other half. My better half." She leans over and kisses my cheek. "Don't be sad, Anushka. I held on to the promise I exacted from him at the train station. Even I know that promises made before the war are no longer binding."

"But Michalina..." I'm determined to continue insisting for her.

"My decision is final." Michalina stands up and takes our Father's hand. "I give you my blessing. Please don't waste it."

I bury my face in my hands and weep.

"Ania, I beg you to join us," Father cries in distress. "Please don't break your mother's heart over a foolish promise to a policeman."

"His name is Anton." Michalina stands up straight and smiles lovingly at me. "And he's not just any policeman. He's the Guardian of Princess Ania's Realm."

I storm at her, enveloping her in a tight embrace and sobbing. The burning in my stomach fades, and my heart is flooded with love.

CHAPTER 25

Anton.
I drag my leg and attempt to walk more quickly, but my limp slows me down. The intense green hue of the fields surrounding me hurts my eyes. These are the colors and the smells that I've come to know and love because she adorned them with her spectacular beauty, but when she's not part of them, they weigh on me. I spot the brown cabin on the horizon and order my feet to move faster.

The physical suffering that accompanied my recovery was nothing compared to my emotional anguish. Every time I closed my eyes, I saw her here, in our safe haven, sitting on a chair in the middle of the field and smiling at the sight of her children. But then the horrible thoughts of all the awful things that could happen to her began popping up. Terrible things could happen to my new family, my only family.

I fix my sight on the cabin and drag my feet. Waking up in the hospital in Belgium was the most horrendous awakening I've ever experienced in my life. I learned that I had been fighting for my life for many months in a ward that few emerge from. The last thing I could remember was the sound of the bombs and the sight of bodies piling up around me. Sniper's bullets hit us one by one, and then came my turn. The first bullet punctured my shoulder, and the next bullet penetrated my arm. The heavy rifle fell out of my hands, and I fought the German with my bare hands. I thrashed him as though he were the soldier who had tried to force himself on the girl who stole my heart. The girl who was my whole world. For an instant, I saw her light blue eyes glistening serenely, and then I knew I was carrying out her revenge. The soldier crumpled to the ground, and I smiled at her, but just then two bullets pierced my leg. My knees buckled, and I sank down to lie beside the devil I had killed. I commanded my eyes to stay open. I reminded myself again and again of my promise to return to her. Heavy boots trampled my chest, and my eyes closed.

When I opened them, all I saw were the white walls surrounding me. I had never seen such a bright white color, and I wondered whether all colors looked like that after you die. But the pain that wracked my body confirmed to me that I was still among the living. Vivid images of a woman with golden hair and light blue eyes flashed through my head at a dizzying speed. Fear about her fate filled my chest, and I knew I had to get out of that room and make my way back to her. When I opened my eyes again, night had already fallen, and an elderly nurse scolded me in an unfamiliar language.

It took what felt like an eternity until I was able to get answers from a Polish-speaking man who was hospitalized in another ward. The information I obtained from him shocked me. The understanding that the war had ended so long ago gave me no respite. I tried to crawl back to her. I tried to throw myself off my bed and crawl to her again and again, but my injuries overpowered me.

I squint and see the colorful flowerbeds that encircle the cabin. My heart fills with precarious hope. I have no idea what or who I will find here, but I know one thing for sure – I will follow her to the ends of the earth.

When I trip over a stone, I twist my ankle, but I grit my teeth and continue walking with determination to the path leading towards the cabin. Suddenly I stop short. The silence alarms me. Where are the children? Where is she? Where is everyone?

All of a sudden, I notice a figure in a brown dress standing with her back to me, watering the flowers around the barn. My breath stops. Even if I had lost my eyesight, I would have known it was she. Her golden hair is in a long braid down her back, her feminine curves have rounded, and anyone else might easily mistake her for her sister. I'll never confuse them. Her quiet strength surrounds her like a radiant halo.

I open my mouth to call her name, but her back muscles tense up, and she slips her hand into the pocket of her dress. She carefully takes out the silver pistol and stands up straight. Her body turns around slowly, and her eyes lock on me. My heart pounds and I understand that my memory did her no favors. She is breathtaking.

Her light blue eyes sparkle with excitement, and the gun falls from her hand. She puts her hand over her heart, and her chest rises and falls heavily.

I drag my feet a step in her direction, and she does the same. I take another step, and she follows suit. I throw my sack on the ground, and she lets out a piercing cry and starts running towards me. She stops a step away from me. Her face is flushed, and her little nose crinkles. She is trying to catch her breath.

I study every feature of her face, and she seems to be doing the same thing to me. I lift my hand, and she lifts hers. I slide my fingers along her jawline, and her fingers flutter over my cheeks. I trace her eyes with my thumb and then touch her red lips, and she moans soundlessly. My chest rises and falls heavily, and I wrap an unruly lock of her hair around my fingers. I tuck it behind her ear and see her eyes become sad. I sigh and move my face up to her cheek. Her panting stirs my blood. "I'm just making sure it's you," I whisper into her ear, "Making sure you are my Ania."

Her hands cup my face, and she presses her forehead to mine and whimpers softly.

I grab the back of her neck, tilt her head to the side and bring my lips to hers. For so long, I've imagined this moment, but now that I have her in my arms, I'm afraid I'll never be able to let go. My lips move close to hers, fluttering over them, touching but not touching.

"Anton..." She whispers my name, and my lips collide with hers. I devour her like a starving man who hasn't eaten for far too long. I clasp her neck and lunge at her mouth. I suck on her lips, bite them, and breathe into her mouth. I push my tongue inside and taste the flavor of heaven. I feel her need with every touch. She slides her fingers into my hair, and my hands glide down her back to her waist. Her chest chafes against my chest, and her pelvis presses up to mine. I am desperate to conquer her here and now. I cup her buttocks, and she gasps and backs away. Her eyes dart across my face in confusion.

I caress her hair, trying to guide her back to me. My eyes don't leave her face, and I follow her every breath. The silence around us is deafening. A troubling question pops into my head, and immediately after it, I'm bombarded by more, and more difficult questions. I look toward the cabin, and terrible apprehension makes it hard for me to determine what to ask first.

"The children?" I ask almost mutely.

"They're fine," she replies in a soothing voice, her eyes sparkling.

"Maria and Luda?"

She nods. "They took the kids to visit Inga and Klaus. They should be back in a few days."

"Ida?"

Her eyes sadden, and my chest quakes with fear.

"Leib came back." She tries to smile. "He took her with him to America."

The news is good, I reassure myself, but I'm afraid to ask the next question. I know she's waiting for it.

"And your sister?" I peek at the cabin again. "Where's Michalina?"

She bows her head and bites her lip.

She doesn't look grief-stricken, just concerned and emotional. I'll be able to handle the news.

"She... she wanted to stay here and wait for you," she stutters and picks up my sack. "She waited so long for you, and then Father arrived."

My eyes open wide in surprise.

"She wanted to wait for you. I swear," Ania repeats the same sentence and pivots toward the cabin. "But her soul is injured and bruised, and she needed Mother and Father's care."

And your soul? I want to ask. Is your soul not equally injured and bleeding after the hell you experienced?

The realization that she stayed here despite everything astounds me. I stare at her back as she walks into the cabin, and I understand that I could never love her more than I love her now.

"Please don't hold it against her," she says without meeting my eyes, "You know how delicate and sensitive she is." She puts the sack on the floor and turns to me, her eyes shining from the tears. "We waited so long for you; I'm afraid she lost hope."

"And you? You didn't lose hope?"

She opens her mouth to answer me but doesn't say a thing. Her eyes race over my face and my body and settle on my injured leg. I was sure she didn't notice my limp, but the pain in her eyes shows that she's aware of it.

"You... You must be exhausted, and I'm rambling on." She scratches her brow. "Please take a bath and rest while I prepare a meal for you."

I want to tell her that the only weariness I feel is from not having her in my arms, and that I need answers to the questions I haven't asked yet, but she points towards the hut and hurries upstairs.

I watch her until she reaches the last step, and then I go out to the back hut. My eyes roam around the backyard. The place looks exactly as it did the day I left.

I take off my clothes and pour a bucket of water over myself. The frigid water from the well rouses me, and I soap myself from head to toe and wash away the dirt from the long trip I took. My injured leg transmits surges of pain up my spine, but when Ania comes out of the kitchen and puts a towel and clean clothes on the chair, I no longer feel any pain. My skin tingles, yearning for her touch. She lowers her eyes and sneaks only the slightest peek at me. When I smile at her, a bright blush rises on her cheeks. She gives me a bashful smile and runs to the kitchen.

Her embarrassment frustrates me. Doesn't she understand that I crossed countries to see her smile?

I dress quickly and go into the cabin. She is standing at the counter with her back to me, industriously cutting up vegetables and throwing them into the pot. I approach her from behind, and her shoulder blades tense up.

"Why didn't you go with on the trip with the children?" I ask, forcing myself not to touch her. Not yet.

"I'm not worried. Maria and Luda are with them," she replies in a shaky voice. "And Inga spoils them like an aunt." She chuckles hoarsely.

"And you weren't afraid of staying here all alone?"

"I'm not afraid for myself. I never have been."

"So why didn't you go with them?" I repeat my question, my lips almost touching her ear.

"Because... because..." she stutters, and then turns to me with anguish in her eyes. "Because I couldn't bear the thought of your returning and my not being here."

I close my eyes, and my heart expands and contracts in the same breath.

"Put down the knife," I command quietly and open my eyes.

"But... But I have to make you something to eat. You must be starving after your travels."

"Put down the knife!"

Her eyes glaze over for a moment, and I remember that this is how she reacts every time she hears what she thinks is an order. I hastily soften my tone, "Please, put the knife down."

She bends her arm back and places the knife on the counter.

"Come with me." I take her hand and lead her to the barn. My limp no longer bothers me, and I don't feel any pain at all. She quickens her pace to keep up with me.

I open the door and pull her inside.

"What are you doing?" She turns her head left and right.

"Not wasting our time talking." I swing her up by the waist and press her back against the wall. A surprised moan escapes her mouth, and I swoop onto her lips.

Her muscles are tense, and her arms are tight. I cup her cheeks and kiss her wildly. Little by little, I feel her body surrender and her thighs tighten around me. I groan into her mouth and carry her over to the hay. I lay her down on the already outstretched blanket, pull off her dress, and take off her shoes. When I stand up, she conceals her breasts in her hands and gapes at me with glassy eyes, as if she's caught in a dream.

"I've fantasized about our night together so many times," I say as I unhook my suspenders and study her body intently. Her skin is rosy in the areas that were exposed to the sun and completely pale in the private parts. Her stomach is flat, her hips are firm, and her breasts are round and magnificent. I stare at her white cotton underwear and feel my stiffness stretching the cloth of my pants. No lingerie in the world would make her look more alluring. "That night, I would have settled for the kiss you gave me." I stretch my lips in a small smile and quickly unbutton my shirt. "I would have settled for your first kiss and wouldn't have dared to ask for more." I kick my shoes off and take off my pants. Her eyes wander to my groin, and a bright red blush spreads up her face and down her neck. "But you chose to give me all of you." I bite my lip and take a long look at her seductive body.

She opens her lips, and I lie on top of her. "Since then, I knew I could no longer settle for less than all of you." I nuzzle my head in her neck and sprinkle soft kisses over it. Her bosom quivers under me, and she spreads her arms to the sides and enfolds me in the heat of her body. I slide my tongue over her collarbone and moan as my lips suckle her nipple. She moves beneath me and gently scratches my arms. I clench my jaw and command myself to show restraint. My lips press against her abdomen, and her hips buck as I lick the upper seam of her underpants. She grabs my shoulders but doesn't dare direct me. She's tense, and I'm desperate for her to let her guard down. My breath flutters over the thin cloth, and her breathing becomes heavy. I remove her underwear with one yank and press my lips to the core of her pleasure. Her hungry moaning is the most beautiful melody I have ever heard. I pleasure her with my tongue slowly and delicately, and when I feel her thighs contract, I rise and bend over her. Her lips part, and she exhales sharply.

I caress her lips with my tongue, then part her hips and situate myself in the warmth between her legs.

Her breathing stops, and she closes her eyes.

"Are you nervous?" I whisper and kiss her again.

She opens her eyes and, batting her eyelashes, shakes her head no, and tries to smile.

"Ania." My voice hardens. "I'm not another one of your suitors. I'm your *only* man."

The nervous smile is wiped from her face, and she scrunches her nose in embarrassment. "I *am* nervous. I'm worried that after you waited so long, I'll disappoint you."

I narrow my eyes and peer at her with concentration. It amazes me that she still doesn't understand that even if she forbade me from touching her and only awarded me with a glance, all my expectations would be fulfilled.

"Do you feel that?" I take her hand and position it at the warm meeting point between our bodies.

She caresses my length and stares as my face twists with pleasure. A different smile, serene and perfect, stretches across her lips. "Are you still nervous?" I can just barely manage to smile back at her. "A little," she admits, letting out a brief, hoarse laugh.

Her laugh overwhelms my senses. I grab her hand and kiss her, then prop myself up on my elbows and begin to penetrate her slowly. She takes a few deep breaths, clutches my midsection, and lets her entire body relax. I plunge deeper, and she squeezes my waist and opens her eyes forcefully. I thrust once more, and she emits a thunderous moan.

My restraint fades.

I conquer her in full force. I penetrate her over and over, hard and fast, while my hands explore her body as if I've never known a woman before her. She doesn't flinch and doesn't try to inhibit me. She grips my shoulders and holds me to her body. I straighten up and lean on one hand. With my other hand I massage her breasts and then let my fingers trail down her abdomen to the sensitive orifice of her pleasure.

"Anton," she calls out my name, and I feel her upper body quiver as she melts beneath me. Her hips twitch, her nails dig into my back, and her mouth opens.

I grab her bottom lip between my teeth and swear I'll never know another woman. My world revolves around her, and I will dedicate my life to pleasing her.

* * *

Ania lies in my arms, relaxed and sleepy. She looks so peaceful; even her breathing sounds different than usual. It's as if she were in another period of her life, transported back to when I visited her at her parent's apartment when the world seemed relatively sane. Before those beasts left behind a bloodstained land.

I arrange the blanket underneath her and leap from the haystack. "I'll be right back," I say as she sits up in concern.

I go into the silent cabin, heat water in a pot, and bring a clean towel and an extra blanket with me. Knowing that Ania is lying there on the hay and I'm not beside her makes me nervous – like if I take too long, she'll be gone before I get back. Her perfect body and soul will fade away and become a mere memory.

I lean on the doorframe and stare at her. She's lying on her back and hugging herself, but her eyes are slightly open, and she's looking at me exactly the way she looked at me in my dreams.

I walk towards her, kneel down, and slide a damp towel over her flushed skin. Her eyes follow my hand, and her chest rises and falls in eager anticipation. There's no trace of embarrassment left. She is bare before me. When I slip the towel between her legs, her hips convulse, and she sighs with pleasure.

I spread the extra blanket over her and lie down beside her. She turns her back to me and snuggles up between my arms.

"Ania." I kiss her shoulder. "Why was there a blanket spread out here?"

"Because we sleep out here," she replies in astonishment.

"But the war is over." I push her hair to the side and kiss the back of her neck.

She shivers and sighs. "I think that over time I came to terms with the fact that you couldn't be mine, but I couldn't come to terms with not feeling like a part of you. I kept on sleeping in the barn so that a part of you – at least in my memory – would always be with me."

I close my eyes and ask myself how it could be possible to love even more when you love the most.

"The night I gave you my body, I already knew I had given you my whole heart," she whispers and rubs her cheek against my arm. "It is important to me that you know that I wouldn't have given myself to you again without my sister's blessing."

I know she needed her sister's blessing, but in the same breath, I want to shake her and tell her that no power exists that could have prevented me from getting her back.

"When I was an innocent little girl, I thought that love caresses the heart," she says in a trembling voice, "but with you, I discovered that love burns the heart."

"Because you're afraid." I wrap my arms around her and press my lips to her head. "You're afraid that our passionate emotions might end at any moment."

She shivers and digs her nails into my arms. "You can stop being afraid." I breathe into her hair, savoring her intoxicating scent, and promise myself to make her mine forever. "Ania, you can stop being afraid because from now until the world ends, I will be your only man."

"Anton," she whispers my name, "I don't know what your plans are, but I need you to understand that I will never leave my children."

"*Our* children," I correct her and hear the sobs that make her body tremble.

"And I won't leave Maria and Luda. They are my sisters."

"*Our*." I almost crush her in my hug.

Sniffling, she wails, "Where were you?" She turns to look at me with tears in her eyes. "Where were you all this time?"

"I was fighting for my life so that I could crawl back to you." I kiss her red lips.

"Don't do that to me again." She beats my chest. "Promise me. Promise you'll never leave me again."

I grab her wrists, press her hands to my lips, and kiss each of her fingers. I dive deep into her wild, light blue eyes. I close my eyes for a moment and then open them and smile at the sole woman in my life.

"I promise."

EPILOGUE

Ania.
The beautiful serving utensils that I bought are arranged on the large dining table that Anton built for us. They don't remind me of Mother's luxury porcelain set at all, but they are ours, and in my eyes, they're the most luxurious. Sarah courageously conducts the tidying of the house, and the other children obey her orders, not daring to object.

I chuckle and stroke my belly. It has rounded this past month, and Anton can't pass by me without reaching out to touch it. I think he believes that that's the way to signal to the baby growing inside me that his father is always with him and watching over him.

I sit down in the armchair and delightedly look at the children dashing from room to room. They have grown so much in the year since we settled on a farm in Louisiana, a state in the southern United States of America. Sarah and Bella have become beautiful girls, Misza has almost all his adult teeth, Gershon has grown taller, and Oleg has added some meat to his bones. The thought that they might have boarded a train to hell still dominates my dreams. Their families weren't so lucky. None of them survived.

I remind myself in the same breath that the children survived. That *we* survived.

I stand up to put napkins on the plates and count the chairs again.

"There's enough room for everyone." Anton's deep voice sounds amused, and I turn to him with an awkward smile. My heart still skips a beat whenever I look at him. His light hair is combed to the side, his brown eyes shine tenderly, his skin is tan, and his quiet intensity emanates from him with a mesmerizing magnetism. He is the handsomest man on earth. He made me his wife on the ship on our voyage to America, we live in the same house and share the same bed, but it seems to me that I will never fully comprehend that this bond between us is forever. I will always be afraid that something terrible will happen and that the universe will try to separate us.

He puts down his tools at the entrance to the house and comes close to me. His eyes study my face, and his hand slides over my belly in a circular motion. He closes his eyes and frowns in vexation. "She tells me her mother is working too hard."

"He or she didn't tell you anything." I slap his hand playfully and laugh.

"I won't let you exhaust yourself." He slides his hand over my stomach once again and leads me to the armchair. "Tell me what still needs to be done, and I'll do it."

I sit down and swing my legs. The house is clean and tidy, each bedroom has undergone a thorough inspection under the strict eye of Sarah, and the table is set and ready to entertain guests. I take a deep breath. From the moment my family members confirmed that they were coming, I've been filled with a fierce excitement that doesn't fade.

"Everything will be fine." Anton stands behind me and massages my shoulders. "Our distinguished guests will lack for nothing."

I know he's right. I made sure that everything was perfect dozens of times, and Maria has been cooking from morning until night. Her presence here in our home has succeeded in cheering me. Not long after we arrived here, determined suitors began to visit the house, and they were forced to withstand Anton's harsh interrogations. But ultimately, it was the young, gentle fellow who runs the butcher shop that managed to steal her heart. She moved in with him a few blocks from our house and spends much of her time with us.

Luda storms into the house and wrinkles her nose apologetically. She is clad in a blue dress and takes off her hat.

"Where were you?" Sarah barks at her, her black doe eyes flaring in irritation.

"Sorry I'm late." Luda bows her head.

I refrain from laughing with all my might. As soon as Luda's feet disembarked onto safe land, she found her voice again, and since then, she's been using it mainly to apologize to Sarah.

"Your room is a mess." Sarah crosses her arms over her chest and defiantly sticks out her chin. Her family ties to my mother are clear as day. "Instead of straightening up, you spend all your time with that guy, and I already told you that I don't approve of you hanging out with him!"

"What guy?" Anton asks in a menacing tone.

Luda's eyes shoot arrows at Sarah, and Sarah rolls her eyes in response. She may treat Luda like she's her boss, but she would never tattle on her.

"Father, I'm taking care of it." Sarah turns to go down the hall, and Luda scurries after her.

Anton's hands tighten on my shoulders, and I feel the pressure in my heart too. I think it'll take a while for both of us to get used to our new titles. We asked the children's permission to submit an official application to adopt them, and at the end of a meeting that Sarah convened, they responded in the affirmative and stopped addressing us by our first names.

"Princess Mother," Anton addresses me by Misza's nickname for me, "would you like to join me in the bathroom?"

I never refuse such propositions, but the suspense that has accompanied me for the last few days won't allow me to relax and enjoy a magical hour of bliss with him. I shake my head no and smooth the material of my dress. I've already bathed and dressed for the imminent visit.

Anton pushes my hair aside and scatters kisses on my neck. I sigh with pleasure, almost tempted to join him, but then I stand up in a panic. "Look at the time!" I admonish him. "The kids have already gotten ready, and you're still scruffy as though you don't even care."

His hoarse laugh makes me instantly calm down and I look at him apologetically. I know he understands and even shares my feelings because his close guard over me has doubled in intensity over the past few days. He caresses my belly once more and goes down the hall.

Maria comes out of the kitchen and puts several trays of appetizers on the table. She drums on her lips with her fingers and examines the table. She is also stressed.

"Everything will be perfect," I mumble, unsure of whether I'm trying to convince her or myself.

The children and Luda walk up the hall single file and then line up so that I can inspect their beautiful clothes. We don't usually make extravagant purchases, but I make sure that they always look clean and respectable. They walk to school together, disband to go to their various classrooms, and always come back together like a small, united army. Occasionally, one of them invites a friend home. Not many endure for long; most feel threatened by the close-knit group, but those who linger get to enjoy my children's pure hearts.

I inspect them one by one, combing Oleg's hair and curling Gershon's sidelocks around my fingers. I was afraid that his unique appearance wouldn't be accepted by other children, and that he might be teased or bullied, but I must have forgotten how powerful my little army can be. The first time an older boy dared to make fun of him, Anton and I were summoned to the principal's office to be informed that violence isn't tolerated at school. It wasn't Gershon who returned home bleeding and bruised, but rather the impudent bully who was bombarded with stones on his way home. At that meeting, I discovered that Anton's fighting spirit still endures. He explained to the principal with a fixed expression and a chilling tone that if anyone dares to bully one of our children again, he will consider the principal directly responsible.

The recollection of that day gets my blood pumping, and I glance at the wall clock, trying to calculate whether I still have time to join him in the bathroom. Unfortunately, the hands have moved too fast.

"Are the bedrooms ready?" I turn my back to the row of children, so they don't notice the suspicious blush rising on my cheeks.

"Every room, with no exceptions," replies Sarah with pride. "Even Luda's room."

A wide beam stretches across my face. Anton toiled for months to expand the house and built beautiful, luxurious rooms for each of them. Still, the bedrooms have remained uninhabited because, every evening, they drag their mattresses into Sarah's room and sleep all together.

"So, what is there left to do?"

"All that's left for you to do is rest," Anton calls from the hall and comes into the parlor wearing tailored gray trousers and a white button-down shirt. His hair is freshly combed, and he's flawlessly clean-shaven. I study him with pleasure, then shake my head and collapse onto the armchair.

We hear the crunch of automobile tires from the driveway, and I leap to my feet. I smooth out the material of my floral dress and inspect myself in the mirror that hangs by the front door.

"You're perfect." Anton hugs me from behind. "You're always perfect."

My anticipation grows when the engine quiets. I want to run outside and storm at my loved ones, but my body is petrified with excitement.

Two raps sound on the door. I tense up inadvertently.

I open my mouth to catch my breath, and Anton opens the door.

"Father." I fall into his arms. He hugs and kisses me over and over and then carefully caresses my round belly. He shakes Anton's hand and picks up the bags of presents at his feet. The tumult of the children's enthusiasm warms my heart. Mother stands in front of me. Her dress fits her perfectly, a fashionable hat is flawlessly positioned on her head, her posture is immaculate, and she scrutinizes me from head to toe. Her eyes dart about restlessly, and she quickly glances to either side. This behavior is the sole indication that the war changed something in her.

"You look almost perfectly fine." She nods and then leans in to kiss my cheeks. I don't hold back and pull her into a tight embrace. "I urge you not to get over-excited," she says with a tremor in her voice and pats me on the back, "In your condition, you have to take care of yourself."

"I tell her that all the time, Mrs. Orzeszkowa." Anton approaches her.

"Perhaps she would listen to you if you treated her like a lady and spoiled her with dresses worthy of a respectable woman." Mother steps back and offers him her hand.

Anton politely kisses her hand. He doesn't respond to her comment, and neither do I. We've both come to terms with the fact that Mother insists on living in a pre-war world. She spent her years in the village mainly tormenting her poor Polish hosts and thus far hasn't shared her fears with us. For her, they were terrible years that shouldn't be recollected or discussed. As far as she's concerned, the damned Germans robbed her of her family and the source of her pride – her boutique – and for that, she will never forgive them. She hasn't asked to hear about my or Michalina's experiences from those years, and neither of us has volunteered any information. Sometimes it seems to me that the war was just a regrettable inconvenience for her.

"I see Maria took care of the refreshments." She claps her hands with delight. "For a moment, I was scared you'd attempt to make them yourself."

She steps forward to survey the table, and I hear a gentle and familiar laugh.

"Anushka, Mother is simply impossible."

"Michalina." I turn to her and hug her tightly. "I've missed you so much." I hold her cheeks and peer at her flushed face. She looks healthy and strong, and her eyes shine with happiness. When I kiss her, I notice the almost imperceptible melancholy shadows that remain in them.

"I told you I was bringing a few surprises," she whispers. "Are you ready for the first surprise?"

I shake my head no. I'm not ready for surprises. Surprises make me nervous.

She moves aside, and a shocked cry escapes my lips. Leib's green eyes peer at me with amusement, and he clasps her from behind quite intimately.

I gnaw on my lip and look back at my parents, who are already seated in the parlor.

"Don't worry." She waves her hand, unbothered. "We're engaged."

"Engaged?" I suddenly feel woozy and sway on my feet.

"Engaged," Leib replies for her. "I'm sure many hearts were broken when I accepted her marriage proposal, but I just couldn't say no."

Michalina pinches his arm and bursts out laughing.

I put my hand on my heart but cannot speak.

"Your mother isn't very happy with the news." Leib winks at me.

"I finally mustered up the courage," Michalina whispers. "I finally realized that I need to insist on my own happiness."

"Mazel tov." Anton shakes Leib's hand and kisses Michalina's cheek.

I'm still having trouble responding. I'm overwhelmed with joy. I carefully touch the triangle pendant hanging around her neck.

I refused to take it back from her. I don't need it in order to remember who I am and where I come from. The message from the grandfather I never knew is imprinted on my heart.

"I'm so happy for you." I hug her again. "For both of you." I try to trap him in my embrace as well.

"Don't get too excited. We have more surprises." Michalina smiles.

I look down and stare at her stomach.

"No. No. Not yet." She caresses my belly.

I smile at her cheekily. "Ida? Did you bring Ida with you?"

Leib swings the door wide open, and my breath catches in my throat. My legs shake, and Anton puts his hands on my hips and holds me steady.

Ida is standing on the threshold, but she's not alone. A man in a black suit with a thick beard is holding her hand. I look deep into his beautiful, kind eyes, which, at present, seem slightly haunted.

"Look!" Oleg shouts. "It's the princess's friend."

I open and close my mouth repeatedly. The air around me thickens, and for a moment, I am back in the ghetto and can almost smell the faint scent of the sweet candies.

"Ania, we're not there anymore," Bruno whispers with a supportive smile, "But there was one thing I had to bring with me." He puts his free hand in his pocket and presents the children with candies of every color. His forearm is exposed, and I stare at the number tattooed there. I cough to clear the lump in my throat and don't say a word. Bruno was also in hell.

The children drop the gifts that Father brought them and run to Bruno, shouting gaily. He hurries to cover his forearm and looks at them with a sad smile.

Bruno holds Misza's hand and then leans down and rubs his leg. "I have to tell you; my leg still hurts from your kick."

Misza gapes at him, and Bruno laughs heartily. Only I am still staring at him, unable to speak a word. His laugh masks such harrowing grief.

"Can I hug you now?" Ida pulls me to her.

I feel my body relax, and the tension slowly dissipates. Her hug penetrates my heart and envelops me with love.

"Why are you covering your hair?" I ask the first question that comes to mind. "Are you still hiding your...?"

"No." She replies with a self-conscious smile. "I don't wear a headscarf to hide my identity. I wear it as a married woman who flaunts her identity." She shows me the gold ring that adorns her finger.

"Married?" I wrinkle my brow.

"I was searching for you, and I found Ida," Bruno says awkwardly, and Anton puts his hands on my shoulders. "But when I saw her, she gently explained to me who the Guardian of the Realm was." He winks at Anton. "And to my delight, I discovered that what I was searching for was right beside me all along." He takes Ida's left hand, the hand wearing their wedding ring, and kisses it.

"You found the fairest of them all." I nod. "I think we should sit down." I gesture toward the dining table.

"Just a minute!" Michalina yells. "We have one more surprise."

"No, no." I wave my hand. "You've surprised me more than enough for one day."

"I promise you won't want to miss this surprise." Ida leaves, and I glance at Anton nervously. He squeezes my shoulders tenderly and gives me a reassuring smile.

"Mrs. Ania Orzeszkowa." I hear a familiar voice, and my jaw drops. I focus my eyes on Anton so he can assure me that I'm not dreaming. "The beautiful Mrs. Orzeszkowa, I am s-h-o c-k-e-d."

Anton stifles a laugh, and I turn my head, feeling like I might faint any minute.

Peter. Peter and Olek! Standing right in front of me.

"I'm dreaming... I must be dreaming."

"You're not dreaming about living in this backwoods town." Peter rolls his eyes. "And you're not dreaming about wearing an ugly floral print dress." He grimaces in mock revulsion and curls his long mustache.

"Peter..." I whisper his name.

"The one and only." He covers his mouth with his hands and bursts into tears.

"I don't believe it!" I let out a scream and barrage him with hugs and kisses. Everyone seems to have moved aside, and no one dares disturb our reunion.

"I don't believe it either." He snivels and lifts me up in the air. "I looked for your name on so many lists I had to start wearing glasses." Peter puts me back down, and Anton pulls me away from him and slides his hand over my stomach. I can see that he shares my intense excitement, but a worry line is etched in his forehead.

"Forgive me." Peter covers his mouth with his hands. "Ida told me you were pregnant, but in my excitement..."

"I'm not sick," I exclaim, pushing Anton's hand away from me. "I'm giddy with excitement, but pregnancy is not a disease."

Olek pushes between us, taking the opportunity to hug and congratulate me. In fact, his quiet, gentle manner brings tears to my eyes.

"I'm so happy." I squeeze Olek's hands and step back. "I need a minute to catch my breath. Just one minute." I lean on Anton and let him lead me to the armchair.

He stands behind me and rubs my shoulders. I look around at everyone, and my heart opens so much that it hurts.

Mother is sitting on an armchair at the opposite end of the room. She's sipping the drink that Luda gave her and is studying the children with a thoughtful look. Every time her eyes land on Sarah, her chest quivers. She knows who Sarah is. I told her when I first saw her upon our arrival in New York, and my heart sank when she greeted the girl coldly as if she were a stranger. I find it hard to understand how it is possible for her not to worship my brave girl. Sarah is the only blood relative left from her family.

Father is sitting next to her, smoking a cigarette. Despite the many new wrinkles on his face, he looks relaxed and calm, almost like before the war.

Ida arranges the candles from her bag on the mantelpiece, and Bruno stands by the window, watching her. Michalina joins her, and Mother frowns in disapproval.

Leib and Olek ask Maria if she needs any help, and only Peter sashays around the parlor, examining every single thing we've put on the furniture.

"I see you've decided to keep the little devils." He points to the children and grins, but his eyes fill with tears, betraying his emotions.

"We're not devils," Oleg retorts angrily. "But we know how to fight like devils."

"So impolite." Mother clucks, and Peter and I stifle a giggle.

Ida and Michalina light the candles and cover their eyes with the palms of their hands; they whisper a quiet prayer, and I inadvertently get up and approach them. They make room for me between them without saying a word. I pick up a match with trembling fingers and light two candles. The children are sitting on the floor, surrounded by gifts and family members, and my belly suddenly fills with intense warmth. I go back to looking at the candles. In the ghetto, there were two. In the village, two became four, and now there are six. Suddenly I understood what Ida was trying to explain to me. Light conquers darkness, and even hell cannot extinguish our candles. I cover my eyes with my hands and say just two words: Thank you.

I lean towards Sarah and gesture to her to go and get the gift that we wrapped together. She nods, but I see the hesitation on her face. Holding the present, she and I walk over to Mother.

Mother looks at the package and then at Sarah.

"Mrs. Orzeszkowa." Sarah puts the package on her lap. "Mother says Grandpa would have wanted you to have this."

Mother clenches her teeth and stares at the package, her eyes feverish.

"Before they took Grandpa to the infirmary, he told me that if I ever met you, I mustn't forget to tell you that he never stopped loving you."

Mother's shoulders shake.

"Grandpa said that he prayed every day for your soul to heal and for you to love him again, too."

I take Sarah's hand and squeeze it in approval.

Mother opens the gift with trembling fingers. Her eyes open wide in astonishment, and she clutches the prayer book to her chest and bursts into tears. This is the first time in my life that I've seen my mother cry.

She runs out of the house, and Father runs after her.

Sarah looks at me, mortified.

"You gave her a good gift." I stroke her hair. "You gave her a gift of love."

Sarah nods and goes back to sit with the children, but her eyes never leave the door. Mother comes back and lets Father help her back into the armchair. She hugs the book to her chest and stares at Sarah as though she's never seen her before.

* * *

We all sit around the crowded table; it is full of delicacies, booming conversations, laughter, and joy. Happiness tainted with sorrow that will never fade away. Every time I raise my hand to pass someone a dish, so many eyes meet mine. My loved ones who came back to me searching for an answer to a question that has never been asked aloud. Everyone at this table experienced the hardships of the war. If we had all sat around a table together before the war, we would have competed against one another for the privilege of sharing our stories and being the center of attention. But at this table, no one volunteers to share the horrors they experienced.

Each person lost a part of themselves. It doesn't surprise me that Ida and Michalina haven't told anyone where I was in the months that I was away from them, and it doesn't seem to shock them that I've kept it to myself. Maybe they believe my decision allows me to imagine that I was never there, and maybe they understand that hell is branded on me – branded so powerfully that if I dared to expose it, my soul would catch fire. I bite my lip and command myself to smile.

The children clear the table. Suddenly Bruno stands up and grabs a half-eaten bun from a plate that Gershon is holding. He hurriedly wraps it in a napkin and stuffs it into his pants pocket. No one says a word.

He sits back down, and his cheek trembles, contorting slightly as he smiles awkwardly. "My Grandma Rosa always said that those who have known hunger will never throw away food."

"To the wise Grandma Rosa." Peter raises his glass, and we all do the same, sighing in gratitude that he managed to alleviate the embarrassment.

Maria's husband brings out the desserts, and I look at Ida and then at Peter and head over to the bin beside the fireplace. Everyone is silent while I rummage through it.

"Has she lost her mind?" Mother whispers in shock.

"Not in the slightest," says Ida excitedly.

I pull the bottle of brandy out from the bottom of the bin and put it on the table.

Peter bursts into loud squeals and claps enthusiastically.

"I don't understand..." Mother scowls, "Does she expect us to drink liquor that was thrown in the trash?"

"Yes!" I say as I pour the brandy into glasses with trembling hands. "It's not merely a drink. It's a promise." I hand the first glass to Ida. "A promise made so long ago that we can now fulfill." I give the second glass to Peter, who gives me his broadest smile. "We would all prefer to imagine that the war never happened." I then hand a glass to Michalina. "But it happened and intertwined our fates." I give a glass to Bruno, and he nods in understanding. "No one will be able to give us back what we lost." I hand a glass to Leib, and he winks at me and rests his hand on Michalina's. "But no one can take away our right to celebrate what we've achieved against all odds." I give Anton a glass, and he presses his lips to mine. I close my eyes, savoring his scent and his touch, before I turn back to the table. I then serve Mother, Father, and Olek. "I raise this glass to Maria." I hand her a glass and pour another one for her husband, who gazes at her lovingly. "I raise my glass to Maria, who risked her life and her sister's life so that we could sit here today. I raise my glass to all the good people who opened their eyes before the forces of evil and maintained their humanity despite its being such a rare commodity in our dark, dismal world." I involuntarily rub my stomach. "May the light spread and dispel the darkness."

Everyone raises their glasses, and muted sobbing can be heard from all around the table.

I pour myself a sip of brandy and tap my glass against Anton's. He gives me such a piercing stare that, for a moment, it seems as though there's no one else in the room but us. "May you never have to promise me anything but your endless love."

"Amen." The answer rings out in a chorus, and the din of clinking glasses echoes from every direction. I taste the brandy carefully, and Anton bends down and kisses my belly.

* * *

The doors of the bedrooms are closed. The house is silent after all the guests have gone to bed, and I tiptoe into the children's room. I look at them, lying side by side on their mattresses, and I lie down between them.

I breathe quietly so as not to wake them, but soon arms and legs wrap around me.

"Mother," Bella whispers, "Tell us the story of the magical kingdom."

"Please," Gershon whispers, and other quiet requests follow his.

"You are too old for that story," I giggle.

"Please." This time it's Sarah asking, as she rests her head on my shoulder.

I stroke her head and close my eyes, again whispering the familiar words that describe our present home in great detail. The flowerbeds, the grassy lawns, the two horses, and even the chicken coop. I continue whispering until their breathing becomes deep and steady, and I understand that they've fallen asleep.

Anton comes in and offers me his hand, and I let him help me to my feet. In our bedroom, I get undressed and cling to his warm body. He caresses me and kisses me, satisfying every part of my body.

I nuzzle into his arms, and he tucks my hair behind my ear and kisses the special meeting point between my right cheek and my ear. "I'm just making sure it's you," he whispers hoarsely, and I shiver and close my eyes. I'm not afraid to fall asleep because, despite the hellish nightmares that haunt me, I know I'll wake up in heaven, swathed in his love and the love of my children.

I relax, and the fog of sleep envelops me as I whisper the story of the magical kingdom for all the children left behind on the bleeding land of Poland, for all the children whose light was extinguished.

"You're with me, and you're safe now." Anton kisses my neck, but I can't stop whispering. "Ania, my love, you can stop now. No one can hurt you or our children."

I clench my teeth and murmur softly, "Do you promise?"

"I promise."

His promise makes me feel calm and at peace. I know it's a transient feeling and that when I wake up in the morning, I'll shield my head with my hands, but at this moment, I'm encased in the love of the only man of my life, and my heart and my home are illuminated.

    They. Could. Not. Extinguish. Our. Light.